the COMMONERS

Shani Denman

For whom tomorrow will never be.

For whom tomorrow is but a day away.

For Jack

Chapter 1 - The Find

Janice's last breath in was more of a gasp. Images from her childhood played like a silent movie behind her frantic eyes, desperate tears running down the sides of her face and settling like pools of misery in the shells of her ears. This couldn't be the end - she had so much to do, so much love to give, so many things to organise, and the ironing, who would do it now? But the end it was. The ironing would remain undone for many days until reluctantly, her husband of thirty years gathered it up, shoved it in a Bag for Life and took it to the ironing shop up the hill. Pressed for Time would prove to be an expensive option he wouldn't repeat.

Janice's killer moved silently away into the trees and hovered for a moment, looking back at his handiwork. He shuddered as the adrenaline spurted through his heart causing a great thumping that erupted in his throat. He breathed deeply and loped into the woods with yeti like strides.

Janice exhaled and her soul passed in one last sob through her anguished mouth. Her eyes turned to those of a doll, still and empty. She felt her body slump into the autumn floor as she rose above it and looked down. How old she'd become, how ugly and old.

'That's not me' she thought. 'When did I get so fat?' She now felt as light as air, tingly and birdlike, with an energy inside her that had not visited in years. She heard her name being called, and turning, she saw her mother and father, Giles the golden retriever and her childhood cat, Pebble. Her heart soared with delight and she found herself in their loving embrace, Pebble snaking around her legs and Giles' head on her thigh, tail swishing to and fro. Then she, and they, were gone - their light sucked out of the woodland gloom in an instant. The leaves swirled momentarily, then the forest floor was still, the air crisp, and the animals of the wood resumed their business.

The night ticked on and there, her body lay until morning when predictably, a dog walker found her.

Holding the straining leads, was a willowy girl of eighteen with large black Kicker boots, a floaty white Broderie Anglaise skirt topped with a huge dark green jumper that swamped her fragile frame. Holly was her name. Her eyes widened as she ran to what she thought was perhaps a fainted lady, only to recoil when she saw the glassy eyes and bloodied chest that failed to rise and fall. She retched and backed away, the dogs yelped and whined, and she pulled them back, wrapping the leads around her slim hands.

Holly looked around for a place to sit, her tummy curdling and her lips quivering. The tips of her slender fingers swiped her fine red hair out of her teary eyes, then retreated up her voluminous sleeves. She took a long breath in, and blowing out through trembling lips, fished her phone with its cracked screen and gothic cover, out of her pocket and rang home. The minutes dragged until her mother arrived, billowing through the woods in a long scarf and big coat, flustered and afraid for her daughter who she found sitting, pigeon toed and hunched, on a mossy log. For all the world she looked like a woodland elf all elbows and knees.

Before Holly could rise, her mother clasped the bony girl to her middle and Holly stretched out her arm, one visible finger pointing from under the dark green cuff like the ghost of Christmas yet to come, at Janice, lying in the autumn leaves, the sun sweeping over her waxy complexion with ethereal light. "I think it's that woman, the one that shouted at you mum, when the dog sniffed the lemons". Actually, they were limes, but now wasn't the time to quibble over citrus. She recalled the unfortunate encounter when her sweet dachshund Margaux had sniffed a box of limes, jabbing her long nose into the crate at Pippins, the grocers. A lady loudly declared it disgusting and unhygienic, that she was intending to buy limes but wouldn't now, after that "filthy dog" had slobbered on them.

"You ain't gonna be eating the skins love" the greengrocer had said, and folded his tall frame down to pat the sausage dog with a large weathered hand. Faye shook herself out of the memory and back to the terrible scene in front of her.

The police arrived driving their vans over the lumpy roots and stones. Limes were forgotten as they were escorted away as the area was cordoned safely off. Officers buzzed back and forth, between their vehicles and the body, rustled in their forensic white suits and questioned Holly on her morning's find. She glanced over as they were erecting a tent around Janice's body and caught a last glimpse of her face, motionless, no cloud of breath above her lips like that of her own, or the dozens of policemen whose morning breath curled and mingled around them like white haired old ladies hovering around a buffet. Holly was given permission to leave and her mother Faye enveloped her in her long wool coat and they walked as one, with the two short changed dogs straining to go back into the trees.

A day passed before the police got back in touch to finalise her statement. This was given to the best of her ability, leaving out any ramblings that were on the tip of her tongue about the woods, trees and the dogs. They half wondered if she was holding something back but didn't press her. She was young, after all. They asked her not to speak about the case to anyone.

When the news broke, the press arrived, swarming all over Kingshurst Village, and parking badly on the grass verges, much to the irritation of the Heritage Committee headed by Stella Mayhew, local shop owner and general busybody. She had been out in her Barbour coat confronting reporters and photographing deep muddy tyre marks in the grass.

Holly suffered nightmares that woke her in the early hours, mist and dead leaves swirling through her dreams, and Janice's face looming near her own, breathing out the swirling frosty morning breath that had been so absent in the woods that day. Then a whispered name, her lips moving, but barely audible. Holly leaned closer, straining to hear, as Janice's face retreated into the mist, the force of which sucked Holly's wavy red hair forward and into her eyes. She would wake batting it out of her face with a cry of "tell me!" The images faded into her mother's soothing words, stroking her hair to wake her. Breakfast nibbled and off to college, these images were forgotten until bedtime, when as soon as her golden lashes met, the characters were waiting in the wings. All attempts at deceiving the dreamworld with jolly thoughts of the dogs, friends and boys were to no avail and for the next couple of weeks the only movie screening at her midnight cinema was this unutterable horror.

Chapter 2 - 10 Miles to London

Kingshurst Village was the last little English village before Kent dissipated into urban sprawl. The only evidence of the capital city's filthy clawing hands were the red London buses that sped through the high street and surrounding narrow roads, skimming the trees and hugging the bends and corners with tramline accuracy.

The small high street cut the common in half and was dotted with interesting and pleasant shops. People visited this village at weekends and strolled the woods and lakes, picnicked on the benches, pondered the stores, peeked into the cool musty gloom of the tiny church and read long forgotten names on gravestones before settling in the tea room and pub to while away a Sunday afternoon.

It had always been a place for visitors and the cosy opportunistic businesses, the card and gift shop, cafe and art gallery stayed open on Sunday afternoons to ensnare these escapees of the outside world, much to the bewilderment of a few long standing locals who moaned about litter and car parking.

Faye had moved to the village as a baby. Her parents had bought a cottage on the edge of the common in the late seventies, and a photograph of them standing on the grass in front of it adorned the mantelpiece. Her father's foot was atop the milestone, hand on hip, as if contemplating the ten miles to London, her mother clutched his arm, and Faye in front, a toddler with a banana smile and bobbed curly hair. She went to the local school where her mother taught art, bought sweets at the local shop, went to brownies in the church hall, and had dance classes and cello lessons.

Life was very pleasant, and her teenage years ordinary and happy, until her father passed away aged fifty, from a heart attack one Sunday afternoon and her mother stricken with grief, waned in sharp moonlike phases. The usually cruel illness of dementia eventually afforded her a peace that was normally reserved for the old and fulfilled. She spent her final days in a care home believing she was at an artists' retreat, painting and drawing small floral pictures until one evening, she passed away, a tiny crescent of a woman, still holding a paintbrush, iris petal left unfinished, life complete.

Faye was at once alone, in her late teens. She had been managing by herself for a while now and of course inherited the cottage with all its contents. There was a good deal of money in the bank from her father's life insurance and although lonely, she managed. She got herself to college, she worked two part time jobs and she graduated. There was one aunt in Scotland who sent birthday cards. Faye instantly knew from the tiny even writing on the envelope that it was from Aunty Anne. There was usually a couple of paragraphs in her cards detailing the latest news of her cousins, a new baby, engagements, exam results, house moves. She could barely remember them, a girl and twin boys, with white blonde hair and pink sweaty faces, upturned noses and chubby little legs. She could never help but liken them to a litter of piglets. They took after their father, who was equally blonde, pink and clammy.

Anne was her mother's sister. She'd moved to Scotland years before to marry Andrew, a doctor whom she'd met whilst hiking in the Highlands. Faye's mother told her the story of how Anne twisted her ankle whilst hiking up Creag Beag, a well known peak in the Cairngorms, and as luck would have it, in a party coming down, a handsome blonde doctor stopped to attend to her. They were married before the year was out. The piglets followed a few years later and once ensconced in the Highland life they were rarely seen south of the border.

Apart from them and a somewhat miserable unmarried uncle who lived by the south coast, that was it. She was glad no-one swooped in to rescue her. She wanted to stay where she was. She had friends, hobbies and the cottage, but it wasn't until she met Ben she suddenly realised how alone she had been. He was a breath of fresh air in her small existence. He interrupted her safe routine with a charming slightly lopsided grin and curly dark hair that flopped over one of his pale blue eyes, fine brows, cheekbones and beautiful dimples. His strong arms and large hands would envelop her completely, and she felt utterly safe with her head on his firm chest, her own arms holding him so close as to claim him forever. Their wedding was small with just a few close friends, pals from the orchestra who she'd grown up with through Junior Strings, Ben's parents from Wales who were very sweet and her own Aunty Anne, Charles and the litter of piglets. St Val's church (as it was affectionately known) was small enough to not embarrass the sparsely attended nuptials and Faye had intended to walk herself down the aisle, but when her Uncle David appeared and offered to give her away, she relented. He drove up from Hastings for the ceremony, but left before the celebrations started, at home in the cottage. She wore a simple long lace gown of palest grey that belonged to her mother and held a small posy of mauve roses with more pinned in her long wavy hair.

They settled into the cottage by the common, and welcomed their daughter one blustery Christmas Eve. Holly was born at home in the front bedroom with the midwife in attendance after two false alarms and dashes to the hospital. Ben had arrived just in time, zooming over the common on his old motorbike and taking the stairs two at a time, shrugging off his leather jacket and instrument case on the way up. Faye took to motherhood well but felt a deep inner fear that nagged her, about being parted from the baby by some mishap or another. She put it down to the trauma of losing her own parents. Later the thought crossed her mind that maybe she'd indeed had some sort of premonition about the future, but for now they were a happy little family.

Chapter 3 - A Delicate China Cup

Faye appeared in her daughter's bedroom door unseen. Holly was sat cross legged on the bed, Margaux tucked into her lap enjoying a thorough tummy scratch and neck rub, her stubby little legs jutting out from her sausage torso. Holly adored her. She instinctively knew when the teenager was in need of attention, barging her way into Holly's teenage angst and demanding a spa treatment. In obliging, Holly would be transported out of her angst, and the little hairy huntress would kill two birds with one stone. This arrangement was a godsend to Faye, who often felt at a loss with Holly, and she was grateful to the little dog for stepping up.

It had been sixteen years since Holly's father had died. The grief was torturous at first, waves so big she felt utterly crushed by them, they ebbed and flowed, dragging ocean debris in and out, disbelief, guilt, sorrow and loneliness like stagnant treacle stopping her from moving on. However, she was determined not to fade away like her mother had. Her network of friends who lived around the common saw to it that she remained present, involved and relevant. She found solace in many things - her cello, being part of the local orchestra, working part time in the tearoom on the high street a couple of afternoons a week, and a morning baking with its owner whom she adored. Her daughter gave her a reason to get up in the mornings and keep busy, socialising with her friends and walking her two dogs on the common. The woodland with all its seasonal changes filling her senses, helped her sleep at night.

"Darling, I'm off to work, will you be ok?" She asked, interrupting the doggy smooch. Margaux and Holly looked up.

"Yep Mum, I'm fine, I've got some reading to do before tomorrow. Holly gestured toward a pile of books by the bed. "That's if this sausage lets me!"

Margaux obliged by climbing off Holly's lap and stretching out on the pink rug, her back paws outstretched facing up. They both smiled at her, she had the cutest dog "toe beans" they cooed in unison, and Holly poked the cute little pads of her paws which she immediately drew in under her.

Downstairs, Faye scraped her thick wayward hair into a high ponytail and grabbed her bag. She slid on her comfy shoes and headed out down the stone path, letting the gate swing shut with a reassuring clunk. Both dogs were opportunists when it came to doors and gates, and there had been numerous times she'd been forced to run across the road to the common in an array of nightwear, random footwear, once with heated rollers, bra and knickers and a cardigan after the canine escape committee. The self closing gate was suggested by her neighbour, a practical man named Todd, who said that much as he enjoyed the fashion parade, he'd rather not scrape a dog off the road. Gratefully, although perturbed by his imagery, she accepted his offer to do the work and the self closer was duly installed. A cake was baked in return for this favour, the deal was sealed and so was the escape route.

Faye marched over the common, following her usual route as the crow flies, past the entrance to Hunters Wood, the pond and a bench, one of many on the common. Today, an elderly gentleman and his equally ancient Pekingese dog were sitting on the bench, and he nodded at Faye as she passed.

The dog growled a strangled little gurgle, "Easy Fella" he muttered. Fella, the conveniently named pooch pulled in his lolling tongue to reveal a single snaggle tooth. Faye raised her eyebrows at the ugly but strangely cute little thing and smiled in reply.

The high street was quiet - rain earlier that day had put off visitors, and even though the sun was weakly shining through, they had clearly chosen to spend their day elsewhere. Although it meant lack of business, she found herself relieved not to have too crazy an afternoon ahead of her at the cafe.

The Decadia Cafe stood detached between the card shop and a solicitors office. It's unusual art deco exterior stood out from its Victorian neighbours. The proprietor was a lady whose tastes were eclectic, eccentric and spot on for her business. Inside were an array of booths each one themed to a different decade. A clever sound system installed by her techy nephew ensured that each zone had an era appropriate playlist. The china was collected and topped up from charity shops, vintage and antique markets from far and wide. There was a high turnover of cups and saucers dependent on who was on washing up duty, if a hen party was booked in or if it was Tuesday. The Kings Knitters, a knitting circle of quirky wool adorned ladies, inevitably knocked something over whilst wrestling yarn, needles, bags and teapots, and were a regular booking. It was Wednesday today and Velvet Miller, the owner was doing an inventory.

"Forty three," she said flatly. "That's seven down on last week." She turned and rolled her large brown eyes at Faye. "Well, I told you I saw a lovely little set of five Royal Doulton in the Cats Sanctuary shop Velvet."

Everyone who knew her was on the lookout for vintage china. "Make that eight, this one has a crack in it" - it was a shame, the pretty little Shelley cup was one of her favourites. Unable to throw it away she placed it on the shelf above the plate rack, briefly picturing herself planting a little succulent in it, but she knew in her heart it would end up in the bin, just on a more decisive day. For now, the little cup sat forlorn on the shelf awaiting its fate.

As predicted, it was a quiet day. There was time for chat as they gave the place a good clean through. Faye's thoughts flickered to her kitchen at home, and how she ought to be cleaning that as thoroughly.

They talked over the recent death of Janice Stanhope, village spokesperson and general busy body, but not as busy a body as her counterpart Stella, self styled lady of the manor. It had been a few weeks and the reporters had got bored, and Velvet hadn't wanted to press her friend on the matter - but curiosity got the better of her and her questions were becoming more direct. Actually it was a relief for Faye to talk it out with someone. The whole thing had shaken her rigid and protecting Holly was her priority, leaving little time to soothe her own nerves.

"The thing is Velve, I just don't understand why she was out there at night.

She didn't have a dog, and it was too dark to be feeding the flipping ducks. She must have been meeting someone. It's really scary to think that someone strangled, and plunged a knife into her" Velvet mimed, plunging a delicate teaspoon at Faye who winced and stepped back with an obliging stagger.

"How could someone, maybe someone we all know, actually do that?" Velvet nodded then shook her head too.

"I know it happens, but for God's sake, not around here! she added. Velvet asked about Janice's husband. He had been questioned a couple of times.

"They always suspect the spouse first" Velvet announced with the knowledge of an armchair detective.

"Is there cctv anywhere that could have picked her up?" Faye asked.

"Well, there's some on the high street and up by the Gallery, but not near the blooming pond. I mean, what on earth would they need it there for? Rogue fishermen?"

Faye imagined Velvet in TV cop mode, leaning over an officer pointing at a blurry screen and saying "there, what was that?

Zoom in, what's that fisherman doing with a knife? Oh, gutting a fish.... Bring him in!"

Her brain burp was interrupted by the bell on the entrance door. There stood a beautiful lady, about thirty five with a flawless, dark brown complexion, her hair in a cropped Afro with the tips dyed a copper that matched her eyes. Adorned with false eyelashes and a glossy brown lipstick, she wore a soft denim jumpsuit with a gold low slung belt and platform sandals. She walked into the cafe and pointed at her chosen booth. The Seventies. She carried no handbag and slid in and sat down in one graceful movement. Velvet scurried out of the kitchen and went to serve her. Faye carried on her list of chores.

A couple came in and sat in the fifties booth. They reminisced over the groovy china adorned with people twisting, like they did last summer. They were faintly rocker billy in attire, turned up jeans and matching short quiffed hair. Tucking into tea and scones they tapped their feet to Bill Haley.

The lady in the seventies booth just sat, inhaling her filter coffee. With her eyes closed, one brow arched and lips a little pursed, she looked as if she was also reminiscing, but with much more melancholy than Mr and Mrs Sideburns who were by now attempting a reigned-in version of the Hand

Jive. Velvet glanced fearfully at her fifties china. Seventies lady hadn't touched her coffee and for all the world looked as if she were absorbing it through the music, the warm aroma of roasted Roberta Flack encircled her as the memories of her mother, large hooped earrings and roll necked sweater, playing records on a little leatherette box record player flooded back, the chunky stylus arm bouncing down onto the vinyl with a pop and a hiss. The brown toffee swirled carpet where she wriggled her toes from under flared orange trousers. The images were vivid - browns and oranges, rusts and yellows, pure 70s. There had been a Volkswagen Caravette in the driveway, and her father talking to the old white haired neighbour over the fence about cars, hand on hipsters. They were happy days - school holidays that went on forever, hours in the garden riding her chopper till her arms ached from the high handlebars. Blowing on a dandelion after stepping out of a lukewarm paddling pool, only to have the fairylike seeds stick to her wet midriff. Watching them detach one by one as she sat in an oversized flowery lounger drying in the sun. She was jolted from her memory by a burst of laughter from the rock'n rollers, who were pointing up at a rather startled bust of Elvis that graced the half landing heading up to the loos. Velvet had picked him up at a boot fair for four pounds. He was a poor representation of the great man with one eye sellotaped in place where a customer had knocked him off, but it was the perfect spot for him, next to the arrow that pointed up to the loo, atop a small cupboard of bathroom essentials. The King of Rocknlooroll she called him. Velvet and Faye laughed to each other remembering, and when they turned back to the cafe, the beautiful lady had gone, bill unpaid much to the astonishment of the girls.

"I think she was in a bit of a daydream Faye" "she didn't even touch her drink" Velvet said sniffing the beverage and checking for lipstick on the smoked glass cup.

"Maybe she had some sort of emergency?" Faye wondered.
"I think it's this place, it happened last week too, the fried egg sandwich man, you know, in the forties booth. He left before you'd made it to the kitchen.

Moving onto milkshakes, the beboppers sipped, talked animatedly about vintage cars and the rally that was coming up. Velvet's ears pricked up, she loved a good vintage car show, her boyfriend was such a petrol head. She'd spent many a Sunday wandering around lumpy fields full of freshly shampooed cars and their proud owners, but now the cafe was open there'd been little time for days out.
The day wore on, the sun moved

carelessly across the common as if it had nothing better to do, the shadows of the ornate lamp posts flipping from one side to another, marking time. Velvet locked up as Faye wound up the awning at the front.

"Go carefully Faye, there's still a murderer out there" Velvet gestured to the common. "See you on Friday lovely" and they parted.

Faye had all but forgotten about Janice for a few hours. She felt a little uncomfortable walking back towards the common, but also irritated that she should feel that way in her home town. How dare someone stir up the equilibrium with a big spoonful of hatred. What's wrong with a strongly worded solicitor's letter or a knock on the door by the police, therapy, mediation - one didn't have to resort to stabbing someone in the woods. It just upsets the whole neighbourhood, she thought. "Thoughtless murdering bastard" she muttered as she passed by the travel agents.

'Seas the Day' was a brightly lit shop, and the staff always seemed to outnumber the clientele; a large lady behind a small desk, shutting down her computer, and a small lady behind a large desk sorting through brochures. The odd collection of items in the window were supposed to entice you within to book a dream cruise, but the ancient binoculars, stuffed giraffe and battered suitcase did little to inspire - even the careworn King Tut mask was tut at best. She was reminded of the half filled charity bag behind the bedroom door, which probably was the only destination for her bikini this year. Her eyes paused on a poster of Italy. A beautiful lady sipping a coffee and glancing sideways at a very stylish man, slicked back hair falling in curls around his ears. Very handsome. Faye occasionally missed having a man. Ben was long gone, and she struggled to remember his features sometimes. The few photos she had of him, she'd seen so many times that his face was just that now, an old snapshot. But she remembered how he felt, how he smelled, his warm embrace and the sound of his voice when her head was against his chest. She took a deep breath and marched on over to the grass as the sun was setting behind the trees.

Holly was on the sofa, reading, headphones on, and she smiled up at her mother as she appeared. Margaux woke from her snooze and from his lookout duty from the back of the sofa, Rollo slithered down to greet her. After a lot of wagging, both dogs resumed their positions, now assured she was in for the night.

"Have they been fed love?" She asked.

"Yes, they kept swapping bowls," Holly called out taking one headphone off. Faye set about preparing dinner. "I'm making a risotto, is that ok?" There was a mumbled yes from the sofa. She took out an opened bottle of Pinot Grigio from the fridge and poured a large glass. The rest can go in the rice, she thought. It would have been so easy to just drink it, but at least this way some of the alcohol would evaporate. Over the years bringing up Holly on her own, there were times when a large glass with dinner had turned into a bottle. She didn't want to go down that road if she could help it. Thankfully she'd managed to keep those moments to a minimum. It wasn't easy being a single mum with no parents of her own for support. She gradually added the wine to the risotto, and the heavenly scent of garlic and mushrooms filled the kitchen with promise. Dinner could be a little hit and miss at times, puzzlingly, if she tried her best. Nonchalance over the hob seemed to do the trick - "never let it know you're hungry" was the advice her mother had given her years ago.

That night Holly dreamt again of the lady by the lake, the mist and the whispers. She didn't wake, but Faye heard her mumbling in her sleep across the landing. The sooner the police got to the bottom of this, the better, she thought, as she drifted off into her own troubled dream.

Chapter 4 - Legend Has It

Kingshurst Village was a popular wedding destination. Many a bride dreamt of gliding down the aisle at St Valentines Church, small but picturesque, draughty in the winter, cool in the summer, a well kept graveyard and pretty lychgate, an ideal backdrop for many a wedding photographer's portfolio and the perfect place name to adorn an invitation.

Although February the fourteenth was the most sought after date, for most of the spring and summer the small church was booked up for weddings.

In the vestibule behind the heavy oak door was a pile of freshly printed leaflets from the History Society, their inky smell mingling with the scent of hymn books and old wood. 'The History of Kingshurst Village' the title read in ye olde font, with a black and white photograph of the little church, and a map of the village printed below. On the last page, there was a paragraph titled 'Myths and Legends'. It was here as a child that Faye read the old story of a King who rode through the woods on his large black stallion, in pursuit of his love whose horse had bolted in a storm. She couldn't remember which King it was, but always imagined Henry VIII and one of his wives, feather bobbing in his hat as he galloped, fearlessly dodging the trees and jumping ditches. It was said that during a storm the galloping of hooves, whinnying of a horse and cries of a lady could be still be heard. The young Faye had loved this tale. There were villagers who claimed to have heard it. "He's riding tonight" she remembered her mother say, nodding at the dark clouds rolling in as they walked home over the common, hair blowing and the smell of rain in the air. Lying in bed after Brownies she tried to stay awake to hear the thudding hooves, but she was asleep before the first rumble of thunder. She smiled at the memory as the rain beat down on the kitchen window.

Thursday! She suddenly remembered, orchestra tonight in the Church hall. The Kingshurst Symphony met every week for rehearsal during the concert season. She hadn't practised for days, the concert was at the weekend and she was still skipping over little sections of Beethoven's Eroica Symphony. She hauled herself up from her morning cuppa and headed into the tiny study where a dark brown cello stood gloomily in the corner. Still in her pyjamas and slipper socks she plonked herself down on a small chair and pulled the instrument toward her. Picking up the bow, she plied it with rosin and ran through some scales before moving onto the more difficult passages of her part.

Once playing, she relished the sound as it rang through her ears and soothed her mind, the wooden chambers within the cello's body echoing with mellow notes and sounds so solid you could almost slice them.

As the rosin scented air billowed up into her nostrils, her head filled with music and she failed to hear the distant neighing of a horse, a faint cry and the rhythmic thud of hooves. By the time the storm reached the cottage the ancient scene had played out, unnoticed in the crescendo of Beethoven's third symphony.

Chapter 5 - After the Storm

A gloomy, suspicious air had settled over the village since the murder like a dark, swirling mist. Rife with rumour, its wary inhabitants carried on their daily lives but in the backs of their minds was a dread. A dread that the crime would never be solved, that the perpetrator would remain amongst them, casually buying his newspaper, having her nails done, riding a bike across the common or sitting on a bus scanning the high street for another victim.

The police were still conducting house to house enquiries, spiralling further and further away from the scene of the murder. Nobody had seen or heard a thing. Janice's last known whereabouts were in her house at teatime. Her husband had described what he termed as "a fairly adequate meal" of "Spag Bol with ruddy turkey mince, I ask you, and Cornish ice-cream with tinned fruit for afters." He described her clothes - navy trousers and a pale pink top with flowers. Her mood, which was "a bit aggitato" which apparently wasn't unusual. The young policeman taking this down privately wondered what Christmas Day would be like in this middle aged, slightly dreary house. Glad he wasn't invited, he carried on scribbling. The net didn't seem to be closing in on anyone.

Detective Inspector Lydia Appleby, an officer close to retirement, flicked through the accumulated evidence after everyone had gone. The strip lighting humming in the old police station shone down unflatteringly on her wrinkled brow and recently emerging jowls, as she frowned in frustration. She'd gone over everything now and had a feeling it was a robbery and drugs related crime. The amount of times she'd rolled her eyes and tutted at thieving dishevelled youngsters who looked older than she, sallow and toothless from their dreadful addiction, to gang related crime and city boy dealers. The scourge of modern man, brought on by himself, no closer to being resolved, and it was heartbreaking. It seemed a thankless task, but somewhere inside her she had to chip away at it, little by little, protecting the innocent and bringing those responsible to justice. Feeling a little surge of superhero, she picked up the files and crammed them into her old brief case, ready to read through again in her dressing gown and slippers with a glass of merlot.

Once home, with the rain still pelting against the windows, Lydia sat cosily by the fireside and spread the papers out on the coffee table. She looked forlornly up at the weather.

The firelight was much kinder on her face, pretty, with high rounded cheekbones, the saviours of only a lucky few aging faces. The flames danced in her clever eyes as ideas darted fox-like through her mind, chasing thoughts and jumping over facts like hedges. It was going to be a long night, and the empty bed upstairs, with its crisp white linen, almost sighed for an occupant as the gentle pop of a cork echoed up the landing.

Chapter 6 - Fabulous Mr Fox

Velvet was closing up the Decadia a little early tonight. Her small hands fumbled with the large key as she bent to lock up, her dark curled hair flopping into her face as she struggled with the bottom lock of the door. She scampered up the steps at the side of the cafe to the flat above to get changed.

* * *

A lovely group of ladies who had been enjoying afternoon tea in the 1940s booth (with Glen Miller accompanying them through their wartime cuppas,) strode down the high street to towards the pub to extend their girls' day out. The Clarice Cliff replica china had a well appreciated airing, and the large colourful teapot had been in overdrive due to the diminutive teacups. They'd been raucously full of beans, but there had not been one breakage and they'd left a large tip left by the sugar bowl. The ancient, slightly leaning Kings Head pub was quiet for a Friday, but it was still early and the merry tea filled throng piled in - some headed straight for the ladies' loos and some to the bar. Three or four gin and tonics later, their laughter had died down to whispers and sniggers. With patting arms, nudging elbows and gesticulating hands they perched around a corner table like a single living creature wriggling on its back. The girl behind the bar glanced up at a sudden burst of laughter. It was Holly, she worked every Friday evening, serving customers, collecting glasses and doing the cleanup at the end of the night.

She turned away from the ladies to serve a young man in a trilby hat and waistcoat. He had a certain flair about him, shirtsleeves rolled and neck unbuttoned a little to reveal a silver chain. He nervously asked for a double brandy, tapped his bank card on the machine and downed the burning beverage in one. The door behind him flung open and a large man in a scarf hissed at him "c'mon Howie, we've got ten minutes before the show!" Howie thanked Holly with a resigned nod, mouthed "see you later" and followed his partner Max out of the pub and up the high street to the glowing windows of the art gallery, their business, and home, above.

The tall Victorian building teetered over the small pavement, with a large bay window, perfect to display artwork. Above was their living room, where resplendent curtains were drawn, and up again, another smaller window with a gabled roof, their bedroom. Beside this was an octagonal turret, where Howie had his studio. With a narrow winding staircase, and windows in four directions it was deliciously light, but small. Storage was a bit of an issue and his artist's materials were stored in towering sets of drawers and piles of boxes - it was otherwise perfect, the artist in his garret.

They had been preparing for weeks for the show.

"Stop flapping Max!" he cried, as they bundled in the front door.

"I'm not flapping, I'm just. Trying. To be. Organised," Max said, calmly punctuating his words with hand gestures, prayer to palms, to Howie's flushed cheeks.

"I know, and I love you for it Max, I'm just so bloody nervous and it's making me worse!"

The pair of them took a deep breath and turned to the empty gallery- empty apart from the most beautiful, flowing art. Achingly sumptuous and fluid, art that connected the viewer to a forgotten part of themselves. The walls were filled with works speckled with gold and silver leaf, fine art elements with glorious coloured movement and light. It was a feast for the eyes, and in five minutes there would be at least fifty pairs of eyes feasting upon it.

"If I forget to tell you later, I'm so proud of you Howie," Max gushed, hand on heart. Howie went to answer, his bottom lip quivering but the door opened, bell jangling, and their first invitee to the Howie Bosun exhibition entered.

Velvet walked in with her boyfriend, Joe, his large hand outstretched to Howie. Her frilled 1950s cupcake dress was iced onto her tiny frame, retro make-up with glossy red lips - she had managed a great turn around from her work dress and apron combo. Joe was more of a biker, scruffy jeans, a large tattoo that went from his wrist, up his arms and up the side of his neck. He was a good two foot taller than Velvet, and twice as wide. She looked as if the retro pin-up girl on his garage wall calendar had come to life one night whilst he tinkered with his engine. He spoke with a surprisingly gentle voice as he congratulated Howie on his work.

"Howie this is bloody amazing, you're gonna be a millionaire, mate." He let go of Howie's hand and patted him on the back.

"Velvet, OMG you look fabulous, as always" Max purred, linking arms with Miss

July 1955.

Before too long, jazz music was quietly playing, and Foxes Gallery was full of people sipping champagne, meandering past the paintings, pointing. From the outside it looked beautiful, twinkling warmly at the top of the high street.

Faye arrived, later than she'd hoped. She kept looking out for Holly who was leaving the pub early tonight to catch the exhibition. A final orchestra rehearsal had gone over a bit as there was some confusion over the running order, giving rise to a lengthy first half. She'd let it slide over her - there was always bickering as the tension mounted towards a concert, and, usually, involving the same people. The woman that ran the refreshments, Sheila, was making a meal of timings, apparently the first half was too long and she wouldn't have enough time to clear up before the second half, making the clean-up afterwards, too late. Faye shrugged off the image of her disgruntled face and took a glass from the silver tray on the Gallery's counter and slugged a large mouthful.

She glanced at the door again for Holly, but there was only a man outside gazing in at the art. It was the man from the park bench, the man with the grumpy Pekingese dog. The same solemn eyes and white tufted hair. He was wearing the same beige overcoat and his once proud shoulders sloped, defeated by age. Fella was standing next to him also gazing in the window, tongue out, tooth on display. Faye fancied they might have a conversation about the art when they got home, the dog looked as mesmerised as he. She smiled and tried to catch his eye, but he turned and walked on. She hated that he might be lonely and made a mental note to engage with him next time they met. It was rather late for a dog walk. Then Holly slipped in the door, waving to the publican who had walked her up the road, her face flushed from keeping up with his long strides.

"Mum, flippin' heck, sorry I'm so late, it suddenly got really busy." Faye realised how relieved she was to see her daughter, it was only a short walk from the pub in a well lit high street, but there was still a nervousness in the air about town.

"I'm glad John walked you up love, I know you didn't want me to ask..." Holly interrupted her mother

"I know, I geddit mum, I'm just glad you didn't come and collect me like a nursery school kid." Faye found it hard letting Holly do her own thing at the best of times, and it was doubly hard with a murderer on the prowl.

They mingled into the crowd just as Max was raising a glass and toasting the man of the hour, a shy sensitive chap with fine pixie features whose cheeks blushed under the spotlight. Howie positively glowed in the adoration, and Max was so proud he flung his arms around him and planted a kiss on his cheek, knocking the flute of champagne against his chest. Howie was too elated to care and brushed the droplets from his shirt and waistcoat as a cheer rose up around him. He'd never forget this evening - surrounded by the people he loved, the art he'd worked so hard on, and the promise of a blossoming career ahead of him.

Later, tucked up in bed, Max and Howie went out like two twinkling lights. Full of champagne and success, they'd sold eleven paintings and had commissions for five more. There were interested parties from other galleries, and an art journalist and critic of some note had been successfully wooed into writing an article about the evening. His colleague had photographed the paintings and taken a few portraits of their shy creator. Max snored gently into the dark as Howie slept on his front, mouth wide open and nose pressed upwards into the crook of his elbow.

The dishwasher swished and sloshed it's way with a heartbeat rhythm around fifty Champagne flutes and the freshly swept gallery was subtly lit below them. The high street was finally quiet.   It started to rain lightly on the town as the clock struck two, and across the road a figure stood silently, jacket pulled up around his ears. He looked up and down the street, and headed up towards Hunters Wood.

Chapter 7 - What Saucery is This?

Velvet's car was predictably cute and retro. Unfortunately it was also, as her boyfriend had termed it, "a heap of shit." The faded red VW Beetle spluttered into view outside Faye's cottage. She heard it from upstairs and smiled. It was Saturday morning and Velvet had the day off. A robust part time lady named Nancy, who was descended from a long line of bomb proof women, was in situ at The Decadia. Her capability and fort holding skills were legendary, and Velvet knew her gem of a business was in safe hands as she tooted the horn for Faye and Holly.

Faye slid the old seat forward for her daughter, hopped into the front and slammed the unexpectedly heavy door. Velvet winced "mind the old girl Faye!"

"Sorry Ethel!" Faye said, stroking the dash. Holly curled up in the back seat with her headphones on, rolled her eyes at the two chattering women and turned up her music. Ethel rumbled off down the road between both sides of the common to the next village, Hawksford.

They pulled up outside a charity shop.

Goods spilled out onto the pavement, and Velvet rubbed her hands together with glee. "Our first stop, let's go bin dipping girls!" "Holly, pass out the 'bags for life'. The girl obliged, unfolding three large bags from the tower stacked on the back seat beside her, and offered them up "God Velvet, you've got bags for eternity in the back here, never mind life!" They giggled and piled out of the car.

The autumn nip in the air was refreshing after a stuffy back seat ride in the Beetle. The smell of old leather seats and vintage engine was mingling in her nostrils unpleasantly and Holly yawned and stretched out, as the others headed towards the shop. Then something caught her eye across the road - a lady in a long flowing dark green coat was entering one of those crystal shops, the kind of place where slightly spooky ladies with lots of jangly silver jewellery go to buy more silver jangly jewellery and come out with a hoard of crystals and an overdraft.

Holly called to her mum - "guys, I'll catch you up, I want to pop in there," and she pointed her slender finger towards the little shop. They nodded, and they parted company.

Inside the charity shop, the hunt was on. They bypassed the baskets of curled handbags, the shoe rack where someone with size nine feet had been having a clear-out of stiletto heels, and headed to the bric-a-brac shelves. There, resplendent on the middle shelf, was a pretty Royal Doulton tea set.

"See, I told you," said Faye. At twenty pounds all in, Velvet gathered it up, milk jug hanging from her little finger, and gingerly took it to the till. The volunteer painstakingly wrapped each piece in newspaper and into the bag for eternity it went.

On a shelf above the china was an ugly little figurine of a farm boy playing a weirdly proportioned cello, a goose looking on at his feet. Faye ran her finger over the curve of the cello and a familiar waft of butterflies tumbled through her tummy. It was concert day and although she was only second cello for this piece, a performance was a performance, and nerves were part of the deal.

"Faye, ready when you are," Velvet said, interrupting her thoughts. Faye took a deep breath and they headed out into the street. Velvet paused. "I'll pop this in the car lovey, you go and find your baby girl."

***

Holly was entranced by the little shop. The owner was a tall woman in her forties, with long dyed black hair with silver angel wings hanging from her ears. The shop was called Luna, which was also the name of the dog, some type of husky, that lay behind the counter, blue eyes twitching this way and that at customers who passed by. It was quite busy, and the faint smell of incense filled the senses as wind chimes jingled by the open back door. The path led out to the sign posted Apothecary Garden, a small courtyard with an array of herbs in pots, more wind chimes, resin fairy sculptures, Egyptian ladies and Buddha in a variety of poses. Bottles of green, blue and amber stood along the metal shelves. The sunlight shone through them onto the patio stones causing a stained glass window effect. It really was a very nice space to be in, thought Holly.

Faye found her daughter by the dream catchers, the beautiful beaded hangings with feathers and webs of coloured threads that promised a dreamless sleep.

"Mum I might get one of these, I'm still getting those dreams" she said, turning to Faye.

"Good idea, I think we should both get one love," she replied.

"Me too! I've been having honkers every night!" puffed Velvet, who had nipped back inside the charity shop to buy the little cello statuette as a good luck present for Faye, stashed it in the car, then caught up with them in the spooky little shop.

They each chose a dream catcher and took it to the counter. The dog looked toward Holly and lifted her head. As they approached the till, Faye said to the owner, "your dog is gorgeous, and so well behaved!" She couldn't imagine either of hers would sit so quietly behind the counter. Holly stooped down at the side of the counter and stroked her ear. She sat up and stared into the girl's eyes with her cool blue gaze and rested her head on Holly's knee.

The shop owner smiled, "yes, she is a good girl, she's a healer too, she knows when someone needs a little help," she said, glancing at Holly. The conversation stalled while Faye and the girls each tapped their bank cards. As she handed Holly her bag, their fingers met briefly. Elsa, the proprietor jumped.

"Sorry, oh the static in this place, honestly, if you could wire me up to the National Grid, I'd power the whole of Croydon!" she flustered.

They thanked her and made their way out of the shop. Except Holly. She'd felt no static, just a little unease about the brief exchange. She paused by the door and looked back at the woman who was staring at her with large, darkly made-up eyes. Shaking off a waft of anxiety, Holly perked up, seeing the other two chuckling women like schoolgirls by the car.

Velvet had produced the ornament. Faye was touched and appalled at the horrid little piece in equal measure.

"...and why is a boy playing a cello in the farmyard anyway?" Holly laughed as she reached them.

"Hmmm tasteful Mum?!" she said sarcastically.

"It was a gift Holly, from your Aunt Velvet," she said, trying to keep a straight face. Velvet let out a snort followed by a belly laugh, "Oh my God, Aunt Velvet? That makes me feel ancient."

Holly raised her eyebrows, plugged in her headphones and climbed into the back of the car, the ancient leather creaking as she grasped the back of the passenger seat.
They drove out of the village and into the country lanes. Next stop was Swanbridge. It wasn't as busy as Hawksford, nor as picturesque, but there were no less than two charity shops here and Velvet parked up the Beetle between the two.

Two shops later, they'd found a whole set of pretty Queen Anne cups and saucers, a stack of chunky 1970s Meakin with large blue flowers (which Faye wouldn't have given house room to,) and a pretty Royal Albert teapot. Velvet carefully entombed the newsprint mummified china into the front boot of Ethel, and packed it firmly with the remaining bags.

"We'll have to take it easy on the way home girls," Velvet said, as she closed the bonnet. Holly was engrossed in her music picking black varnish off her stubby nails in the back, and Faye sat, ornament on her lap, and closed her eyes as Velvet turned the car around. They rumbled off, heading for home, 'Mission Replenish' complete.

Chapter 8 - A Symphony of Heartbreak

Upstairs in the cottage, an unscheduled crisis was developing. Faye had planned to wear her long black lace dress, her usual concert attire, but as she sat on the edge of the bed, the dress seemed to pull uncomfortably over her tummy and thighs. She took a look in the mirror and realised to her horror that there was no way she could sit and play in it. A row of bulges had appeared that hadn't been there before, and the seams strained and tugged uncomfortably.

"Holy shit, what the actual....." Before she could regain her composure, the dress was off over her head and tossed on the floor in disgust.

She marched into the bathroom and pulled some old neglected scales out from under the old roll top bath. Blowing away the dust she set herself upon it, watching the dial swing through the numbers, but she couldn't read it. She crouched down squinting and to her dismay nearly a whole stone had attached itself to her person, and in shock, she lost her balance and rocked backwards off the scales and onto the bathroom floor. The bump to her coccyx brought tears to her eyes.

Back in the bedroom, the wardrobe was under attack. Hot and bothered, and with one cheek in, one cheek out of her knickers, she leaned into the darkest corners, her hands fumbling through the clattering hangers, stopping at everything black. At last she pulled out something long enough and loose fitting, but as she held the hanger under her bust she realised in the mirror that this was the dress she'd worn to Ben's funeral.

The tiered black fabric fell sadly onto her lap as she crumpled onto the bed. The grief swept over her like it had happened yesterday. She crawled up the bed holding her breath and climbed under the duvet, pulling it over her head. She let out a guttural wail. It had been a long time since she'd cried like this, sadness and longing lurching through her whole body as if to remind every last cell that they were without the love of her life. She fell into an uneasy sleep, nose snuffly from crying, and awoke later, with both dogs standing over her protectively. She felt heavy and disoriented, with only twenty minutes to get to the church.

Pulling herself together, she splashed water on her puffy face, popped her head through the neck of the dress and watched it fall around her body in the mirror. It actually felt lovely on. The very reason she'd chosen it for the funeral all those years ago, light matt, silky fabric with a few small ruffles, and lacing at the front. She slipped her shoes on and tied her hair back as she went down the stairs. A quick slick of make up in the cloakroom a squirt of perfume and she was ready. The dogs looked mournful by the lounge door as she reached for the handle of her cello case.

"Oh alright you two, because you were so sweet looking after me," and she detoured to the kitchen to get a couple of chewy sticks and tossed them across the hallway. Sorrow forgotten, Margaux and Rollo dashed to the living room rug to devour their catch. Faye lumbered out of the house with the large instrument, and made for the high street.

On the common, was a dog walker. A slightly scruffy long haired man in a leather jacket and jeans, he nodded to Faye.

"That's some guitar you've got there," he quipped. She laughed politely, noticing his tattoos and earring. The dog was a large black poodle cross of some kind, sporting a bandana. His owner had a weathered lined face and soulful watery grey eyes.

"What's he called?" asked Faye.

"Hendrix" said the man, and the dog looked up at him on hearing his name.
"He's lovely, enjoy your walk," she said soldiering on with the cello knocking into her legs.

"Rock on, girl!" he called after her.

***

Velvet, delighted with her haul of china was up to her elbows in suds. Holly was on drying up duty and they were on the last cup.

"Right missy, we've got to get to the concert or your mother will have my guts for garters." Holly looked puzzled at the old fashioned phrase. They cleared up, hung up their aprons, touched up their make up and neatened their hair in the small bathroom mirror.

Velvet was nearer Holly's age than Faye's, she was somewhat like a big sister to Holly, yet a younger sister to Faye. Whatever they were, it worked and they craved each other's company and revelled in it when they were together.

The girls arrived at St. Valentine's as

the audience were still mingling in the aisles and entrance. A rather red faced official looking lady with glasses on a string, and a Kingshurst Symphony card dangling between her large bosoms, was loudly asking people to take their seats because of "Health & Safety."

"Sheila's on form tonight," muttered the lady on the door, who was checking tickets and chattering amiably to the public. A man carrying a dubious looking box of wine rolled his eyes and quipped, "give Sheila a lanyard, and she takes a mile!"

"Holls, look there's your mum, is she ok? She looks a bit lost". Faye was standing unpacking her cello in the far corner of the church and did indeed look a little lost. Her eyes were glazed as she adjusted the spike underneath the instrument, her thick curly hair flopping out of its restraining ruffle into her face. As she stood, cello resting against her shoulder, she scraped her hair back into place and spotted the girls in the aisle. This seemed to bring her to, she smiled and managed a discreet wave.

At last in their seats, the audience clapped in the orchestra, the floppy haired conductor and the leader, a balding gent in glasses with a hole in his patent shoe that gaped as he walked across with his violin. He sat down and collected himself, and the conductor raised his baton and the concert began.

Velvet wasn't really into classical music as a rule, and sometimes found these concerts hard to sit through, having been brought up on a diet of 1950s music. The church pews were very hard on the buttocks and she found some of the more meandering pieces a bit of a trial. She'd let her mind wander into a mental inventory of her vintage china collection. Holly loved to watch her mother play, the sway of the orchestra as they swept through the opening piece, Elgar's Nimrod, from the Enigma Variations. The flamboyance of the conductor and the earnest faces of each musician belied the huge emotional wave they produced as one. The soul stirring piece reached its climax and she felt the hairs on her arms stand on end. Faye gulped back a few tears as the last bar floated out into the rafters of the little church. Tonight was going to be tough - once triggered, grief had a habit of raking up the emotions for a day or two. She knew she'd settle back down until the next time but weathering the storm was tricky, and people didn't always understand. It was nearing the anniversary too, that dreadful rainy night; the knock on the door of the cottage, how she'd opened it wondering why Ben hadn't taken a key to be faced with two police officers, a rumble of thunder, and a fork of lightning silhouetting them briefly against the illuminated rain. They informed her that Ben's motorbike had hit a tree, possibly avoiding a deer. There were no witnesses. With their little girl asleep upstairs, they sat her down, and she'd melted into wrenching sobs, slithering off the sofa opposite the two police officers who perched awkwardly in their uniforms, radios turned down to faint fuzzy voices.

The world had kept on turning. Their daughter had grown, and every day, Ben seemed further and further away from their daily lives. Faye had occasionally considered dating but the notion of losing someone again had prevented her from forming any serious attachments. She had made a life, a contented life, broken only by episodes of grief that she managed to wade through, bravely.

A Mozart overture and a short minuet later, and it was time for the interval. The audience drifted into groups of drinkers and non drinkers, as the unchilled budget orange juice table and luke warm winky wine table opened for business.

Mrs Lanyard manned the refreshments with military precision. Over in the kitchenette was Nancy, stoic as ever, furiously washing the thick rimmed glasses and replacing them into a sectioned box as soon as they were drained of their contents.

Tensions were high to get this little operation complete before the orchestra struck up again as no-one wanted to stay behind for too long after.

"Blimey," winked Faye's neighbour, Todd sipping the white wine, "I'd say notes of wood and an undertone of brasso!"

Velvet and Holly sniggered, returning to their pew, and sat down with a wince. Velvet eyed up the prayer cushions but to be honest they looked as hard as bricks. She shrugged off her jacket, folded it, and slid it underneath her bottom, small comfort but it was something. Holly copied and they clapped in the orchestra and conductor for the second half.

Having regained her composure, Faye manoeuvred the bulky cello and sat down, also with a wince, but more due to the scales incident earlier.

The conductor lifted his arms and Beethoven entered the building. Sweeping this way and that, and taking the conductor's hair with it, the audience relished the sound of the Eroica Symphony. Max and Howie were in the front row, transfixed. As it came to a close they waited with bated breath for the conductor's arms to drop to his sides before belting out a loud "bravo!" which startled the ancient double bass player, who dropped his bow sending it clattering down the music stand to the floor.

The conductor, face flushed with pride turned bowed deeply, his combed over hair briefly departing his shining scalp like a swinging loft hatch. He rose, and gestured to the orchestra to stand and take their bows.

"Wooohoo," shouted Holly, as the clapping reached a crescendo. The orchestra were happy, the conductor, hair restored to its factory setting with a smarming hand, was too - but there were two people in the church who weren't. One was Sheila, whose lanyard had wielded little power tonight. She scowled as she stacked the orchestra chairs afterwards, slamming them into each other and made heavy weather of pushing them into the transept with a screech of metal on tiles. The other was a murderer. He lurked at the back of the church, slowly doing up his coat, all the time keeping one eye on his prey. He smiled politely at an elderly couple holding open the heavy wooden door and slipped out behind them. It had started to rain as he dropped down the steps and disappeared into the gloom of the churchyard.

A merry group assembled in the King's Head after the concert, in time for last orders. Faye and Velvet sat huddled in the corner, Max and Howie on one side with Holly, Nancy who had hung up her tea towel for the night, and a couple of musicians from the orchestra. Jim, the trombonist, whose long limbs awkwardly folded under and over the table, sipped a pint, and Jenny a clarinettist who was considerably smaller, nursed a diet lemonade as her dark, shining bob swung to and fro when she laughed.

Faye was a little quieter than usual and Velvet put her arm around her friend and asked if she was ok. Her eyes filled instantly and she nodded, and whispered to Velvet about the dress upset earlier. Velvet hugged her tight, knocking her glasses down her nose and into her gin and tonic. They giggled

"I really like that frock anyway Faye, you should always wear it for concerts, I bet it feels so happy to be out of the wardrobe and out on the town."

Velvet always had a cute way of putting things. Glasses back on, Faye sipped her drink and began to feel a little brighter.

The conversation turned to the murder and how incredible it was, that the town had resumed its activities, and residents had ploughed on regardless. There was talk of suspects and still people wondered why Janice had been in the woods that night. How the mighty Stella coping, running the village single handed without her gossipy sidekick? Faye sucked in a hesitant breath, she didn't like to speak ill of the departed.

Sitting alone in a booth backing onto the main area of the pub was Detective Lydia Appleby. Officially off duty, she was listening to the conversation and sipping a glass of pinot noir. She was no more enlightened by the gossip than any of them, but listened nonetheless. Then a comment piqued her interest - she heard Velvet say "she wasn't actually very friendly, nearly everyone in Kingshurst Village has had a run in with her at some point." Lydia raised an eyebrow - perhaps Janice had seriously rubbed someone up the wrong way one too many times.

The landlord rang the bell for closing and the pub began to empty out. Friends walked friends home. Holly and Faye linked arms outside the pub behind a struggling Todd, who was regretting his neighbourly offer to carry the cello. The wind had billowed up across town and buffeted the large case against his legs. Velvet peeled away and her boyfriend Joe was on the doorstep waiting for her. The rest of them reached the common, and crossed over. For a moment Faye thought she saw a figure over by the trees on the far side. It sent a chill through her but she kept it to herself, not wanting to alarm her daughter. She found herself fumbling for her keys to open the cottage door which swung free as soon as the lock was conquered.

"Oh my goodness Holly! What a night! Todd, thank you so much my lovely, for carrying that all the way back."

Todd stowed the cello safe in the

hallway, and departed with a faux salute. "Right you are Ma'am, g'night all!"

Faye watched him negotiate the garden gates and nip safely into his house before she closed the front door.

That night, the wind raged through the empty streets, whistled through the trees, whipped the chimneys and battered the roofs of Kingshurst Village. Holly dreamt again of the swirling leaves and retreating eyes of Janice. By morning the wind had dropped its flailing limbs and stomped back in retreat. The sun was meekly glowing behind thin misty clouds, crows cawed on the common and the resident geese honked as they emerged from the woods where they had sheltered overnight.

A pre-breakfast scream was heard throughout the town.

The scream belonged to Mr Lanyard. Or precisely Mr Cray, when he discovered his wife, Mrs Sheila Cray, slumped over a crate of glasses on the garden path of their bungalow.

By the time the police left the gloomy scene, it was late afternoon. Mr Cray was in deep shock. His daughter stayed with him and stunned neighbours rallied around. It appeared his wife had been strangled with the aforementioned lanyard, at approximately eleven o'clock the night before. She had lain, undisturbed, with her carefully rollered hair flopping over the back of her head, slowly uncurling in the wind and drizzle to resemble a used mop.

Detective Inspector Appleby had been called away from her Sunday breakfast, consisting of a black coffee and two hearty paracetamol. She calmly followed text book police procedure, but underneath she had a growing unease about this crime and a desire to follow her instincts. Different method, but a similar victim, a middle aged woman, and from what Lydia had gleaned, a woman with an unpleasant personality. She had a nasty feeling, and it wasn't just the paracetamol and caffeine burning into her empty belly.

While the forensic team did their work, Lydia stood on the garden path seemingly fixated on the moss around the flagstones, her thick soled shoe easing a green sodden chunk of it free. Her mind was whirring.

"Ma'am, we're all done here, I'll get the findings to you as soon as possible." Roused from her moss mining, Lydia thanked the young forensics officer without eye contact and headed back into to the bungalow.

It was a miserable day all round. The orchestra members were shocked and Nancy was upset - she knew Sheila wasn't the easiest of women, she could be quite sharp with her at times over the wine glasses, but she still cried genuine tears when she heard the news.

The local amateur dramatics society The Kingshurst Players cancelled their one night only production of Murder at the Vicarage as a mark of respect. No one wanted to venture out in the dark after such an event, and besides, Ursula, the grande dame of the village hall stage knew that it wouldn't make a bean as ticket sales were down, as it was. Better to defer until next year. The sets and costumes weren't going anywhere. The troop were reluctant to cancel, except Ursula's husband Charles, who had come out of retirement to play the Inspector. He was heartily relieved as he hadn't learnt his lines anyway and had written prompts on the inside of a hat that he kept dropping.

Faye was fast asleep on the settee after her busy Saturday of ups and downs. Todd woke her knocking on the door with a pumpkin he'd grown himself in his flourishing vegetable patch. The dogs hadn't even bothered to bark as they recognised his scent through the gap in the door but backed off when they saw the huge squash under his arm.

"I thought Holly might like to carve this for Hallowe'en, might keep her busy?" he said, thumping it into her stomach. He then dropped the bombshell of another murder.

Bewildered, and still holding the pumpkin in her arms, she closed the door with her bottom and sat on the stairs with a bump. How was she going to break it to Holly, who was just turning a corner with the bad dreams. The murderer must have followed Sheila home, from the concert, she concluded. Closing her eyes she scanned the audience in her mind, but all she could picture was Max and Howie in the front row grinning at her.

Holly appeared over the banister above, her long red hair dangling like spun gold in the morning light. She clocked the pumpkin in her mother's arms.

"Oooh is that for me?" She asked. Faye took a deep breath and called her down.

Chapter 9 - All Hallows Evensong

Once again the village was dragged from the pretence of normality that had tucked its way around the bruised residents like cotton wool. Talk of a meeting to be held in the church hall was brewing. Nancy had already offered to do teas but the Reverend declined her offer, much to her disappointment.

"We won't be there for that long Nancy, and the press might even be there, we'll make it as short as possible."

Taking pity on her crestfallen face, he suggested she would be the perfect person to hand out leaflets at the door. Satisfied with her role she raised an eyebrow and headed towards Stella Mayhew who, having peeled off her ageing Barbour jacket to reveal a large bosom encased in leopard print silk, had begun deftly unfolding tables around the edge of the hall. She stopped for a moment to hand Nancy the leaflets from a picnic basket.

Faye sat in the Decadia after closing and pushed a piece of apple cake around a pretty Wedgwood plate, with a fork. Usually she'd have hoovered up the unsold slice in a flash, but the butterflies in her tummy had made off with her appetite at the thought of the village meeting. The sinister reality of what was going on in Kingshurst Village, was upon her. Velvet and Holly were chattering in the kitchen, planning a shopping trip to a recently opened vintage store in Swanbridge.

"You'll love it Holly," she enthused, "real retro stuff apparently, 50s 60s and some really cool 70s bits!"

Holly loved shopping with Velvet, her enthusiasm was catching. Faye clocked that her friend was distracting Holly beautifully. Prompted by her empathy she rose out of her slump to join them.

Finishing up in the cafe, they made their way to the church hall. Most of the villagers were in attendance. As predicted, the press were at the back, clunking about with cameras and microphones. Faye had recognised the BBC reporter outside doing a broadcast, his hair blowing sideways in the wind. Inside the hall a collection of local villagers, concerned parents, business owners and local busybodies took their seats, the sound of moving chairs on the varnished floor groaning periodically above the low chatter.

There was a sharp knock on the table at

the front. The room fell silent. The Reverend stood, Stella hovering by his side. He raised a hand and addressed the gathering.

"Good evening ladies and gentlemen, residents, the police and the good people of the press," he clasped his hands behind his back and continued.

"Unfortunately, as you no doubt have heard, another suspected murder has taken place in our village. We shall get onto that shortly. But first may I draw your attention to the obligatory fire regulations." He went on to remind everyone where the exits were, his gesturing mirrored by Stella who stood like an air stewardess elaborately marking the side doors with her hands, face as stern as a school mistress. The Reverend did a double take at her and paused to collect himself. There was a snigger from the front row - Joe was the culprit and Velvet jabbed him in the ribs.

The Reverend continued. "I will, of course, be available to speak to anyone who is anxious about recent events, my door is always open - but tonight may I introduce Detective Inspector Appleby who has joined us from the Metropolitan Police." He stepped to one side and politely ushered Stella off centre stage.

Lydia Appleby stood up and took her place in front of the gathering. "Thank you

Reverend. Ladies and gents, I'm sure you have a lot of questions. My colleagues and I will be here for an hour after the meeting to hear anything you may wish to tell us, likewise any questions you may have, we urge you to ask at the end. Please come forward with any information you have, anything out of the ordinary you have seen or heard. But for now, here is what we know."

She proceeded to give an account of the approximate time, location and nature of the murder, the whereabouts of the victim that evening, and the subsequent horrific find the next morning. She stuck to the facts as she knew them. The audience fidgeted uncomfortably on the plastic chairs, listening to the grimly served up details. The press snapped the odd photo. At the end of her talk a member of the press raised their hand.

"Jack Pearson, Evening News. Ma'am is this killing linked to the recent stabbing? Do we have a serial killer on the loose?"

There were gasps and muttering from the audience. Lydia had been expecting this question.

"No official link has been made, we are awaiting the forensic report, and we will update the public as soon as we know more." And she closed the question down.

There followed a number of arms

shooting into the air and shouts, but Lydia stood her ground.

"Furthermore, FURTHERMORE," she raised her voice until the crowd quietened. "I urge you all to be vigilant, move safely in groups of two or more around the area, particularly in the hours of darkness. Check in with loved ones and inform the Police of anything out of the ordinary."

There were more shouts as she exited the spotlight under a flurry of flash bulbs.

Chairs were dragged and tables budged into place by Stella's ample hips until what resembled a school parents' evening was in place. The police sat behind their makeshift desks and people hovered about not wanting to be the first in the queue. After a tumbleweed five minutes of leaflet reading the villagers edged closer one by one to speak to the officers.

"I don't want to talk to anyone really" said Max, eager to leave. "Pub?" They all nodded, heading towards the exit. Only Nancy remained, in a professional capacity as leaflet distributor, giving out slips of paper with the police contact details at the door. Velvet gestured to her the universal drinking mime for pub, and Nancy nodded and winked back. Before too long they were piled into a booth glumly sipping their drinks. Holly was behind the bar. Joe reached into his pocket and pulled out the slip of paper. He flattened it on the pub table and they all stared at it.

"They better find this little fucker before I do," he said. Velvet rolled her eyes.

"Or what? Who made you The Equaliser all of a sudden, Joe?" He wrinkled up his nose.

"I just couldn't bear it if..... well you know..." her face softened.

"I'll be careful. We all will, won't we girls?" They nodded miserably. Faye decided to wait for Holly's shift to end - even though the landlord saw her home, she suddenly felt very unsettled and wanted to walk her back herself - the nights seemed to be getting darker and the spooky season was nearly upon them.

Hallowe'en had always been a big thing in Kingshurst. The "trick or treaters" were relentless but with recent events the Village Association had a rethink. They organised a pumpkin hunt in the high street - every shop would have a pumpkin in their window, and children could go in to collect a treat. A safer, more controlled version. Some complained that the freedom and excitement would be lost, but all in all, most people thought it was a good idea. With upmost efficiency, head of the committee Stella planned the event, and organised sponsorship from the various businesses on the high street.

In the days coming up to Hallowe'en, pumpkins in varying themes started to appear in shop windows. There would be an award for "best pumpkin" and the competition was fierce. No Pinterest page was left unsearched in the quest to create the most elaborately carved vegetable.

The day itself came and went with a sigh of relief. Nobody was really buying into the grimness of the season for obvious reasons. Velvet and Holly sat in the Decadia watching the last of the pumpkin hunt stragglers winding their way up the high street. Velvet felt sad not to be dressing up this year in her cute retro witch costume. She'd settled for a black dress and blacking out a tooth with mascara.

"Next year we'll have a party at the Decadia, we can really go mad and bake loads of proper ghoulish cakes Holly," she said, biting into a shop-bought fiendish fancy.

"Oooh this tastes like ear ache" she moaned to the bewildered teenager. Sometimes Velvet had the strangest terminology. She fidgeted in her own flung together costume, a pair of striped black and white tights and a short black dress, her old Doc Martens and a black jumper.

"Velve, you know that lady, the one I found, do you think she knew who it was that, you know, killed her?" She asked, unable to look Velvet in the eye.

"I think she may have Holly, I mean, there had to be a reason she was in the woods at night. She must have been meeting someone, maybe it was a love affair gone wrong?" offered Velvet, trying to reassure Holly that it wasn't a random killing, but equally unsure as to whether she was saying the right thing. She'd never had to justify a murderer before.

"Ewww at her age," said Holly in disdain, adding "O.M.G., gross!" Velvet laughed, "there's no age limit on passion Holly, and the older you get the more urgent it can become!" Holly pulled a face and shuddered.

Velvet shrugged. "Come on you, Joe will drop you home. Thanks for helping me out today." She got up and crossed to the counter, opened the till and handed Holly a thin bundle of five pound notes.

"Thanks Velvet, I'm saving up for some new boots." She tucked the notes into her bag and waited by the door for Joe. He pulled up outside on his motorbike, she climbed on the back and he barely felt her weight. She held tight as he carefully moved off on to the road across the common, checking his mirrors around the little bends and looking back and forth at junctions. He knew Faye was wary of the bike, and he promised he'd always be extra careful dropping Holly home. Respectful of his promise to her, he crept along the road at a snail's pace and came to a stop outside the cottage. She jumped off, thanked him with a wave, ran to the door and let herself in. He watched until she was safely inside, then turned the bike around and headed back to the cafe with a little more speed.

The wind blew up the high street, carrying the tumbling leaves with it, past the grinning pumpkins and gloomy shop windows. Above, a full harvest moon sat glowing in the sky. It shone down over Kingshurst watching steadily as people blew out their candles, munched on left-over sweeties and flicked their kettles on after a half hearted Hallowe'en.

Chapter 10 - Now is the Winter

Autumn was in retreat, its vivid oranges and yellows giving way to mushy browns and greys. Winter reached out its frozen finger and flicked the heating on with a clunk. The recent winds had stripped every last leaf from the trees, and on her dog walk one late November morning, Faye, took a different route across the common. Around the lake she walked, wind buffeting the water into a choppy sea more fit for gulls than ducks. The paths were still soft underfoot, a light echoey thud sounded with each step as if beneath the brown powdery carpet of soil lay floorboards, and a room below with puzzled occupants looking up wondering who was passing above.

Holly stayed home working on a project, headphones on and pieces of paper scattered across her bedroom floor. She had acknowledged her mothers elaborate mime of walking the dogs with a thumbs up. Faye was glad to step out into the breezy cold air. The radiators had been on full blast and the house was stuffy. She pulled her coat up around her chin, and rearranged her scarf around her head and shoulders. The dogs darted in and out of the bushes, following scents and pricking their ears at the slightest rustle and distant voice. On they went, reaching the clearing in the woods, switching from leafy mulch to mossy grass and pebbles underfoot. Faye stopped at the side of a swampy area. She felt safe enough with her fierce companions.

When Holly was little they called this area the 'magic swamp' - here the trees were crooked and gnarly, bent twisted limbs entwined, trying to escape the rising water which rose and fell throughout the year. Some summers the ground was bone dry, and other times of the year the ducks ventured over the common and used the pond like a holiday retreat. It never grew lilies or pond weed, no fish lived in there and the ducks lost interest within a few days and returned to the village pond. Today the water was quite high. The streams and springs under the ground often got clogged with forest debris and the recent rain had topped it up. The dogs sniffed at the water's edge, Rollo jumped back, startled at his own reflection. The weak winter sun caught the upper sides of the twisted trees and the breeze rippled their reflection and his, in the dark water. It was an eerily beautiful place.

She turned to walk on, the breeze blowing a piece of hair into her face, she swept it away, and looked up to see a lone deer standing in the shadow of a large oak tree. She froze, the deer stared at her, his nose twitching and ears flicking back and forth, scanning the woodland for danger. She didn't alert the dogs, although they were both rooted to the spot, sniffing the air intently. She took the opportunity to snap their leads back on.

The encounter lasted no more than a minute before the animal stepped back into the shadows and disappeared. Faye felt a flutter of dread at seeing the creature, she had never felt the same about them since Ben's accident. She knew it was irrational and kept her feelings to herself, deer weren't usually cast as the harbingers of doom, but to Faye, this is precisely what they were. Sighing deeply, she wandered on, the dogs pulling at their leads.

There was a reluctance to go deep into the woods these days, most people skirting around the edges, and walkers were less inclined to catch an oncoming eye and changed course upon spotting another person. So, when Faye heard a voice, she jumped, clutching her scarf to her chest. There on the bench by the lake was the old rocker she'd seen on the way to the concert. His dog Hendrix sat by his side, studying the comings and goings on the water, his curly haired ears jiggling as he turned his head from one side of the pond to the other. His owner introduced himself this time.

"Rick Falconer," he gestured to himself with an impish smile, raised eyebrow and shrugged his long hair back over his shoulder. "And you're Faye," he added, lazily crossing his booted ankle over his skinny knee.

Faye felt her tummy turn and replied politely, "have we met?"

"No, but I promised I'd keep an eye on you love" he said with a wink.

Although not said in a sinister way, Faye was alarmed, sensed by the dogs who started to growl and bark, jumping about in front of her .

"By whom, may I ask?" she called over the din, untangling herself from the knot of leads and harnesses. But there was no reply. He'd gone. Just upped and gone without offering an explanation. She turned this way and that but there was no sign of him, or Hendrix. A wave of unease sent her reeling back through the woods, her foot momentarily dipping into a little hole dug by some animal or other, which sent her stumbling forward and into the open of the common. A few deep breaths and she regained her composure but her strides were peppered with little skips as she hastened towards the high street.

"Sorry, did I scare you love?" She spun around to see Rick now sitting on a bench by the road.

"No, erm I, well yes! What did you mean, what you said back there?" She stammered. Hendrix looked from him to her, fully engaged with the conversation, frizzy ears once again quivering with each turn of his head.

"I knew your husband, love. Ben played sax on a few of my album tracks, I promised I'd look out for you if there was any trouble, you know," he gestured to the village, "and with all this shit going down, I thought I'd better step up, you know, keep my promise."

She was confused. When would Ben have made such a request? She decided at that moment that this was just a scenario that Rick had somehow cooked up in his drug riddled brain. So, she politely replied:

"Well I appreciate the sentiment, but I'm fine, I have friends. I don't need 'keeping an eye on' - but thank you. Enjoy your walk, take care," and she started towards the shops.

His watery grey eyes crinkled up at the edges and he smiled, raised a hand in defeat and stood. "You take care Faye, no harm meant."

She flinched inwardly at his use of her name but resisted looking back until she'd crossed the road. When she did, he'd already gone.

Slippery sod, she thought, and made a mental note to look him up later and check out the album. Any chance to hear Ben play, however small the snippet, felt like his hand on her heart. To hear the very air from his lungs shaped into music, the breaths between the notes hanging in the ether like crystals on a chandelier. Oh that she could reach out and pass her hand through them, glittering and cold, for a few moments. That upon holding one, it would warm against her skin, just like his cold lifeless cheek warmed against hers in the funeral home, when she sat perched on a chair, arm draped over his body. Her eyes filled with glossy sadness. She blinked back the memory as she reached the high street, drawn to the glowing colours of the green grocers.

The vibrant fruit and vegetables lit by the bare bulbs hanging above, warming the gloom of the morning, beckoned her, like a sanctuary.

There were hints of Christmas - sprouts were in! She felt a flutter of excitement, or was it dread? She could never quite make up her mind about Christmas. She'd loved it as a child but without her parents and Ben, bringing up Holly had been even harder at this time of year. But, as with other things, friends rallied around, and they were seldom alone through the Christmas holidays. Cosy nights in, Christmas movies, invites and trips out. There was so much to look forward to, that the grief of missing loved ones could be soothed just enough to get through until January, when the grey days of the new year held their own challenges.

She feigned looking at the fruit and vegetables, while Ted the grocer was talking loudly to someone about getting chestnuts in for December. He clocked her with his dark hooded eyes and asked, "you alright there love?" His weathered hands scooped up a dozen oranges. She nodded - her own hands that were examining a large cooking apple had ceased to belong to her, she didn't know how long she'd stood with the misshapen green Bramley, until Velvet called across to her from The Decadia.

Faye made it across the road, limping slightly from turning her ankle in the woods. She burst into tears and fell into Velvet's arms, the dogs wrapping themselves around the pair.

Howie and Max, who were on their way up the high street, dodging between the shoppers, saw them. They joined the embrace and bundled into the cafe. No questions, no advice, just good honest hugs. They knew that Faye sometimes had these moments, they knew that words were futile and that sometimes she just needed love and kindness. They had loved Ben too. He'd been their first friend when they moved to the village.

Over the years, there had been those who tried to fix her grief, the main intention to make things more comfortable for themselves. Faye recalled the moment she realised that with bereavement comes a never ending round of forgiveness. Forgive them for not understanding, for saying the wrong thing, for not saying anything, or for making the most ludicrous assumptions.

It was trench warfare, and one trudged on, day after day - sometimes lying in the mud, breathing in the earthy smells, head full of dead leaves; then out of nowhere, memories like rays of sun would shine warmly on her face as she grappled the stoney walls and rose to bask in their heat. Snipers were always waiting with bullet shaped ill-thought out remarks. Forgive.

The banal phrases in cards - "he's in a better place," "he's with God," "at least you had Holly," "you'll meet someone else" - like labels tied to ugly cuddly toys thrust upon her, that they expected to be spread out on her duvet of bereavement as comforts. Forgive.

The self serving phrase by one acquaintance 'getting used to the new normal' was like slipping a dagger into her ribs. Forgive. Her friends had dwindled down to the people holding her now, who understood that grief was natural, that there was no cure, that love and patience were all that was required. To sit with her in her grief and allow it to pass.

So, she may not be the same girl she was, her behaviour may seem odd at times, her priorities altered, her perceptions askew; but her resilience and her empathy had grown tenfold.

They valued her friendship, her intuition and her self deprecating, honest humour. She and they were blessed.

Tragedy had brought them together like a thread woven in and out of their clothes, pulled by some unknown force, drawing them closer, connected for always. She was worth all the trouble it took to love her.

Chapter 11 - One on the Stroke of Midnight

It was Christmas Eve. Holly's 19th birthday. She was busy preparing for a small party, with some of her college friends in the cottage. Twinkling fairy lights were strung around the cosy lounge, and the Christmas tree in the corner glowed red, green and gold, intruding into her pink birthday decorations - the curse of being born at Christmas. She gazed at it and dived back into the bag of pink.

Christmas birthdays had their upside, party food was available in every supermarket, Prosecco was on offer in the mini market and people were in party mode. Velvet had baked a cake and was with her mother in the kitchen, shrieking with laughter about something. Holly felt blessed. Her friends started arriving, gifts were piling up under the 'birthday tree' (now jauntily re-purposed with pink baubles and a birthday banner sash diagonally draped like a pageant queen.)

Faye had been laughing straight for the past hour. Her cheeks ached and her eyes were streaming. Velvet, fuelled only with Prosecco and Pringles had been icing the cake, and whilst being a great baker, the precision required for cake decoration was not in her repertoire. The pair of them had been attempting a cake that Holly had seen on Pinterest, Faye had her iPad propped up against a bag of flour. Said elegant rose gold and pink towering creation glowered haughtily at them both from the screen. Their effort was indeed rose gold and pink with the attached chocolate shards, but for the life of them, adding Happy Birthday Holly and a stylised 19 was proving impossible. There were blobs of discarded, scraped off attempts all over them, and the table.

Going in for another try was Faye, this time with one foot on a kitchen chair, tongue between her teeth, and one eye closed. She hovered above the cake and squeezed the icing bag one more time.

"Yes yes that's it, slowly, slowly Faye, good!" Velvet gasped frozen to the spot, hands clasped, a dusting of icing sugar across her left eyebrow. Faye reached the end of the wording, and dabbed the nozzle against the cake to finish. Lifting it away whilst exhaling slowly, her chest was fit to burst.

"That's it.... I've done it, thank gawd for that, I thought I was gonna pass out Velve," she blurted, and with that, the nozzle came out of the bag and icing erupted in huge swirls onto the floor in front of them. The dogs dived in for the cleanup. Velvet held the door open and Faye ceremoniously carried in the cake, followed by the dogs. The handful of girls and one boy were dancing and singing "Murder on the dance floor…. "   Sophie Ellis-Bextor's pretty vibrato voice carried through the house. They turned, saw the cake and made great whoops of delight. The dogs retreated to their bed under the kitchen table, curled around each other like autumn leaves. Rollo's eyebrows twitched alternately as he watched the dancing through the doorway, whilst simultaneously keeping an eye on the cake.

"Happy bRithday?! Exclaimed Holly. "Ohhhh Emmmm Geeee mother!" They hooted with laughter, Faye bent double with the giggles, apologising profusely.

There was a knock at the window, Max and Howie waving a bottle and a present, and behind them was Todd from next door who gave a double thumbs up, two giant packets of crisps dangling from his folded fingers. Faye let them in and Holly headed over for hugs.

The adults left the kids to it, after extracting themselves from the dancing, all except Max, who moved 80s style fearlessly among the youngsters, glass in hand.

In the kitchen Margaux was shamelessly licking icing off the corner of the table with her long tongue, back legs on the kitchen chair and her stubby front paws on the table top. Faye scooped her up and handed her to Howie who fed her the end of one of the 'pigs in blankets' he'd swiped off the baking tray. The squidgy morsel went down in one. Faye cleaned the table and laid out the nibbles. Velvet opened the cheaply procured Prosecco, and there were giggles as Howie realised they'd bought the same brand that was on special offer. Todd proposed a toast to being single, albeit enforced. Faye sighed and agreed it was nice to make one's own decisions - she'd long decided she'd never marry again, Ben was her one and only. Todd drained his glass and plunged his hand into the crisps he'd brought. His wife Moira had left him a couple of years ago. She'd packed a suitcase and walked out one evening when he was out at the off licence buying wine. She sent a single text saying he'd never see her again, she'd met someone else, someone with money, ambition and a villa in Portugal and not to try and find her. He obliged wholeheartedly, reeling from his lucky escape. She'd never shown him much tenderness. He couldn't do a thing right when they were together and he spent more and more time in the garden, wrapped up in winter, pottering in the shed just to keep out of her way. His only fear was that she would return, wanting money and turn his quiet tax accountant, gardening life upside down.

Moira had never really spoken to Faye, choosing instead to turn her head away whenever she'd tried to engage. Faye felt for him, all alone, he seemed a sensitive soul. She'd made him dinner a few times, and the odd cake. He had once asked her out on a date but she'd declined, he was a bit old for her anyway and when she said no, the relief that swept across his face was palpable. He later explained that he felt he ought to give it a go but actually he didn't really fancy her. They'd had a laugh about it and no more was said. Normal neighbourly service resumed.

After a team game of charades at the table by the adults, a conga of teenagers headed by a very sweaty Max burst into the kitchen. They all joined and the side kicking eel snaked its way around the little house, Todd flailing around at the back hanging on for dear life with the dogs barking and skipping behind.

It was late when Joe arrived to pick Velvet up in her beloved Ethel. Parents picked up their youngsters after drawn out hugs. Todd bowed deeply on the path "milady," he said to Faye "I bid thee goodnight and a Merry Christmas, as I do believe the church clock doth striketh the midnight hour!" His mock Shakespeare fizzled into mumblings as he staggered backwards through his garden gate.

Max and Howie's rendition of Silent

Night faded out over the common as they headed towards the bright lights. Indeed the church bells rang Christmas Day in, as a small congregation gathered for Midnight Mass in the distance. Then all was calm, all was silent at the cottage.

Then, as the world stood still for just a second, Faye, standing totally alone in front of her house, saw him. On the grass opposite, there in the darkness, stood Ben. She felt an enormous thump of her heart, and she held her breath, frozen to the spot, her eyes wide as if trying to gather all the information in the darkness. His curly hair silhouetted against the town lights, the slope of his shoulders. She opened her mouth to call his name but no sound came out. At that moment Holly called, "Mum, come in, it's freezing," and in the split second she glanced around to see her daughter draped against the front door, she turned back and he was gone. Her heart felt as if it had been on pause, a breath finally escaped her lips and hung briefly in the air as she walked back to the house. She didn't tell Holly, who was deliriously happy from her party. Guilt flooded her mind that she'd raised a glass about being single. She busied herself clearing up the kitchen, periodically looking out onto the dark common. Holly opened her presents dreamily on the sofa. Most of her guests had managed birthday wrapping paper despite the time of year. Bath bombs and perfume, a book about vintage make-up, a delicate necklace and bracelet set, gothic looking nail polishes and earrings. She gathered up her stash and headed upstairs happier than she'd felt in a long while.

Faye took a chamomile tea up to bed and stood sipping it close to the bedroom window. She saw nothing, just the stars in the night sky, a lazy crescent moon hanging above the festively lit village, and her own floral tea scented breath against the pane.

However much she told herself it was the Prosecco, she knew. She knew it had been Ben. His spirit, not just an image of him she had somehow projected. Whatever it was, she felt him near, her hair twitched at the roots around her ear as his invisible hand stroked her dark glossy hair. She peacefully felt a shiver down her spine but she also felt loved.

She climbed into bed and slept in his invisible embrace until Christmas morning, when the pale yellow winter sun shone through a retreating mist on the common. The streets of Kingshurst Village were quiet, cars frosted over and shops closed as families rose and gathered inside their houses to open gifts, eat fancy breakfasts, or prepare heaps of vegetables - others slept on oblivious, nursing hangovers. Mums who had been up half the night re-settling excited children staggered back upstairs, ricocheting off the banisters, after putting twenty five pound turkeys in the oven. Children who had been wakeful, listening for Father Christmas, snoozed in deeply whilst their exhausted parents stole an extra half hour's sleep before all hell broke loose in front of the Christmas tree.

There were two houses where two widowers sat quietly at their breakfast tables waiting to be picked up by relatives. Two men whose Christmases would never be the same. Two bewildered gents who were unaware that they'd crossed the mind of most of the village and prayers had been said for them at midnight mass.

At twelve thirty, once again the family of friends re-grouped at Max and Howie's apartment above Foxes Gallery including Nancy who hadn't spent Christmas with them before. She'd smuggled in her own crocheted dish cloths, looking forward to plunging her hands into the kitchen sink later after the King's Speech.

"Merry Christmas my darlings," bellowed Max, as he poured the wine.

"Cheers to the chefs!" Velvet toasted, raising her glass and sipping the dry white Pouilly Fumé, Max's favourite.

Crackers were pulled, hats were perched, jokes told, and daft cracker prizes discarded as soon as the food appeared. The meal was a triumph. Roast turkey and all the trimmings. Howie, a little weary from his dawn raid to put the turkey in the oven, had been drinking champagne since trimming the sprouts. He slumped a little in his chair, his hat sliding off his head and floating lazily down to the floor. He missed his mouth with a sprout, gently dabbing the green vegetable onto his cheek stamping it with gravy. Velvet gazed up and down the table at the merry pink faces and even Todd, who had at first declined the invite, was thoroughly enjoying himself. "Toddy, have another potato old chap!" said Max, stabbing the crisped shining carbohydrate and plonking it on Todd's plate. He didn't refuse, they were his absolute favourite. Max returned to telling Joe, earnestly about the Benedictine monks who had once made the smoky crisp wine that he was slugging down, his large hand dwarfing the glass. Random toasts were made, "to friends!" "to sprouts!" "to Velvet's antique gravy boat!" - a cheer erupted - "and to all who sail in her!" quipped Todd to which he added awkwardly, "err, the boat, not Velvet of course!" Finally "to absent friends!" - sighs followed that one. Faye thought about last night on the Common. It felt like a dream. She'd kept it to herself. Her little golden moment. Her Christmas present from him.

Dinner over, Nancy sprung into action and cleared the plates for Max to make his entrance, flaming Christmas pudding aloft. Howie followed with the brandy and matches, just in case the pyrotechnics failed. An hour later and all that shopping and prepping, timing and fretting, concluded in eight very full, very festive, squiffy people. At three pm, the elderly King, the father of the nation, entered via the flat screen television and wished them all a Merry Christmas and a Happy Healthy New Year. His Majesty said, "grief is the price we pay for love" and never was a truer word spoken. The merry throng of friends raised a glass and heartily agreed,

"God save the King!"

Nancy chimed in with a "here, here" as she sidled steadily towards the kitchen sink.

Chapter 12 - Betwixtmas

It was Monday, or was it Tuesday? Whatever it was, it was one of those bleary food and movie filled days between Christmas and New Year, where the most exercise taken, was crossing the lounge between the Quality Street and the sofa. Where one meal rolled into the next and consisted of placing random items from under foil onto a plate.

The group of friends had laid low for a few days, the weather was bitter. Then one afternoon the sun came out. Smart phones beeped in unison around the village as a group text was received

"Anyone up for a walk, cos I have eaten own body weight in mince pies, need to shift some sugar!" The author was Howie. He hovered with one foot on the bottom step staring idly at the shoe rack, two pairs of wellie boots bent with misery at having been neglected. His artists eye picked out the colours of the shoes while he awaited a reply. His phone buzzed. "Yes, need to move my fat butt off the sofa before it melds with the cushions," replied Velvet, whose bottom was far from fat.

Max replied from upstairs, "meeee, but bring me up a turkey sandwich first!"

Howie wasn't about to start making sandwiches. "No way Max, get your peachy arse out of bed and get down here, it's one o'clock!"

Max groaned but smiled to himself. 'Peachy eh? I've still got it,' he thought, looking at his pyjama clad backside in the mirror.

By quarter to two, five of the group had assembled on the common. Velvet and Faye blearily hunched together, holding one dog lead each. Max and Howie were bickering over who had the door keys and Todd appeared on his front step blinking into the sun like starved bear emerging from hibernation. He waved across to them and loped down the path, his long scarf momentarily stopping him in his bear tracks as it caught on the picket fence.

The winter sun was low in the sky and gave little warmth to the ramblers. They chatted and laughed, reminiscing about Christmas Day, potatoes and pudding.

"How is Holly? Asked Velvet. Faye

replied, "not bad, she's got a friend over, they were upstairs listening to ancient records on my mums old box record player, it was an awful Barry Manilow single blaring out of the spare bedroom as I left!"

She felt a twinge of guilt making fun of her parents record collection from the seventies, but there were indeed some absolute corkers amongst them. Faye used to love the old record player, red leatherette with a blocky little arm and needle that you could set to auto, stack the singles on the spindle in the middle and watch them drop one by one onto the turntable as the arm moved robotically onto the vinyl. The pop and hiss, then music would burst through the built in speaker right through her middle it felt, leaving her no choice but to dance around the spare room to the old tunes. She was so happy when Holly found it, aged thirteen and spent a whole weekend working her way through the seven inch singles. The magical effect wore off after a while but every now and again she had a little record session. She heard the two girls giggling and the clumping of dancing feet as she left. Her mum would have loved this, she thought, heart full for a moment. She didn't often think of her mother these days. It seemed so long ago she died, such a lot had happened since. She felt guilty about that too. Guilt was bereavement's little side kick, it seemed. She rarely felt one without the other chiming in - like the gift that keeps on giving.

When the walkers reached the woods they passed the spot where Janice's body had been found. There was still a police notice asking for information. It sent a chill through them all.

"Has anyone worked out why she was up here?" asked Howie, "She must have known her killer, to be consorting with them in the woods at night?"

The others answered with blank faces. They didn't linger, and moved on into the trees, up and along the mulchy paths, with deep breaths, linked arms and tangled leads, teetering through the muddy patches. Max and Howie marched through them smugly in their wellingtons. The dogs, tummies low to the ground on account of having short legs, were particularly grubby by the time they reached the other side of the woods. Todd lagged behind a little, he was feeling a bit rough around the edges. The toll of too much rich food and drink over a short period was catching up with him. He wasn't used to it, living alone he barely cooked and when he did, it was a limited repertoire of simple foods. He woke up that morning convinced Christmas Day's selection of vegetables had worn off, and scurvy had set in. They reached a stile behind the church and he hauled his scrawny frame over.

Max turned back and frowned. "Are you alright Todd? Steady fella," he quipped, offering his arm, which Todd took gratefully.

"I'm just feeling a bit weary," he huffed. "Actually, I think I need to sit down, my head is spinning."

With that, Max wheeled him around to the nearest bench, a very old barnacled oak seat in the churchyard. Todd sat down and heaved a sigh. The others had carried on, oblivious.

"Todd, is everything ok? How long have you been feeling like this?" Have you booked a doctors appointment?" Max fired questions at him not waiting for a reply.

"I think you need an MOT pronto! Phone the GP in the morning - you could have a well man check up!" Todd raised his hands, palms up, towards Max "Whoa, steady Max, I'm just feeling a bit under the weather, honestly, no need to worry."

Despite his protestation, Max dashed off a quick text to Howie up ahead. "Todd having funny turn, catch u up in pub," but that was enough to make the herd of friends turn and thud back across the churchyard.

Faye slapped a motherly hand on Todds forehead to check for a temperature. Velvet sat beside him taking his hand. Howie crouched in front of him. Todd squirmed with embarrassment, "I'm ok, honestly guys, I just feel a bit rubbish after all that food and drink."

Only after they had grilled him thoroughly for symptoms which included fuzzy vision and numbness in his face and feeling very queasy, did they help him up and head for home, any ideas of the pub discarded.

They reached the cottage. "I'll take him in some dinner later," said Faye, trying to picture what was in the fridge. They nodded. "I can still hear you know - honestly guys I'm ok," said Todd, and promptly collapsed onto the grass, unconscious.

The ambulance took only ten minutes to arrive, flashing, and squealing its siren across the common. Todd came around with the crew attending him, and after a brief question and answer session he was loaded into the flashing vehicle. Max volunteered to accompany him. Howie had taken his keys while they waited, and let himself into the house to grab a hospital bag. He filled a drinks bottle that was on the kitchen drainer, and grabbed a packet of biscuits. It was so quiet in the house, so tidy, so clean and so terribly empty. He dashed into the bedroom down the hall and grabbed the half read book from the bedside table, reading glasses, a pair of pyjamas from the airing cupboard, and some underwear from the drawer. He felt like the world's biggest snoop but couldn't resist glancing this way and that as he gathered the loot. Grabbing toiletries and box of what looked like current medication, he darted back to the kitchen and unplugged Todd's phone charger which stretched onto the table lying in wait for its counterpart from the socket behind the kitchen door. In doing so, he knocked a collection of shopping bags off the hook on the door. He came face to face with something that stopped him in his tracks. It was a newspaper clipping from the local rag.

The headline read "Battle Axe Murders, Police Stumped" followed by two head shots of the victims and a write up of recent events, the emboldened first paragraph read:-

The murders of two local women known for their 'battle axe' personalities and brusque manner has stumped detectives and shaken the local community.

It wasn't so much the article, but the placement of it. It was pinned to a noticeboard on the back of the kitchen door, surrounded by photographs of the woods, the common, other newspaper clippings, and even a few dried pieces of fauna presumably from the surrounding woodland.

Howie froze at the grim collage for a few moments, his breathing heavy from rushing about. He looked about the kitchen as if to find an explanation. Perhaps Todd was an amateur sleuth or maybe just a bit of a ghoul? The other alternative was too disturbing to comprehend. Surely he wasn't capable of murder. He decided then and there not to mention this to the others. Todd was a friend, he was unwell and anything other than support at this time would be inappropriate. No, he would keep this unsettling discovery to himself for the time being, and draped the cooking apron and collection of bags for life, minus one for the things he'd gathered, back onto the hook behind the door and left the house.

At the front gate he met the others. The ambulance had already left.

"They've gone to King's College Hospital. Max asked if you could meet him there."

Howie nodded bleakly, and the small crowd dispersed promising to keep each other updated on the group chat. Faye took Howie's inability to meet her eye as an attempt to stifle an emotional eruption and thought no more of it.

Oblivious to the drama, Holly was in

the kitchen making a festive pasta bake with green and red pasta bows they'd got in a foodie hamper from Max and Howie. Faye had lost her appetite, but was pleased to see Holly busying herself by the stove. The resulting washing up looked a little alarming, but it was a small price to pay. Faye was about to tell her the update, but hesitated. Holly was very fond of Todd. He was a steadying presence next door and they often chatted about her studies. She'd called him Dot when she was little, picked him daisies from the garden and fed them through holes in the fence with her chubby little fingers, as according to her, his perfectly manicured lawn was "bare." No, there was little point in worrying her until they knew more.

At the sprawling building that was Kings College Hospital, Todd sat up in a bed miserably waiting to see a doctor. Max was sitting in a chair beside him fast asleep and snoring. He'd left the house earlier as quite the country squire, but now, face lolling to one side, mouth open and his tall frame collapsing in on itself, buttons gaping over a festive dinner belly, knees splayed and welly boot tops gaping to match his mouth, he resembled some sort of monstrous tweedy nest of chicks waiting to be fed. He certainly looked more like the patient than Todd, who glanced helplessly up and down the busy A&E ward.

His head had started to pound uncomfortably in the last hour and he wished he'd made it home before having his little turn, then no one would have made all this fuss.

Eventually a gaggle of scrub-bedecked medics gathered around the bed as his name, address, symptoms and vital signs were checked yet again; the drip he was hooked up to reviewed; and the doctor who looked approximately twelve, told him that what he had probably suffered from, was a migraine - perhaps brought on by all the rich food and drink of the season. He'd had one years back and now the fuzzy vision, weird sparkles out of the corners of his eye, and throbbing head made sense. However, he was dehydrated and his blood pressure was quite low, so they decided to keep him in for the night, for observation.

Max had resumed his country squire elegance, unfurling from the chair and nodded along with the doctors. A clipboard toting nurse asked about his next of kin, and Todd looked a little embarrassed. He didn't want to bring his estranged wife into the equation, so rustled up a niece. They nodded and left. About an hour later he was wheeled down to a ward. Max followed the bed through the miles of grey and green corridors feeling more and more depressed at each welly boot squeaking corner. He texted Howie as he walked. 'Todd on Balmoral Ward, just heading there now.

Are you on way? Can't abide this place. Need a drink, M', followed by a wine glass emoji.

Upon sending and receiving this text, both Howie and Max simultaneously pictured the small, tired but immaculately clean little hotel they once stayed at in Scotland, grandly named The Balmoral Castle Hotel. Sadly it was neither a castle, nor grand, nor anything resembling Balmoral, the royal residence in the Highlands. They stayed for two nights one November, the floorboards groaned and creaked as they had tottered tipsily to their room on the second floor, the large room key clattering in the lock as they stood giggling trying to open the door. The bed was comfy but small, and the decor dated - the en-suite bathroom was tiny, but the view was fabulous. Across the lane, was a bridge and a loch, with trees in their autumn foliage reflecting into its still water. It was breathtaking, yet they slept through breakfast the next day and missed the mist rising off the loch and the osprey leaving overhead for warmer climes, eggs, bacon and fried haggis.

When Howie parked the car as near as he could to the looming hospital building, it was already dark. He found his way through the maze of vaguely signposted corridors, and as he entered Balmoral Ward, his stomach lurched. What if his face betrayed him? He took a deep breath and walked towards the Wellington boots sticking out from behind the curtain.

The man in the next bed looked alarmingly lifeless, his mouth open in a perfect circle, from which a column of rough snoring erupted. This, and the softly flashing lights and rhythmic beeps from the monitor ,the only clues that he was indeed alive.

Todd was very pleased to see him and was touched that Howie had put together a bag with his overnight things. Howie suddenly felt a little foolish and hugged Todd gently. Max was relieved to see a pair of his trainers appear from a second bag.

"Oh thank you Howie, you are so thoughtful darling, what would I do without you, my knight with white Nikes!"

He immediately jettisoned his uncomfortable boots, wriggled his cramping toes, and slid his feet into the white lace ups, relishing the feel of the arch supports.

Howie gazed at him, and picked up the discarded wellies. Max was always so appreciative of his efforts, no matter how small - he noted everything, and made sure Howie knew it. Nothing went unmentioned. It was one of the things he loved about Max the most. He made his mind up at that moment, standing in the grey hospital ward, a welly boot in each hand, amidst the beeps and snores and rustling biscuit wrappers, that he would propose to Max at New Year, down on one knee, for the world to see.   Even Todd's offer of a shortbread finger at that moment failed to distract him from this momentous decision and accompanying daydream.

Chapter 13 - Auld Acquaintances

It was New Year's Eve. This year everyone was invited to The Decadia Tearooms, and Velvet had laid on a buffet. She and Holly had been preparing food for what seemed like hours, but actually the singing along to old songs and dancing amongst the tables had taken up a large portion of prep time. Joe had strung fairy lights in their hundreds and the place twinkled invitingly.

The town arrived. Coats were shoved onto the dark bannister by the dozen, and the music was thumping. Booths were snapped up by groups of friends and dancing started almost immediately in the spaces in between. Velvet came out of the kitchen, cheeks flushed from wrestling a dishcloth out of Nancy's hands.

"Go and enjoy the party woman! You're not working tonight!"

Joe slid into view and took Velvet's hand and they began jiving along to Elvis Presley's Jailhouse Rock. They finished, amongst whoops of appreciation. Holly asked

Velvet to teach her the jive, they stepped to one side and the lesson began. Faye smiled at them contentedly just as Joe took her hand and pulled her to him, and walked her through the steps too. She had a vague recollection of jiving with her father years ago. It all seemed familiar and before she knew it they were dancing away, his large hands around her waist and hand, his big booted feet more nimble than she ever could have imagined. It felt good to dance with someone bigger than her. She felt tiny being twirled around and passed from hand to hand in the large span of his arms. The song ended and they parted, laughing, breathless. He said she was a natural, and she felt absurdly proud. Velvet claimed him back for a slow smooch, her arms entwined around his chunky neck, bending him down level with her face, nose to nose they giggled, and although Faye had absolutely no designs on Joe, she felt the tiniest pang of envy. Single life had its moments to be sure but, boy, that had felt so good. Feeling spare and alone, she headed outside for a breath of fresh air.

Outside the front of the Decadia, Howie was sneaking a vape. He jumped when she said hello.

"Are you ok Howie? You seem a bit on edge?" He shifted from foot to foot and shivered as clouds of gingerbread steam billowed around him. "Yeah, I'm fine my darling, you?" he said, unconvincingly.

She nodded and wrinkled her nose in reply. "It's been a funny old year, what with one thing and another." He agreed.
They perched on the windowsill of the cafe leaned against each other and looked up at the stars blinking their last of the year.

"I'm going to make a New Year's resolution Howie, I need to get another part time job, or I might have to sell the cottage," she looked down at her party shoes, as if they held the answer.

"Oh lovey, are things that bad?" Howie tried to make eye contact with her.

"Not yet, but I'm really tightening my belt now. I suppose everyone assumed because I was left the cottage I'd be ok, and I will, but it might have to be somewhere else, which makes me sad." Howie put his arm around her.

"Come on, let's see this year out and we can have a proper chat about it in the New Year - I'm no financial expert but I'm happy to crunch the numbers with you, and we can talk to Todd."

The cold night air was starting to seep through their party clothes. Howie shoved his vape into his pocket and his fingers fell upon another object, a small, square box in which a diamond and platinum gent's ring nestled, awaiting the right moment. His stomach did a small flip as they returned to the party.

A pair of eyes upon them glinted from the shadows.

Over the common, Todd had sat this one out. He arrived home from hospital that morning by taxi and went straight to bed, but doing nothing was driving him bonkers. He wasn't ready to start working again, he had letters to write, plus the less jovial year end was looming, the tax one. He groaned thinking about the endless tax returns he would be submitting on behalf of his clients. He had a long bath, popped on the comfy tracksuit he'd worn home from hospital, and shuffled down the hall, intent on reading a book on the sofa by the fire - Death on the Nile by Agatha Christie.

As he made himself comfortable, fire crackling, cushions propping up the parts that needed propping, he opened his book to read. However, despite scanning from margin to margin, the words rising from page to eye refused to lodge in his mind, instead they swirled around and sank back into the Nile.

He gave up and closed it with a snap. Staring blankly into the fire he wondered what the others were up to now. Probably nibbling at the buffet or dancing. He wished he felt better.

He reached for the remote control and the TV sprang to life. Jules Holland sat looking scruffier and older than he'd remembered, at the piano, jazzy music spilling out as his hands slithered up and down the keys.

"Oh good God no," uttered Todd who had a dislike of jazz, it was far too unpredictable. He flicked over to Die Hard. That would do "Yippee ki yay mutherfuckers" he mused and sank back to watch Bruce Willis padding around in bare feet and a vest. Thinking of his own vest that lay beneath his tracksuit he marvelled at the versatility of the garment. Twenty minutes later he was fast asleep. He woke with a jolt to Hans Gruber's confused face falling to his death at Nakatomi Plaza. He shuddered and looked at the time. It felt as if he'd been asleep for hours, so deep was his nap. Perhaps he was right not to go, he was obviously more tired than he thought.

A little peckish, he rose from the settee and headed to the gloom of the kitchen. The light from the fridge cast a warm glow over him as he stood eyeing the collection of leftovers. His appetite ebbed away and he settled for a few grapes and a slice of Brie. Wishing he'd put slippers back on, his cold feet carried him over to a box of unopened crackers on the table. He pulled out a chair and settled to eat his snack. The creamy Brie and salty crackers were comforting, a pop of fresh fruity tang from the grapes awoke his senses and he looked about the kitchen, nostrils flaring slightly with the deep breaths as his mouth was occupied, his eyes falling upon the back of the kitchen door. He reached over and pushed the bags aside revealing his cork board. As he chewed, his eyes roamed over the information he'd compiled. Remembering something, he reached into his pocket for a newspaper cutting he'd torn out in hospital that morning.

Unfolding it and smoothing the creases on the table, it read:

KINGSHURST KEEPS CALM AND CAROLS ON
Despite the recent killing spree by persons unknown, the villagers of Kingshurst Common continue festivities in a bid to raise spirits of the local community.

The article went on to describe how Mrs Stella Mayhew, Common conservator and village events organiser (Todd guffawed at the self proclaimed title) had organised carol singing, children's crafting and old folks' Christmas parties. There was a group photo of crinkly oldies in cracker hats holding a plate of mince pies. Behind them was Stella, large lipstick smeared grin that went down at the corners instead of up. Todd reached over the table held the scrap of paper on the notice board and pushed a drawing pin through Stella's wide forehead.

A fox called its ugly cry on the common. His large outstretched tail followed his snaking body as he weaved his way through the undergrowth. He reached the clearing and dashed across the frozen grass towards the town hoping to find more scraps from the recent festivities. It had been rich pickings this week. He hovered in the shadows between store fronts. Two people were standing outside the cafe. He watched them as they returned shivering to the party.

It was nearly midnight. The music had been hushed and the countdown began. Howie took a deep breath and positioned himself next to Max. Across the cafe Joe had lifted Velvet onto one shoulder and was effortlessly bobbing her up and down to the decreasing count. As the bells rang out from the live radio broadcast he fished a large ring out of his pocket and thrust it in front of her. Stunned, Howie froze in the middle of the party. Velvet squealed with delight and slithered down into Joes arms. There was clapping and kissing midst the new year's greetings. The music blasted out once more.

Max turned, hands outstretched to wish Howie a happy new year and was surprised to find him on the floor. Howie looked up, his face a mixture of humiliation and irritation.

"What are you doing down there? C'mon you, I think you've had a bit too much Prosecco!" Max said, as he hoiked him up by his armpits.

This certainly wasn't the finale to the year Howie had been hoping for. "Happy New Year," he said weakly. Max squeezed him tight and said the same.

"Onwards and upwards! Shall we see if Toddy is still awake?" Howie nodded miserably. They left the party after doing a round of hugs and headed across the road and onto the grass. Out in the cold once more Howie started to see the funny side of what had just happened and sighed to himself, there'd be another time. Max was singing ABBA's Happy New Year in baritone huffs of breath which clouded the night air. They staggered haphazardly over the common to the garden gate. Todd was indeed still up, he heard them come around the side of the house and flung open the kitchen back door.

"Happy New Year boys! Come in!"

He was absurdly pleased to see them - the evening had left him maudlin and forlorn. He ushered them towards the whisky decanter where a fine single malt was waiting to greet the New Year.

Chapter 14 - January the 93rd

The ghost of wages long spent was haunting bank accounts up and down the country and January dragged on like a dead body in a heavy carpet. Velvet snapped shut her laptop and groaned.

"How am I supposed to plan a summer wedding without any blimmin money?"

"It doesn't have to be huge does it?" Faye suggested, "I mean as long as the people who matter most are there, small and sumptuous is better than big and cheap?"

Velvet nodded "absolutely, no big cheap wedding for me!. Small and cheap possibly..." she sighed.

"What I need, is a bit more business though, this place is awfully quiet Faye" she gestured to the empty cafe. "We need bums on seats. Oh and while I have you here, do you think Holly would be a bridesmaid? Or would she think that was seriously uncool?"

Faye grinned, "she's already brought it up! Are you kidding! She just thinks you're not gonna ask her because she's taller than you!"

Velvet laughed "I don't care! Everyone's taller than me!"

The door to the cafe opened and there in an array of scarves and hats were the knitting group, bags and all. They squeezed there way through the entrance, bundling their way between the tables.

"Yoooo hoo! Only us, Happy New Year girls!"

Velvet was relieved, she didn't think they'd be back till next month, but here they were, ready for a tea and cake marathon. It set her to thinking, maybe she could appeal to more group activities. She waved them through to their favourite booth and with her mind buzzing she headed for the kitchen.

Faye made her way over to the chattering ladies with her pad and pen. As she took their order, she glanced out of the front window. There were three faces she recognised. Rick the rocker, the lady who ordered the coffee and left without drinking it, and the old chap with the ancient Pekinese, all standing looking in the window at the cakes.

Velvet always kept a small display of china, some flowers and a series of domed cloches under which she placed yesterday's cakes, as props in the window. Faye's voice trailed off from thanking the ladies as she eyed the strange line-up. Perhaps they were coming in. Maybe it said 'closed' on the door? She turned on her heel, and went to check. Thinking of Velvet's business she opened it and called out "we're open," but there was no reply, they'd already walked away. The sign was the right way around too. She looked up and down the road, a little relieved as she'd not relished the thought of conversing with Rick Falconer again after the last encounter.

When she returned to the cafe, a young man was sitting in the 1940s booth. Surprised, she went over to take his order.

"Tea, and a couple of crumpets if you have them love," he said. He was wearing clean overalls, the sort a mechanic might wear. His short curly hair, pushed back on his forehead, sprung to the side in a rebellious spiral. He had a thin moustache, a handsome face and his eyebrows knitted expressively as he spoke.

"I say, you don't happen to have any jam do you?" His light cockney voice made her want to reply in the same tone but she restrained herself and asked which flavour.

"Strawberry, raspberry or lemon curd?"

"Blimey it's like Christmas bleedin' day in 'ere! Strawberry thanks!"

Bemused, she rustled up the appropriate china and cutlery. Velvet popped two crumpets into the industrial toaster with a clunk.

"I've never seen him before, nice looking guy, bit of a Dambusters vibe - I mean, there's retro, and just plain odd!" She rolled her eyes - "it's my own fault, I have literally given all the oddballs a place to congregate!"

Just then, the door opened and Holly walked in. "Except her" laughed Velvet. Holly accepted whatever the joke may have been, and asked if it was ok if she parked herself up for an hour to do some work.

After delivering the crumpets to Stan, who introduced himself with a small salute, Faye overheard him offering one to Holly. She watched out of the corner of her eye as he charmed his way onto her table, stared intently at her smiling, savouring every mouthful she took. Faye walked up to his booth and audibly slapped the the bill on the table and went to report back to Velvet.

"Ok Velv, he's now flirting with my daughter!" They peeped out from the kitchen door. Holly was munching away on a hot buttered crumpet, still with her headphones on oblivious to the young man sitting opposite her. He was still chattering away and seemed blithely unaware that she couldn't hear a word he said.

"How odd. I think I'd better say something" Faye said but Velvet caught her arm.

"No, don't interfere, maybe she likes him, he's kinda cute!"

"Oh, I didn't really think of that," said Faye, hesitating. "I'll text her... in case she needs rescuing." Privately horrified that her daughter was old enough for any sort of romantic liaison, she typed "Are you ok? Do you need me to interrupt?" and sent it with a whoosh.

Holly replied "I'm fine, just need to finish this work, thanks for the crumpets!"

Faye frowned and showed it to Velvet. "I don't even think she's noticed him, she thinks I put them on the table!"

They went back to the kitchen door to

spy on the youngsters, but Holly was alone. Stan Stan the Crumpet man, was gone, bill unpaid, object of his affection unbothered. The two women in the kitchen looked at each other with disbelief. Velvet slumped against the door. "Another bloomin weirdo! I told you, it's my fault - this place attracts them!"

Down the high street at Fox's Gallery, Max was deliberating in the window. They hadn't got around to changing the large, heavily framed winter scene from the display following Christmas. It was time for something more reasonably priced to suit the January pocket. He selected some small local watercolours and a couple of vibrant abstract pieces in spring colours to bring a bit of warmth and colour to the grey day. From upstairs he heard a loud clatter followed by an expletive.

Above in his garret, Howie was sulking. The light was poor and the paint looked drab in any colour. He'd begun dwelling on the proposal fiasco at New Year. The fact he was suffering from artist's block did little to improve his mood. He played about with ideas, but all he made was a mess of his studio and a lot of washing up. He picked up his brushes and palette, disgusted with himself. Balancing pots of painty water on its slimy surface, he made his way to the narrow spiral staircase that led down to the landing. He burst into the small bathroom and ditched everything in the sink with a loud clatter.

"Aaaah you little fucker," he shouted, upon realising one of the pots had overflowed during the descent and a small river of watery mixed paint from the pallet had run down the steps the entire way. He returned to the stairs armed with bunches of toilet paper and started mopping the trickling stream of paint which meandered all the way from the studio.

Max appeared at the foot of the spiral stairs and gazed up at Howie.
"Oh dear, having a bad day?"

Howie peeked behind him under one arm. "You could say that, can you pass me a bit more loo roll?" Max assessed the situation as he dived into the bathroom. He glanced at the full sink and fetched more tissue, passed it to Howie, then returned to the bathroom and started the clean up. By the time Howie had stemmed the flow, he was nearly finished.

"Oh God you didn't have to do that Max, I made a hell of a mess!" But Max knew when Howie was down, that a little help and support was crucial. Howie stood in doorway resting his head on the frame. The cool wood soothed the throb in his temple.

"I feel like crap. My creativity, my artistry, all my get up and go, has got up and gone…"

Max turned took the painty loo roll from Howie's hands and flushed it.

"….gone down the bloody toilet!" continued Howie, gesturing to the swirling vortex of paint and water. He slid dramatically down the door frame with a groan into a crumpled heap on the floor. Max crouched down and stroked his hair.

"You, my love, need a holiday!"
Howie looked up pleadingly.

"Tomorrow morning we'll go down to 'Seas the Day' and book something. We'll close for a week. January is doing bugger all anyway," carried on Max.

A small tear trickled down Howie's face and plopped onto his Christmas sock.

"Come on fella, this won't do," said Max, as he helped him up and led him down to the kitchen. "Lunch time!"

Warmed by a steaming bowl of homemade soup and a hunk of crusty bread, they sat at the table discussing holiday destinations, the day salvaged at last.

The Common was cold and hard. The grass crisp underfoot, frost that had lasted the sunless day, its silvery hold on all things natural and man made, clung with fern like fronds. Holly and Faye strode back towards the cottage, breathing in icicle sharp air and pumping out warm clouds as they walked.

"You mean you never even heard him prattling on?" Faye said.

"Durrrr mother, I had my headphones on! I was reading, I didn't even see him over my laptop screen! Can we drop it now, you're creeping me out?"

Holly shot her mother a look that told Faye the conversation was over. Holly slammed her large headphones back on and walked ahead, folding her arms in front of her, backpack swinging on one shoulder. Faye felt puffed out trying to keep pace, and dropped back with a large sigh.

She didn't want to frighten Holly, but the encounter had left her feeling very uncomfortable. A thought had popped into her head. Perhaps slippery Stan was the murderer? Expertly sneaking about stealthily, charming women, ordering crumpets all over the place. She quickened her pace to catch up with the girl who was disappearing into a mist rolling out over the common. A crow cawed loudly from its perch in an ash tree, took flight and flapped its jagged wings over them.

Back in The Decadia, Velvet was having a very different set of thoughts to Faye. She made a mental note to drive over to Hawksford in the morning. There was someone she needed to speak to.

***

The day ticked by and the evening wore on. The last bus from London swept onto the high street and stopped by the church. The doors opened with a squeal and out stepped a man into the darkness. The doors squeezed shut behind him and with a huff and a groan the bus pulled away like some large animal having spat its unwanted prey onto the pavement.

He turned and watched his brightly lit ride disappear up the road, pulled his coat about his ears and his hat down over his brow - a large hand knitted hat, bobble long since gone but still wearable and warm beyond belief. The alpaca and wool blended yarn proved impenetrable to the cold night air. He walked up the high street in long strides, carrying his case, not looking in any of the shop windows, but at his feet as he went, head down, breath trailing over his shoulder like steam from a train. He was fit, and the slight hill of the high street didn't bother him.

He reached Pippins, the greengrocers, and stopped, set his case down, and retrieving a key from his pocket he let himself into the door beside the shop, which led to a small flat above. Two sets of stairs and another door later, he was in the warm, hanging his coat and hat on a hook in the hall. He wiped his damp brow, flopped down onto the small settee and flicked the television on. The late night news was in full flow but his eyes didn't focus on the screen. Instead, they settled on a picture on the mantlepiece. A lady smiling, strands of hair across her face, battling the wind on some beach or other. In the light of the screen he sat quietly entranced in a memory, the flickering glow momentarily animating her eyes. He flinched as a pain seared across his heart. Rising, he sighed and switched off the TV, plunging her happy face into darkness once more. It was past midnight and he had to be up in a few hours.

Chapter 15 - Breakfast Epiphany

The next morning, as planned, Max and Howie were out bright and early. The travel agents weren't yet open so they made their way to the Decadia for breakfast.

They were surprised to see just Nancy there, sleeves rolled up, dashing in and out of the kitchen. It was fairly busy, as Velvet's morning menu was very popular with the locals. They slid into the 1960s booth. A few minutes later Nancy appeared with her notepad. They ordered their usual - avocado on toast with a poached egg, wilted spinach, a hash brown and two extra hot cappuccinos. She dutifully wrote it down.

"Velvet having a lie in then?" asked Max with a smile.

"No, she was down here at seven, but she had somewhere to be so I said I'd be ok just on my own - but actually, it's getting a bit busy." She looked disappointed in her own admission of defeat.

"Oh bless you Nancy, I'll give you a hand if you like," offered Howie.

Nancy looked slightly aghast and put both palms up in front of her.

"No, it's fine, I have Holly on standby," and she turned and headed to the kitchen, her apron strings stressing on her behalf as she shoved the notepad into the front pocket.

The boys exchanged glances, hoping they hadn't caused offence. They sat in bleary silence, Howie looked out into the street but the windows had misted up. He wiped a small patch and peered out. Across the road at the grocers, a door to the side opened, and out stepped a tall slender man. He strode across the road, his long limbs seeming not to synchronise. The effect was that of a baby giraffe. Howie smiled to himself - how someone so poorly co-ordinated managed to play a musical instrument was beyond him. The bell on the door sounded as the giraffe entered one limb at a time. He took a seat on the other side of the door.

Eventually they ate. The clock ticked around to nine and Howie alerted Max that the Travel Agent was opening, and they rose from their booth and settled the bill at the counter.

"That was perfection, Nancy," purred Max. Nancy smiled in quiet triumph that she'd risen to the challenge unaided as she rang up their order on the till.

On the way out of the Decadia, Howie put a hand on his partner's shoulder.

"Mind yourself Max," he said, gesturing to the long muddy booted limb that sprawled out of a booth. The owner quietly folded it up under the table, but didn't look up from his menu.

Inside Seas the Day, the boys sat at the large desk whilst Melissa, as it read on her badge, spread a few brochures in front of them.

The navy blue and diamanté talons she'd had done for New Year clacked on the keyboard as she handled over the literature. Geraldine, the other employee, eyed the men suspiciously from behind her computer, swept her frizzy brown hair behind one ear and exhaled a disapproving sigh.

Aware he was being watched, Max turned around slowly and gave her a broad smile. "My boyfriend and I would like a bit of winter sun, so you can put the ski holidays to one side," he said, readdressing Melissa.

She rose to get a few more brochures, her concave frame teetering in high heels over to the display, hipbones sticking out of her tight skirt as if searching for food.

"We need a double room, seven nights, somewhere hot, with plenty of gay bars," he added loudly.

Howie closed his eyes and stifled a laugh, Max never could resist a little bigot baiting. Geraldine raised a penciled eyebrow, pursed her brown lips until they resembled a prune and prodded the keyboard with a short pudgy finger.

Twenty minutes later, a week on the island of Fuertaventura, at a beach front hotel was booked. Afterwards, as they walked up the high street, a storm broke out in Seas the Day, Melissa's nails twinkling as she gesticulated her fury towards her colleague who was now prawn pink in the face, which clashed horribly with her brown lipstick.

***

In Hawksford, Velvet was sitting in an uncomfortable armchair, one that promised so much upon first glance but rose up to meet her lowering bottom with a firm thump. Her brow was knitted, and her tummy a little fluttery with nerves. At last her host appeared, Elsa, owner of Luna, the shop where they had bought dreamcatchers. She smelled of cigarette smoke, incense and coffee. She held two mugs of it and placed them on the table between the chairs and sat herself down. Velvet glanced enviously at the puffy Indian embroidered cushion with tiny mirrors sewn into it, as Elsa tucked herself around it until her long skirt hid it from view.

"Now, what can I do for you, have you had a reading before, love?"

She talked with her hands, every syllable she uttered had a matching hand movement, her voice soft and low, with a smoker's growl at the end of each sentence.

Velvet took a deep breath and began to explain her thoughts and worries. She hadn't realised how much things had been pressing on her until now. She ended by explaining about her worries over financing the wedding.`

Elsa was sweet. She lay a hand on Velvet's.

"Love it's alright, you've really been bombarded haven't you? Let's say a little prayer together and I'll gather my thoughts."

She reached for Velvet's other hand, and they bowed their heads. She quietly uttered a prayer asking for guidance and clarity from above and beyond. "Let's get started," she said, and closed her eyes. Velvet felt the air leave the room, and a silence thick as custard enveloped them both until Elsa spoke again.

Chapter 16 - Roses are Red

January thankfully gave way to February but winter refused to give way to spring. Kingshurst Village sat in its place between London and the garden of England, suspended in frost and mysterious murders, its inhabitants rallying hard to get on with their daily lives.

Valentine's Day was looming and Max had placed a local artwork of the beloved St Val's Church in the gallery window, and some romantic figure paintings. Whenever Velvet walked past, her tummy turned over - the wedding date was booked for the third Saturday in May, and there was so much to organise.

She and Joe had been to see Reverend Fields, who privately disapproved of non church attendees getting married there, however, he recognised Velvet's contribution to village life, and as he had no wish to find an alternative cafe for his Saturday morning brunch, that, and considering the general good character of the couple, he agreed to marry them.

The search for a vintage dress was on. Strangely, every dress she'd found online was far too large. She had assumed young women of the 1940s and 50s, were war starved waifs but apparently the vintage brides in the five kilometres surrounding the village must have been sturdy land girls. Scrolling through images of headless brides on eBay was beginning to make her own head spin.

A large wood pigeon landed on the sill of the cafe. He eyed her through the window, his iridescent head bobbing. A car sped through the high street, and startled, he took to the air in a flap, collected himself and expertly glided over the rooftops adjusting his wings and head to change direction towards the gardens, where bird feeders were plentiful. He landed in Todd's. The little hanging cages were always fully loaded with nuts and seeds. Squirrels sat fatly on the high fences and the birds took turns in swooping in for a snack. Filling up the bird feeders was yet another job Todd had set himself, to escape the hostile attentions of Moira. He had never got out of the habit, and kept a detailed log of feathered friends in an old note book by the lounge window.

Why she had married him was always a mystery to him, but to her, it was obvious. He, a bachelor with his own home, proposed, she accepted and he couldn't believe his luck as he unwittingly provided her with an escape route from a strict father.

Her rather foul temper appeared a couple of weeks after the wedding and had floored him completely. Still reeling from the shock, he retreated to his garden and created a small village - the shed, networks of gazebos, patio and garage.

It was still very tidy out there, but the house was now his, and he reclaimed it with vigour, systematically redecorating the place from top to bottom. He glanced out of the window and smiled at the feathered visitor.

The house was quiet, so he switched the radio on. The pigeon took off and headed back to town landing on the postbox across from the card shop where Joe was picking out a valentines card for Velvet.

"To my Fiancé on Valentines Day," read the caption on the front, and he ran a chubby thumb over the aptly velvet flocked card. It was his turn to get a waft of butterflies. They had only been engaged a few weeks and he was already inwardly groaning at the wedding chatter - his mother one end of the phone, Velvet in his ear, and his sisters dropping huge hints about bridesmaids dresses.

He was delighted to be marrying the love of his life, but as for wedding plans, he wanted only to focus on the best man, ushers, and if he could afford it, the wedding car.

The card shop was owned by Stella Mayhew. She stood guard over the latest in a long line of young trainee assistants - being a woman of very little self awareness, these sacrificial lambs timidly handed in their resignations at regular intervals.

"That'll be two ninety five," said the girl robotically. Stella rolled her eyes and the girl added a "please" and smiled. Joe paid up and tucked the card into his leather jacket pocket. He crossed with Nancy on her way into the shop.

"Alright, Nance?" he asked, as he squeezed between the narrow shop door and her. She blushed scarlet and headed for the Valentine's aisle. He smiled, wondering who she was buying for - Nancy had been single for as long as he remembered. It would be nice to see her with someone.

There was another customer in Papier d'Amour. He lingered by the 'condolences' section. Moving silently, slowly up the aisle towards the pink and red glow of the Valentine's display, he had just reached Congratulations on your Engagement when the staffroom door opened and Stella's daughter Cheryl strode out into the store.

"Mummy, you really need to make a decision on the summer stock, I need to get this order in pronto!"

He fell back to weddings, and caught his trouser leg on the racking. Stella scowled at her daughter and hissed,

"Not whilst there are customers in the shop Cheryl, oh give it here then!"

She snatched the catalogue, and perching on the stool behind the till, her large hips eclipsing it, she licked a red nail polished finger and started to leaf through the glossy pages. Cheryl rolled her eyes and returned to the back of the shop. The lurker picked a card at random and pretended to study it but upon realising it said "To The Man of my Dreams on our Wedding Day," hastily stuffed it back.

Nancy hadn't managed to actually to touch a card yet and was still standing, red faced, trying to read the captions on each one. She huffed and puffed, then one caught her eye. A teddy dozing lazily in a cushioned pink heart, the wording read:

Is there room in your heart for me?

She slid it out of the rack and pressed it against her chest, as she made her way to the counter. Stella nudged the young assistant who stumbled forward and in the same robotic tone asked:

"Have you found everything you were looking for? Perhaps you would like one of our Valentine's plushies?"

She gestured awkwardly towards a basket of hideous stuffed vegetables with grinning faces, their white stringy arms clutching puffy hearts. Nancy stammered a "no thank you," and in the agonising time it took the girl to put the barcode number into the till, whilst brandishing her choice of card to the entire high street, Nancy turned to the carousel of sparkly alphabet key rings and spun it intently. She tapped her card on the machine and took her purchase and left with a nod.

"Milly, please smile when you draw the clientele's attention to the vegetable plushies, it's no good you standing there with a face like a slapped cocker spaniel!" Her whistling sibilant 's' was having a grand outing today.

"Stand up straight girl, proper smile, show us your incisors! Buttocks firm, pull that flabby stomach in, stick them little boobies out, that's it," she said to Milly, who now resembled a vampire with wind.

Stella picked up her catalogue. "Cheryl, put the kettle on, I need a coffee." She pushed past the girl. "I think we'll stick to Yours

Especially and Artisanal Soupçon."

The remaining customer pressed his temple, the hissing s sound was getting to him. Quietly appalled and overwhelmed , with the smell of hairspray, card stock and some vile perfume she'd sprayed down her crinkled cleavage that morning, he fled the shop. The flatulent vampire watched him leave then crumpled onto the stool behind the till.

The postbox just across from the Papier D'Amour was seeing a lot of action that week. Brazen lovers who confidently tossed their cards into the slot, furtive school lads, singletons, teenage sweethearts who kissed the envelopes before releasing them into the void with a plop, all fed the old postbox, which sat on the Common, with their loving intentions. It greedily gobbled up the lot.

There were two weddings scheduled in the church for Valentine's Day, one at twelve thirty and one at three thirty. The Reverend had managed to persuade both couples to share the church flowers as the colour scheme was to be red roses for Valentine's.

He hinted to them it would save on costs, but in fact his motive was to reduce the comings and goings of Stella, the self appointed church florist, who was a law unto herself. The fewer dealings with her and her daughter, the better, as far as he was concerned. If only someone else would step up, he pondered, but no-one dared. The displays were unimaginative and symmetrical, and he longed to see the creative fluid floral arrangements his mother produced, back when he was a young curate. He pictured the trailing ivy, picked from the churchyard, roses, lsysianthus, and anemones in rustic containers with touches of gypsophila, pussy willow and twisted hazel. Instead, he was greeted with plastic pots and over used crumbling green foam, stuffed to capacity with carnations, chrysanthemums, pungent lilies and sprigs of gypsophila jammed into every gap. The last thing he wanted, was to be un-Christian, but when he entered the church and the pong of lilies struck the back of his nose like an elastic band, he yearned for the old days. With less than a week to go, he wondered if there was some way he could put Stella off and do them himself.

Way above the church, an EasyJet plane caught the light, its windows gleaming momentarily in the winter sun. Aboard were Max and Howie, buckled up and awaiting their first drink. Their well deserved holiday had begun, and they sat back and closed their eyes after an early start. The pair had slept badly, knowing that their alarm was set for four thirty - and when it did bleep loudly into the darkness, the urge to slap it quiet and snuggle back down was irresistible. But of course, they didn't, they got up, pinned a closed notice to the shop door, excitedly wheeled their suitcases out onto the dark high street, and jumped into a waiting taxi.

Chapter 17 - Violets are Blue

Postmen were stalked up and down the country. Many people of course, didn't entertain the remotest care that it was Valentine's Day, but the romantics ate their breakfast with one eye on the garden gate, keeping an ear out for the dog barking at the flap of the letterbox, or sat nonchalantly on the back of the settee subtly glancing out the window, like Holly.

There was a boy at college, tall and slim with curly dark hair, who had put his long black coat around her at the bus stop. She had protested out of embarrassment, but the warmth and heaviness of the wool on her shoulders, and the woody citrus scent of him emanating from the large collar as he pulled it up around her freezing face, his hand momentarily brushing her cheek, was enough to transform her tummy into the butterfly house at London Zoo. It was irrelevant. of course, that he then turned to his mates and made a stupid quip about goth girls always being cold and it was just as well he had his dad's coat. The dye was cast, and she lay in wait for the postman.

Velvet and Joe were in each other's arms, of course. They exchanged cards in bed and stayed there all morning.

"Shall we go and have lunch at the pub?" asked Velvet.

"Ooh yeah, I like your thinking," said Joe, whose thoughts instantly turned to the huge portions of lasagne and chips at The King's Head. Velvet's, of course, had nothing to do with the pub grub and everything to do with getting a good view of the weddings in the church across the road. She made sure her wedding notebook was in her bag so she could write up any ideas.

Holly stood dejected in the hall looking at the white envelopes on the mat. The dogs had finished their reign of terror on the postman, which ceased as he reached Todd's gate and was no longer on their turf. She huffed at the red envelope in his hand as he walked up the path next door - really? The dogs heroically trotted in through the back door, quest complete.

Faye came down the stairs and called perkily, "anything for me?"

"Yep, they are all for you. Just looks like boring stuff though - I reckon Todd's got a Valentine's card, so unfair!" and she walked away without picking them up. Faye remembered the date and smiled.

"Hey, fancy a bit of lunch out love?" she said, stooping to pick up the post. Holly was right, the post was just a bunch of window envelopes with typed addresses. Nothing personal, but then she wasn't expecting anything of a personal nature. Those days seemed long gone. She and Ben used to exchange cards and a little gift on Valentine's day, but she saw it as a day for other people now. One letter peaked her interest though. It was from her solicitor. She hadn't used one for years, not since making a Will after Ben died. Curiously, she turned it over in her hands and reached for a key on the hook to use as a letter opener. What was inside took her completely by surprise. It was a letter from a solicitor in Hastings telling her that her Uncle David had died. Why had no-one rung her? There was a copy of the death certificate stating he had died of natural causes, his heart. He had already been cremated, as instructed in his Will, and there would be no funeral. He had named Faye and Holly as his beneficiaries, to inherit the entirety of his estate, which consisted of an apartment in Hastings on the south coast, and the contents thereof; his car, and all other personal belongings. Stunned, she reached for her phone and scrolled through for her Aunt's number.

Anne answered after about three rings, sounding flustered. "Hello, Dr MacKenzie's Surgery?"

Faye whispered "Aunty Anne, I've had this letter about Uncle David?" There was a pause, and Anne sighed.

"Yes, I've just received it too, it seems he passed away on the first of February - I can't believe no-one contacted us sooner Faye, what is going on?" Anne broke down in tears.

Her brother was very dear to her as a child, but in later years they had grown apart, and he had become quite remote from the rest of the family and kept himself to himself.

"Aunty Anne, I'm so sorry, this must be such a shock to you, and, well, the, erm, letter from his solicitor says he's left everything to Holly and I! I don't understand, surely you are his next of kin?" Faye stammered not sure if it was too soon to mention the will.

"Ah, that much I do know - David was very keen for you and Holly to inherit because of what happened to both your fathers, Faye. He felt it quite keenly when Ben died, he liked him very much, and said that as Holly was brought up without a father, the least he could do was give her a legacy."

Faye was bemused. "She'll have the cottage though!" She suddenly wished he had taken more of an interest in them - then she remembered how little money she actually had in the bank, and mustered a "well, that was very thoughtful of him."

Anne knew though, and she could read Faye pretty well. "He wasn't a warm man Faye, he never could express himself even as a child, but he still felt things deeply, and always wanted to do the right thing - even if it was from a distance. Who do you think paid for Ben's funeral love?"

Faye took a sharp intake of breath and sat down on the stairs with a bump.

"Wha.. what do you mean? The record company, the company paid for it, the man, said it had been covered, I remember, the funeral director, patted my hand and said it had been covered, th-that I didn't need to worry", why didn't anyone tell me?"

She felt the hot sting of tears in her eyes, indignation like a burning spear starting to rise up in her tummy. As the words came out she realised the man never actually named the benefactor, that she had reached that assumption on her own. The shame that she had never thanked Uncle David, and then the horrible feeling that it was now too late to do so. She tried to gulp back the tears erupting from her.

"Calm down Faye, its alright love, I was remiss in not telling you, but he wouldn't have wanted a thank you," she said, again reading her reaction so well.

"He was a proud man, he would have been very uncomfortable with you gushing over him. He was probably relieved you thought it was the record company, lovey."

"I'm so sorry Aunty Anne, I was phoning to console you, not the other way around," Faye said, pulling herself around and wiping the tears from her face with the flats of her hands.

Anne could picture her doing so - she remembered her as a child, crying after a scolding; pink cheeks, stubborn little palms wiping away tears, dolly fingers outstretched as if their touch would make her crumble. At this moment Anne regretted being so far away. She'd forgotten how vulnerable Faye was. Her life was so absorbing in the Highlands, her husband and children, her sister's family so far away, little dolls house figures in her mind, far away in their little English cottage.

"Look Faye, let me talk to Andrew, I think maybe we should go down to Hastings, together, maybe find out what happened and get to the bottom of this. I absolutely have no problem with you and Holly inheriting, the children will have more than enough when we go, from Andrew and I, but I think maybe you need a family member with you to sort this out.   I'm due some holiday, I'll come down. Listen, I've got to go, I haven't told Andrew the news yet - let me ring you back later," and she was gone, a click as she hung up her old green wall telephone in the hallway of the Highland house. She turned from the phone, looked again at the letter in her hand and called to her husband down the tartan carpeted hallway.

Faye stood up and tucked her phone into her jeans, debating whether to share the news with Holly yet, but Holly already knew, she'd heard her mothers strange tone and had been standing in the doorway listening. She rushed forward and hugged her mother. Together they sat on the stairs and talked the whole thing through. Impressed with the adult way her daughter dealt with the news, Faye realised Holly was growing up. She didn't remember much about Uncle David, but she was touched at his generosity and agreed that they would keep all this to themselves for the moment until they knew more. For the first time in years Faye felt as if she wasn't the only grown up in the house. That she could at last share a bit more with her daughter and not shield her from everything.

"Mum, we'll get to the bottom of all this, with or without Aunty Anne, don't worry.

***

Next door, Todd stood frozen in his hallway, the red envelope burning a hole in the doormat. He felt as if all the blood in his veins had sunk into his shoes, and he couldn't move. She was coming back, she wanted to patch things up, it couldn't be? After what seemed an eternity, he shuffled forward and picked up the letter. There was a heart drawn childishly on the back - he turned it over, to see his name was written in faint hearted biro. There was no postmark. Sweat started to pop out of his top lip and he turned and took the letter into the kitchen to open. Sitting at the table he used his toast knife to open the envelope. Inside, was a Valentine's card. He took little notice of the picture and opened it. The writing looked familiar, perhaps she disguised it? But why? It read:

Roses are red,
Violets are blue
I think that our friendship
Could be more, do you?

He stared open mouthed at the rhyme. There was a question mark underneath and some kisses. He looked again at the envelope, it was definitely for him. "Well I'll be buggered," he said out loud and set the card on the table.

Over in the pub, Velvet and Joe were installed in the booth by the window. Joe was sipping a pint of ale, and Velvet was mid-sip of her gin and tonic, when she saw a white Rolls Royce pull-up outside the church.

"Ohmigod, it's here Joe!" He glanced over at the door to the kitchen, expecting it to be swinging open with two steaming plates of food held aloft.

"No! The brides car, she's here!" She tugged at his sweatshirt, and Joe rolled his eyes, his pint spilling - but actually, he did feel a little zing of excitement, and joined her looking out of the window.

It was a little windy, and as the young girl edged forward to step out of the car, the breeze took her veil up into the air above her head, but it remained pinned in place. Patting it back down, her father tried to help, but clearly she didn't want him squashing her exquisitely coiffed hair, and she backed up banging her head on the roof of the car. There was an exchange of words and he stepped away, allowing her to stand up and smooth herself down. The photographer snapped his first photo of a father-daughter moment which belied the previous one, all smiles and into the church they went.

Velvet drank in the scene; the dress, the flowers, the shoes, the veil, the hair, the car - every detail. Fishing out her notebook she scribbled furiously. The food finally arrived, and Joe hadn't even seen it coming - maybe this wedding lark was more absorbing than he first thought. They tucked into the steaming mass of lasagne, peas and carrots, with a stodgy portion of chips on the side. It was enough to make his Italian Nonna faint. She would have scowled at this Anglicised monstrosity, hand on heart muttering in her native tongue.

They were just finishing when the wedding party came out of the church. The dress was lovely - full length, off the shoulder and nipped in at the waist, with a full taffeta skirt. The bride seemed much calmer, smiling broadly, with the family surrounding her laughing and happy. Two teenage bridesmaids stood sulkily in lavender dresses, shoulders rounded, heavily made up with false eyelashes you could sweep up confetti with as they sneaked drags of their boyfriends' cigarettes, standing nearby in pencil thin suits. The photographer called "bridesmaids!" and both blew out the smoke straight up like two lavender chimneys. Then, miraculously transformed into two pouting goddesses, shoulders back, cleavages forward, they posed either side of the bride, their endless bathroom selfies finally paying off.

The wind had died down and the sun was beginning to shine on the nuptials. The photographs seemed to go on forever; bride and groom on their own, with his parents, with her parents, with all the parents, with the grandparents with the bridesmaids, without the bridesmaids, with men, with just women, and with the children, most of which were doing circuits around the gravestones to the side of the church.

It was a chaotic, noisy event, peals of laughter and church bells - a recording, of course - it was a long time since the actual bells had rung. Villagers looked on in delight, the Reverend Fields, less so - he smiled in a way that said "I'm very happy for you, but now please go away." Velvet noticed him, and felt a pang of guilt that she hadn't sought his spiritual guidance instead of Elsa's. He was very nice, but may have branded her a witch and ducked her in the village pond.

At last, the wedding party departed. Badly parked cars moved slowly off curbs and accelerated up over the common after the Rolls Royce. The high street was quiet again. The church warden came out with a broom and swept the confetti into the rose bed near the lychgate. Within minutes, the local birdlife swooped down to eat the biodegradable rice

paper morsels.
Velvet made a note.

"What did you think Joe?" she asked, tapping the pen on her chin.

"Decent motor Velv" he replied.

***

Valentine's Day in Fuertaventura was warm and hazy. Max and Howie were fast asleep on sun beds by the pool, books face down on their chests, sunglasses on, and cocktails drained on little tables. They had done very little on this holiday, and become almost institutionalised in their habits, turning up for meals and drifting from one part of the resort to another. It had been absolute bliss so far. No decisions to be made apart from the buffet. The agonising choice over wine and the tricky decision over which bread to pop into the rolling toaster at breakfast, were welcome diversions. The landscape around them felt alien; with its black sand, little Christmas cake walls with white painted tops, strange bell bottomed palm trees and the occasional stray cat curled up in a ball, eyes peering out at them as they passed on the way to mini golf. The resort was very quiet, the harbour picturesque, its collection of fishing boats and tourist vessels bobbed gently as they wandered past. It wasn't the warmest time of the year to visit but getting a tan wasn't top priority, this trip was about rest and relaxation. There were local cheeses and liqueurs to try, and the honey rum became a firm favourite.

Howie woke to find the sun had broken through the haze, and he breathed in the sweet air - suncream and coconut mingling with pool, and laundry scent from the fresh towels. He looked at Max who was snoring softly, mouth open. Howie smiled, took out his phone and filmed him for a few seconds catching one nice, loud, barrelling snore. He added it to the group chat back home. Within seconds there were laughing emojis and hearts. He chuckled.

"I know what you're up to Howard," murmured a low voice next to him. Max's own phone had buzzed numerous times in his pocket and woken him too. "Revenge is best served cold, Mr Bosun!"

"I'll be ready for you, Foxy," purred Howie in reply. Howie had his own agenda of how tonight would go - dinner, romance and a proposal. He had brought the ring with him, in his suitcase, hidden in a pair of socks.

Next to the pool was a large, woven willow pod sun lounger. They'd had their eye on it all week, but every day it was occupied by the same couple: a pudgy middle-aged pair, her with an immense bosom spilling out of a bikini, him with a large taut midriff, which popped out from under his rib cage and was met by a pair of skimpy trunks which sat like an egg cup under his round belly, bronzed from regular holidaying. They managed to secure the pod from early in the morning until late afternoon, and they lay, all day, limbs entangled, like a pile of artisan sausages at the deli - reading, sleeping, and drinking. Every time the boys came down to the pool they looked to see if it was available, but it never was - 'the Pod People' as Max had named them, were always there. It didn't really bother Howie, he was happy that they had more to do with themselves than lie in the same place all day, but it was starting to irritate Max.

"I can't believe how selfish they are," he would say at regular intervals, along with "I'm not going to say anything Howie, you're absolutely right, what does it matter?" - but as the week wore on, the injustice of the Pod People grew.

Max came up with a plan. He would set his alarm for 5am, come down to the pool and set up shop in the pod, go back to sleep, and await their disappointed faces. He awoke,

peeled himself out of bed, blearily padded down the little pathways to the pool with his towel and book to find they were already there, lying smugly with their towels over them, looking at their phones.   He had nonchalantly styled it out and gone for a swim, wincing at the freezing water, all the while incredulous at their nerve. The next night, he slept through the alarm he had set for four thirty, and the night after that, he awoke at four with the dawn chorus, tripped over one of the little Christmas cake walls outside the villa and limped back to bed. Operation Tit Willow was not going to plan. Howie hadn't appeared to notice the nightly escapades, he slept like a log, full of margaritas and wine. Max decided that perhaps it wasn't worth the hassle, gave up on the idea, and resorted to giving them thunderous looks whenever they passed by. The selfish sausages were oblivious, and continued their dominance over the willow pod, ordering their drinks from their phones and never leaving it unattended.

Hundreds of miles away, the second wedding of the day was taking place in Kingshurst Village.

St Val's was filling up again, with a small party of trendy people. The bride arrived in a less ostentatious form of transport - a small vintage car. Joe knew the make and model immediately, as the cream Morris

Oxford came to a stop, the chrome trim gleaming in the sunlight. "1955 I reckon," he said. Velvet stood up to get a better look. The driver got out and opened the passenger door, to reveal a tall, slim bride in her thirties. She wore a simple gown of heavy Duchess satin, tulip shaped, tea length, and held a round bouquet of red roses against shiny, dark green foliage. She had no father with her, no bridesmaids, and she walked into the church alone. It seemed a little forlorn after the previous bumptious crowd.

"Oh bless her Joe, she's all on her own," said Velvet, dismayed. But she needn't have worried - forty minutes later, out came the bride and groom with a party of deeply stylish adults - it was a very grown up wedding.

"I wonder where they are having the reception? Probably some expensive restaurant or a fancy bar somewhere," said Joe, wincing inwardly. Money was a bit tight for their nuptials, and he was going to suggest the Decadia, but thought better of it now.

**

Across the miles, the day wore on and at dinner, Howie shifted in his seat. He still hadn't found the right moment to pop the question. The restaurant was decorated for "El Dia de San Valentin" and Max was blathering on about wine to the waiter, and the people on the next table were looking - he reviewed the situation and decided to wait until after dinner, and perhaps propose on the walk back.

Dessert demolished, they made their way past the comfy chairs, by the infamous pod, chuckling about the pod people.

"Hand me your phone Howie, let me take a selfie?" Howie obliged and before he could muster a pose, Max pushed him playfully into the pool. The shock of the cold water rushing into every orifice took his breath away, and he spluttered to the surface and gasped at the night air.   Max stood roaring with laughter on the edge of the pool, videoing the entire event on Howie's safely dry phone. The pool attendant-cum-barman, angrily shouted in Spanish to them, then broken English saying they were not allowed in the pool after sun down.

Max turned and apologised, "lo siento, lo siento Señor, fue un accidente," stifling a giggle.

"Help me out then you git," seethed

Howie, trying to climb out of the side without having to do the walk of shame from the steps.

"You see my soggy friend, as I said, revenge is a dish best served cold!" Howie could see the funny side, and he laughed. The video, of course, went straight to the group chat. A few dings later, and everyone had replied, giggling. Howie chased Max through the network of paths back to their mini villa.

"Let's get you out of those wet things," said Max, with a wink and thoughts of any other type of proposal were forgotten.

At three thirty, Howie awoke with a plan. He extracted himself from the tangled bedlinen, gathered some bits together and tiptoed down towards the pool. The pod was empty. He'd beaten them to it and he'd known all week what Max had been up to! With stolen roses from the poolside bar tables, he scattered petals in the pod, positioned himself in the centre with two mini bottles of cava swiped from the mini bar. An hour passed he sent a text to Max "Meet me by the pool," and then he dozed off. At four thirty, like clockwork, the pod people, brazen as usual, strolled up to the poolside. They looked at each other in surprise to see their usual spot taken. After exchanging grumbles peppered with a few expletives they turned and walked away. Howie slept on, and then at about six o'clock, Max was there, standing with tears in his eyes, looking down at Howie. He lay, like a starfish, a rose petal rising and falling from his left nostril as he breathed, with a little bottle of cava in each hand and a small box placed on his chest. As if he could sense Max, he woke and smiled up.

"Will you bloody well marry me?" he asked sleepily, and Max said
"Yes, yes! I will!" and dived into the pod.

Howie opened the box and a little rush of pool water tipped out onto them from the night before, and they laughed.

Max was serious for a moment. "Oh my God, you were going to ask me last night, and I pushed you into the pool! Oh Howie, I'm so sorry!" he clapped his hand over his mouth.

"Oh forget it Max, I've been trying to ask you since New Year!"

They marvelled at the view of the glowing horizon from the pod, the stars still twinkling between the woven willow branches. As the sun rose, a new chapter was beginning for the Fox Bosuns, or the Bosun Foxes, the Bofoxuns, or the Foxbuns. Whatever they decided, the pod was theirs, the day was theirs, and it began with a beautiful sunrise.

Chapter 18 - Beside the Seaside

There was a knock at the door. Faye fumbled into a dressing gown, and stumbled down the stairs to answer it. Expecting a delivery driver to have dumped a parcel on the step and retreated, as they seemed to do these days, she opened the door and looked down, but was greeted by a pair of very sensible shoes, sensible trousers and a Black Watch tartan poncho.

"Oh my goodness, Aunty Anne!" exclaimed Faye, "what are you doing here?" She beckoned her in and stood speechless in the hall as Anne put her bags down. She'd obviously come to stay.

"I'm sorry, I didn't ring, the phone lines were down because of the snow and I just made a decision and packed a bag. I thought about ringing you from the services on the motorway, but I didn't want you flying into a panic and making up beds and what have you... so - anyway, here I am," and she stopped speaking and looked a bit embarrassed. Faye wouldn't have minded one bit making up a bed and she was suddenly very glad to see her Aunty - she was so much like her mother, it made her want to cry. She flung her arms around Anne and they hugged for a good long time.

"I'm so glad you're here, I really am, it's been too long." They made their way into the lounge and they sat on the sofa holding hands and catching up with all the news.

The next day, they set off for Hastings, three women from different generations of the same family, in Anne's large comfortable gold car. The old Jaguar literally purred along the country lanes, and as she stepped it up a gear for the motorway, the low noise of the engine reached a hearty growl. It felt luxurious to Holly, compared to Velvet's old Ethel, and she stretched out in the back with her headphones on, listening to an old Kate Bush song and daydreaming of Henry of the long black coat.
Suddenly, Faye remembered she hadn't spoken to Velvet and she was due at the cafe the next day for baking. She dived into her handbag for her mobile phone.

"Excuse me chaps, I need to ring Velvet!" She made the call.
"Ok, thanks Velve, sorry I wont be there for

baking day, try not to poison anyone without me!" She laughed at the standing joke between them.

Anne glanced over, to her eyeing the phone.

"I really should get one of those phones, I'm such a dinosaur..."

Next door to the cottage, Todd was getting used to being a doggy daddy. Rollo made himself at home, stretched out on the back of the sofa as he watched the girls drive away, and Margaux sat barking away next to him. She was now inspecting every corner of Todd's living room, hound nose down. Todd pottered in the kitchen, finding homes for all the dog food and paraphernalia that came with them. He found himself giving a running commentary to the dogs, and it felt good not to be alone in the house.

When the girls reached Hastings, it was lunchtime. They parked up on the seafront and got portions of hot chips and salty, crunchy, battered cod from the fish and chip shop. They made for a stone bench, the pebbles of the beach crunching underfoot and tucked in to the piping hot food. After a few mouthfuls, Faye spoke, her bottom lip glistening from the oil.

"Anne, did you ever visit him down

here? I have no idea where he lived. He never invited us down here - I wonder if he had a girlfriend, or a boyfriend?" Her thoughts spilled out, one after the other. Anne waited to finish a mouthful before replying, dabbed her lips with a napkin and spoke.

"I don't believe there was anyone in his life. He was engaged a long time ago, but it didn't work out and he ended it. His flat is just up there, behind those shops - I came here once, but we went out to lunch so I didn't really see anything but the hall and kitchen. It's not anything special from what I remember. Anyway we'll soon see, let's finish up here, get to the solicitor's and pick up the keys."

Anne turned her attention to her last few chips, and Holly stared out to sea, the wind teasing her long red curls around her face. She separated a hot chip from a strand of hair, and popped it into her mouth. Faye tapped her on the shoulder and motioned towards the car which sat like a golden sphinx on the seafront.

The solicitors were business-like, and handed over some paperwork, a copy of the deeds and two sets of house keys. Faye was self conscious that she smelled of fish and chips, and had hastily wiped her hands on her jeans as they walked in the door. The solicitors offered their condolences, and explained, as per the will, that David had requested that upon his death he would be cremated, interred at the local cemetery and his next of kin would not be notified until after this was done. He didn't wish for any money to be wasted on a funeral or flowers. They had no choice but to accept this and respect his wishes, and they left the office knowing that however odd this seemed, it was what he wanted.

Back in the car, they cruised through Hastings along the sea front behind into the town, leaving the beach huts and funfair behind them. It was out of the tourist season and very quiet. Anne glanced at the address again, and Faye directed from the map on her phone. Again, Anne looked enviously at the phone.

"I didn't know you could do that with one of those!" Up higher and higher into the cliffs they drove, the gold car gleaming warm against the grey rocks of the winding road. Eventually, they pulled up outside a large Victorian house with white painted gables and a crunchy gravel driveway that the old Jaguar crept over slowly, stones popping and grinding under the fat tyres.

"This is very nice Anne, I wonder how many flats it was made into?" pondered

Velvet. The old house had once been a single dwelling, but sometime in the 1970s it had been made into flats and sold off. There were six electronic doorbells to the side of the front door, with names on. David was number four.

Anne rung the bell just in case - "you never know," she whispered.

It was quite a tense moment, but no one answered. The outer door key opened the door, and they walked quietly up the large staircase, looking around them. It was pleasantly decorated and quite recently. So far so good. They reached the front door and let themselves in. The flat smelled of cleaning products, aftershave and laundry. It was spotlessly clean, and the interior was stylish and modern, not at all what Faye was expecting. David clearly wasn't a miserable old miser living in a grotty flat, this was the home of a decisive, intelligent man. There were hundreds of books in the living room, neatly categorised on extensive shelves. On the coffee table were large polished fossils, ammonites and seashells, a guitar propped up in the corner, and a small desk with a laptop, papers and a fountain pen. They stood there in wonder. The large clock on the wall ticked loudly in the stunned silence of the room. Holly spoke first.

"This, is well nice Mum, he was so cool!" She pointed at the guitar - "I can't believe it, why did he keep all this to himself, I'd have loved to have hung out here with him."

Anne shook her head, "he was a funny old thing Holly, very private. I think he was happiest on his own, just living the way he wanted, no interfering family or responsibilities. Its a shame though isn't it?" She looked about her and sat down on the sofa. Faye nodded in agreement and sat down too.

"It's a beautiful home, he must have been very content here." Holly explored the kitchen. The view from the window was fantastic; the dark blue sea, tiny ships in the distance, and the tops of the shops and houses down in the town. The call of seagulls drifted up from the coast.

They explored the rest of the flat - much like the living room, it was tasteful and masculine with artistic touches; a trendy leather chair here, a large curved standard lamp there, the bathroom stylish and functional, minimal personal belongings on show, just a razor, toothbrush and a bottle of aftershave on the bathroom shelf. There would be no huge clear out to be done, no skip in the driveway or bags and bags of charity donations. Even his clothes were stylish and few. The sparseness of the whole place was a welcome relief to them all.

Faye stood in the hallway looking guiltily at the mail they'd picked up from the doormat.

"I feel like such a snoop," she said. It was mostly junk mail and bank letters. "Here, you have these Anne, I don't feel right opening them," She handed Anne the cache of letters. Looking about her, Faye's eyes fell upon the hooks by the telephone, in particular the set of car keys hanging there.

"Anne, Holly, look, the car! I forgot about the car, I wonder what it is?" The girls crowded around the keyring. There were two keys, one with the word 'Ford' and one with a pewter horse dangling from a chain.

"Maybe he's got a Ford van that pulls a horse box?" Holly said, looking confused and slightly disappointed with the old style key. They put their coats back on and headed back down to the driveway. Outside they ventured to match up the key fob with the right car. Holly marched towards an old silver Ford Fiesta parked by the steps.

"It must be that one," she said. They tried the key, but it didn't fit. Just then a neighbour came out and they backed off guiltily.

"Can I help you?" The woman said, not unpleasantly. Anne stepped forward and extended her hand.

"Erm, yes, sorry, I am David's sister, David from number four - this is his niece, and her daughter... We were just wondering which car was his?"

The lady looked relieved and shook her hand. "Oh I see, I'm sorry for your loss, he was a nice chap. Kept himself to himself, never said very much, but seemed a decent sort. The car, his one, is the one under the tarpaulin, by the hedge. He didn't drive it much. I'm Alice by the way." Anne gave her name and they chatted on for a little while.

Holly wandered over to the dark shape by the hedge, she hoped it wasn't a total wreck under there. Whatever it was it was old, quite boxy looking, but she'd make the best of it and maybe they could sell it and put the money towards a small run around as her first car. Joe had already given her a couple of driving lessons around the supermarket carpark last summer. She'd had her eye on a little Fiat 500 that was for sale in the high street. The wind blew her red hair around her face. She tied it back with a band from her pocket. The weather was taking a turn.

The neighbour went back to her chores, and Anne and Faye wandered over to Holly, gravel crunching underfoot. "Well, let's take a look then, shall we?" They worked out how the tarpaulin was secured, and started to uncover the car. From beneath the dark stiff fabric, a beautiful, pale blue 1965 Ford Mustang convertible emerged. It was flawless. The colour was the blue of Holly's eyes, which were now popping out of her head. It was so unexpected a find, she didn't know what to say. Clearly it wasn't the type of vehicle suitable for a first car, but goodness it was beautiful. The raised galloping horse logo on the bonnet caught Holly's eye, it felt cold under her fingers, and now the keyring made sense. They stood around it in awe, took a few photos with their phones, and then it started to rain very lightly, so without even consulting one another, they covered it back over as fast as they could and headed back inside. None of them spoke, walking back up to the flat. They went inside and closed the door, then all burst into laughter and excited chatter.

"A HORSE box? laughed Anne.

"Well I don't know anything about cars!" giggled Holly.

"Oh my god, Joe is going to have a blackout when he hears about this!" said Faye, explaining who he was to Anne, all the while thanking her lucky stars that he was in her life and knew about this stuff.

After spending a few more hours at the flat going through paperwork, guffawing at the value of the car once they had looked it up on the internet, they decided to go out for dinner and then back to the small hotel they had booked for a couple of nights. Faye was last to leave the flat and she turned, stroked the door frame and mouthed the words "Thank you, Uncle David," to the empty hallway, and closed the door.

A single woody note from the guitar in the corner softly resonated through the apartment in reply.

Chapter 19 - Stella By Starlight

Stella was dead. Dead as the false nails on her limp hands, her glassy eyes transfixed on her killer as he receded into the night. She was sitting on a park bench, wrapped up in a Barbour waxed coat, and in her mouth, an envelope, from a greetings card, screwed up into a ball. Her William Morris scarf had fallen casually around her collar, with nonchalant folds of silk belying its grim dealings with her throat. She remained exactly like this as the night gave way to day, the crows cawed and the dogs barked in back gardens, school children were eating Coco Pops, and commuters downed their coffees.

It wasn't until quarter past ten, that two girls on horseback, riding across the common, realised something wasn't right with the lady sitting on the bench. One of the horses, a dark shiny cob with shaggy legs shied as they approached, his full mane rippling as he reared, large muscular legs stamping. The young rider got him under control, apologising to the woman, who didn't reply, and appeared to just stare into the distance. The other girl tried talking to her, but nothing. She dismounted her chestnut mare and to her receding horror realised the woman was dead. They flagged down a postman, his red van screeching to halt, assuming there had been a riding accident. One by one, the villagers heard the news. Stella's daughter Cheryl, with a stony tear-stained face, was led to a police car. The young shop girl was told to close up for the day, which she did within seconds of it pulling away, exhaust fumes billowing, closed sign swinging in the door frame.

Detective Inspector Appleby sat with her head in her hands - the Chief was getting irritable, impatient for a conclusion to this case. She and her team were doing their best, but there was so little evidence of the killer. Not a footprint, not a fingerprint, not a trace of saliva or even a hair. He or she was being extremely careful. Each victim, a strong willed woman with unpleasant tendencies, according to the locals. It seemed everyone was a suspect - nobody liked these old bags. The daughter was in shock, no solid alibi, but there was enough evidence on her laptop to place her on it late into the night. She thought her mother was down in the shop the next morning, and the shopgirl thought she was upstairs in the flat and had opened for business. The ex-husband was in the Algarve, and there was no money missing from anywhere,   A new approach was needed, and soon. She reached for her cigarettes and secreted one in her pocket along with a lighter, and headed for the fire escape.   Once outside, she lit it and inhaled deeply, the vile chemicals seeping into her veins but clearing her mind. Perhaps, a decoy battle axe might work, she wondered. Someone to throw their weight about, make a noise in the village, create a stink, catch the killer's eye and see if they took the bait? It was a risk, but she knew just the person for the job.   She was strong, quietly clever and an actress to boot, albeit amateur. Convincing her, as well as the Chief, was the next hurdle.

***

"Absolutely not, I'm not throwing myself under the bus," Ursula paused with dramatic effect "or under a killer for that matter!" She crossed her legs and then her arms.

Lydia understood her reluctance of course, but went in for another try.

"You would be the hero of the day Ursula, the star of the town, play the greatest role of your life - and   - you'll be the village saviour!"

"The village idiot more like, what do you take me for?" She scoffed at the policewoman but the word 'star' was taking effect. She softened and uncrossed her arms. "What would it involve?" "How dangerous would it actually be?" she asked, raising an eyebrow and stroking a false eyelash back into place.

The Chief was harder to convince. Putting a civilian in danger was always a red flag but they were running out of options and he didn't want to be remembered in his retirement as the Chief that let a serial killer slip through his fingers. He pictured a television documentary some time in the future with images of him getting into a patrol car, or striding towards the court house with papers in his hand, the narrator stating his name as the weak link in the case.

After a few tense meetings it looked as if DI Appleby was onto something. He'd back the idea as long as there was top notch surveillance and if it worked, that he take credit for the plan. She was on board with that, she sought neither fame or ambition at this stage.

"You won't regret it Sir," she said, with some regret that she'd even thought of it in the first place - suddenly the risks were starting to leave an unpleasant heaving in her stomach. A glass of red wine for dinner would help with that, she thought.

Chapter 20 - A Star is Bored

The very next day, Ursula was preparing
for the performance of a lifetime. It may
take a few days to set the trap but she
was now totally on board and, if successful, it
could pave her way to the West End.

She was tired of church halls, tired of
home made costumes and photocopying flyers
in the post office. She longed for the
professional theatre, a proper dressing room,
a director that didn't have a day job, a decent
lighting rig and not someone's little brother
operating it. She'd had a taste of this in her
childhood - her mother had been on the
London stage, she'd watched from the wings,
entranced at her magical transformation from
mother to goddess, she'd sat in the stalls with
her bead box making bracelets for her friends,
the stage hands and the crew, who obligingly
wore them. Her afternoons between shows
spent wandering around the orchestra pit
examining the instruments, peering into a
cello to see the vast wooden hall inside, play
conducting behind the podium, and peeping
into the enticing doors and pockets of the

crushed velvet linings of the violin cases.

She ran errands between dressing rooms, uninhibited dancers wearing next to nothing plying her with sweets they wouldn't dare eat to pinch a pair of tights from another chorus girl. She played with her mother's make up while she was on stage, creating uneven wings at the corners of her eyes and round blush circles on her cheeks. The lipstick brush loaded up with colour never seemed to go on evenly, and by the time her mother came back her lips were thick with it. She was regularly scolded for messing about with her mother's precious 'Max Factor Professional', but it was irresistible to the seven year old girl. These memories, her mother, the excitement of the theatre, all swelled in her bosom whenever she performed, but it was never quite the same, - she yearned for those golden days.

Now Stella was gone, Ursula was to take her place in her community as helpful but overbearing busy body. Stella had done a lot of good in her time, but eagerness had been replaced with ego. She had become an ugly pastiche of the woman she once was.

Ursula picked up the phone and made a few calls from a list compiled by Stella's daughter, slotting herself into the roles around town that Stella and her counterpart Sheila inhabited. She was full of compassion for their loss, of course, but made sure she appeared indispensable to them. The scene was set. Curtain up.

Far from the murder scene, Faye, Aunty Anne and Holly were purring along the A21 back to Kingshurst. They chattered animatedly in the car, a stark contrast to the journey down. Holly was quite excited about their inheritance. To Faye, it was a relief that Holly would be taken care of in the years to come, and the savings she'd managed to scrape by for the future could now be used for other things. A new sofa for a start - the sagging beast with threadbare arms and a faint whiff of dog, needed to go. The bathroom was tired and some of the windows needed replacing badly. Faye felt very blessed indeed.

The village felt small and packed together after the space of the countryside. They pulled in by the cottage, and Todd opened the front door immediately. Margaux had alerted him to their arrival, and frankly he was glad. Much as he'd loved the company, the little sausage dog had driven him to distraction with her barking. Rollo was much more his style of dog. Magnificent in his ability to shut the world out and nap without moving for at least three hours straight, but funny, playful and affectionate when he was awake.

The transaction was done, two dogs and their belongings in return for a bottle of wine and a stick of seaside rock, with the words Hastings Rocks having been expertly rolled through it by a ruddy weatherbeaten woman in a hairnet brandishing a large pair of candy shears.

Howie and Max were also making their way home. They landed at a dreary Gatwick airport, the taxi driver waiting for them holding up a card which read FOX-BOSUN.

"I still think Bosun-Fox sounds better," Max laughed, and the debate continued to the car and remained unsettled until they were dropped off at the Gallery.

"Home sweet home," said Max, unlocking the door. Everything looked small. The stairs looked narrow, the rooms, pokey - always an after effect of having spent time in large airports and a spacious hotel lobbies. It didn't take long for them to shrink back to village sized people, a cup of breakfast tea that didn't taste of hotel kettle, a slice of marmite on toast and behold, England was home once more.

Chapter 21 - Winds of Change

Ursula sat Lydia down next to her on the chaise longue in her bougie lounge.

"Detective, Lydia, let me tell you something," she breathed, "one of the challenges of putting on plays, is moving the set around without destroying the magic between writer, actor and audience. Professional theatres have all manner of machinery, ropes, pulleys, electronic moving parts, knobs and levers. In the church hall, the only moving parts are Melanie and Geoff, clad head to foot in black. They work their little backsides off between scenes, flying in and out, whisking away chairs and tables, sliding in wobbly scenery, but however efficient they are love, they are still there, seen. We need to step this up, we need to 'go pro' dear. We need West End, Broadway, and we've got West Wickham and Broadstairs". She sat back on the chaise longue her monologue hanging in the air between them.

Lydia was speechless, she hadn't

expected Ursula to be so insightful, but she was right. To flush this murderer out, they needed to set the scene more realistically, and at the moment Melanie and Geoff were stamping across the stage in hob nailed boots.

"It's time to involve a few locals, get some scenes played out in public." She reached for her notebook and started making a cast list.

***

Faye was lying on the sofa, and Holly was painting her toenails, perched on the footstool. She rarely bothered with nail polish as her nails were kept short for playing the cello, but as Holly pointed out, she didn't play it with her feet, and besides, short painted nails were on trend at the moment. So, she'd agreed to both. The dogs had departed to the kitchen the minute the bottle was opened, their noses twitching disapprovingly. The afternoon sun was shining in the living room window and Faye closed her eyes. Anne had gone home, she'd stripped the bedlinen off the spare bed and tidied around before she packed her car and drove off in the early hours. It was a long drive back to Scotland, and she wanted to avoid the traffic and the weather, which would be turning later in the day. It had been such an emotional and wonderful weekend, but Faye was utterly wiped out. There was still a mountain of sorting out to be done, and Anne hoped to come back again in a few weeks.

Faye was just nodding off when the doorbell rang. "Oh blast! Who is it" she groaned. "I'll go mum," Holly bounced out into the hall and opened the door. There stood Velvet and another lady. Holly, recognised her as Detective Inspector Appleby but was confused at her presence on the doorstep with Velvet.

"Can we come in Hols, is your mum in?" Holly let them in, "Mum, Velvet's here" she called as she led them into the lounge. Faye sat herself up and saw Velvet first.

"Hiya lovely, poisoned anyone while I was away?" she asked blearily, then caught sight of Lydia.

"Oh! Blimey, hello... we have a standing, erm, joke."

Inspector Appleby raised an eyebrow and smiled. Velvet broke the awkward silence. "Faye, as you will remember, this is Detective Inspector Lydia Appleby. She came to me yesterday with some ideas, I suggested we team up, seeing as we work together. Anyway, I hope you don't mind me volunteering you too."

Velvet looked knowingly at Faye trying to convey some sort of message. Bewildered, Faye motioned for them to sit down. Still with toe separators wedged on her feet she glanced at Holly. "We'll just finish off in a bit mum, I'll put the kettle on."

"Faye, I assume you know about Stella?". Faye looked blankly at her, dread creeping in. "Erm no, what about her? They hadn't heard anything. Velvet had assumed they would have heard from Todd. They broke the news, Faye felt her tummy curdle, this was really too close to home now.

Lydia took a deep breath and asked, "Mrs Marshall, Faye, where were you this weekend, and do you have any witnesses?"

Taken aback, Faye told her, and she looked at Velvet, "what is this all about, what, do you think I have something to do with it?"

Lydia continued, "I simply needed to clarify that before we go any further. What I need from you now is the assurance that you won't divulge any of our conversation to anyone."

"I suppose so, but what about my daughter?" Faye replied, as Holly came into the room with a tray of tea and set it on the table. Lydia looked at Velvet who nodded.

"She's totally trustworthy Lydia, I've known Holly her whole life." The room was crackling with tension. "Sit down Holly, this concerns us all."

They talked long into the evening. Faye and Velvet found Lydia to be very likeable and unexpectedly funny. Her straight laced appearance and professional attitude when working masked a big personality that surprised them both.

The plan was to set up a couple of incidents in public areas, with Ursula as the star turn. She would be unreasonable, rude and boorish in a bid to flush out the murderer. She would be followed closely, the subject of a stake out, every time she was out alone. Lydia had approached Velvet at first because of her busy cafe, frequented by many of the villagers. The other venue was to be the next concert at the Church, and so forth. Faye's tummy lurched again, but this time because she'd missed the last rehearsal, had been asked to play First Cello, a step up from her usual position in the orchestra, and hadn't practised her part nearly enough. She made a mental note to get her cello out of the case and set up ready for the morning. They switched tea for wine and a rustled up cheeseboard.

Holly agreed not to divulge any detail of the conversation to anyone. She then headed up to bed feeling extremely grown up.

"So whats the next step?" asked Faye. "We will set up a group chat online, between us and Ursula - I'll do that now, and arrange a secret meeting to go over the details. Outside the village, maybe in Hawksford.

"I know someone there," piped up Velvet, "the spooky magic shop owner, Elsa, she's really nice - I spoke to her last week and she has a back room in the shop where she does readings for people. We could go there?"

"Readings?" Lydia asked.

"Yes, she's a psychic," Velvet replied.

"Oh, I see." She paused to think. "Well, yes, that does sound a good place," agreed Lydia.

Faye looked at Velvet desperate to ask why she was there, but left it for another time.
Ursula popped up on the group chat with a ping. She was in agreement, and they set a date, venue to be confirmed. In the meantime, Velvet was to contact Elsa and book the room. She wasn't quite sure how she was going to explain things, but she'd fudge

around the reason somehow.

In the hallway, the three ladies stood in the semi darkness, and felt empowered, until Joe arrived to walk Velvet home, and to their annoyance, their vulnerability was exposed once more. Outside, the wind was whipping up as Lydia lit up a cigarette with some difficulty, and followed them across the road at a distance. The Common was pitch black, apart from Joe's phone torch, the village lights kept their glow to themselves and the darkness edged right up to the high street and tried its best to envelop it. Velvet shuddered and held tight to Joe's arm. She couldn't wait to get home to their cosy flat above the Decadia. He didn't know all the details of what was going on, and he'd be livid that she was involved so deeply - he assumed they were just using the cafe as a stake out. She didn't like keeping things from him, but he'd only worry. Hopefully this would all be over in time for the wedding, and the whole village could put it behind them. But for now, Lydia was behind them, walking with her head down, scarf wrapped around her ears, smoke billowing to the east carried on a wicked wind. Joe glanced back and whispered to Velvet, "She's a funny one isn't she, is it something I said?"

That night, the wind grew so fierce it edged out roof tiles until they smashed onto pavements below, turned over bins and sent their lids spinning down garden paths, and a large ash tree lurched its great roots out of the earth with a groan. In the early hours it had crashed right across the high street, blocking the road and entrance to the pub.

Faye tossed and turned all night as the storm whipped through the woods, thinning out the trees of all their dead wood, swept over the green and buffeted against the cottage windows. The animals of the common took to the undergrowth and birds clung to their perches deep in the hedgerows.

Morning came, and the wind dropped, the sky was a mixture of yellow and pink, and strange grey wispy clouds hung, exhausted from being blown this way and that.

The traffic was redirected from the high street as a little bit of chaos reigned outside the Kings Head.

The publican, John, and the Reverend Fields stood in the street like demon and angel deciding the fate of the fallen tree. They parted company as the tree surgeon arrived to chop the giant monster into chunks, shred its sorry branches and cart it away. The noise of the shredder and chain saws seared through the town.

"Nothing stays the same does it?" Said Joe to Velvet. "Look at that, it's been there as long as I remember, what a shame!" he added as he swept some dried mud off the pavement outside the cafe into the road.

They stood in the doorway watching the goings on at the other end of the high street.

"There go my customers," Velvet muttered, her eyes following the bus as it detoured around the common. She hoped her knitters would be in today. She'd managed to spread the word to other groups in the area and now the Decadia was the proud hostess of two rival bookclubs, the Square Granny Crochet club and Pat's Paper Craft club, a group of ladies who came with a bewilderingly large array of materials and left with a small handful of embellished greetings cards, none of which would stay upright on a mantelpiece due to their bulky frontage. However, they all drank gallons of tea and coffee, ordered brunches, lunches and cakes galore. She was pleased that trade was picking up, but just not this morning. Remembering she had a phone call to make, she nipped out into the hallway and picked up the receiver on her old Bakelite telephone.

"Hello, is that Elsa? Yes yes, It's Velvet, from last week, yes, fine thanks... yes, I was just enquiring if I could use or hire your little room out the back for a meeting? It's a delicate matter, I can't go into the details, but we need somewhere small and private to talk, away from home. Would that be possible?" She cringed at the end of the phone, twirling the spiral cord around her fingers, awaiting a reply.

"Yes I suppose so lovey, I don't usually hire it out, but I tell you what, I'll trade you for a couple of slices of cake? I know you bake fantastic cakes? Would that be ok? I wouldn't have a clue what to charge otherwise."

Elsa licked her lips remembering the moist piece of chocolate cake she had demolished at the Decadia last year, and awaited her answer.

"Deal!" came the reply, and they set a date for half past ten on Thursday. Velvet hung up the heavy receiver with a clunk and launching back into modern technology, pulled her smartphone out of her pocket to update the group chat.

The next two days dragged. As promised to herself, Faye practised her cello. She loved Rachmaninov's second piano concerto and there were a number of little solos for the first cello - a role that had been thrust upon her as Deirdre, the ancient cellist had a chest infection she couldn't shift. She was utterly petrified. A visiting Russian pianist named Alexei Volcov was gracious enough to play, for a fee. He would be staying at the Kings Arms which had two guest rooms above. The orchestra were quite a-buzz about him, and from his photograph he was, in the words of the bassoonist Melanie, "very dishy" - her long face growing even longer as she pouted her lips and winked an eye.

Faye perched on her chair in the spare room, her bowing arm at the perfect angle, staring intently at the music on the stand. Her baggy knitted socks, a gift from the knitting ladies at the cafe, sank down around her ankles as she played, clouds of rosin rose about her as she went over and over her part. Only when her tummy started to rumble did she put down the bow and lie the cello carefully on its side. Her hands ached, and she shook them out and massaged them on her way down the to the kitchen.

The dogs were waiting for their walk.

"Ok little ones, come on then," she smiled, and found their leads, stuffed her lumpy wool-clad feet into her wellingtons and headed out of the cottage. Lunch would have to wait.

It wasn't as cold as it had been, the wind had dropped to a gentle breeze and the sun was making a passable attempt at warming her face as she stepped over the road to the common. The dogs strained on the leads and she pulled them back to heel a number of times before they settled into walking next to her.

As she crossed the grass, she saw the bench where Stella had died. The grass had been trampled into a muddy patch around it, presumably where the police had worked on the site. She shuddered, and a rush of anger rose from her chest and erupted from her eyes as a couple of hot tears. This was her home, her daughter's birthplace, her husband died here, it had been her parents home, and whoever this monster was, he or she was scrawling a very ugly chapter into their legacy.

She was determined more than ever to help Lydia set a trap. Thursday couldn't come soon enough.

Chapter 22 - Thursdays Girl

Lydia walked into the shop. She felt so out of place in the alien surroundings. A waft of incense reached her nostrils, a smell she had detested since childhood, when, during her catholic upbringing, she'd stood in church trying not to inhale the acrid fragrance as the young priest walked past swinging the thurible on its clanky brass chains. She remembered him smiling apologetically at her obvious distaste for the smoky contents. She pushed the image aside and walked up to the counter. Elsa looked up from her book.

"What can I do for you, love?" she asked, with a smile.

"I'm here for the meeting," said Lydia, looking around her at the unfamiliar objects.

Elsa nodded, and led her through a beaded and shell curtain which trailed over her shoulders then swung down into the doorway with a series of taps and clicks.
Velvet and Faye were already there.

Ursula arrived in a flurry of leopard print fur, moments after Lydia. They all eyed each other a little nervously.

"I'll leave you lovely ladies to it then," said Elsa, with a knowing look. "Just remember, to err is human, to forgive, defines."

"Divine," interjected Lydia.

"Thank you, isn't it just? I decorated it all last year," she motioned to the wall behind Lydia covered in stencilled angels and dragonflies.

Faye stifled a giggle but Velvet put a hand on her arm.

"Thank you Elsa, it's really lovely, we'll get started - enjoy the cake!"

Elsa floated out of the back room in a cloud of lavender room spray with one thing on her mind - she flicked the kettle on, and rummaged in the drawer for a fork.

The four women sat, on two mismatched chairs, a beanbag and a shop stool.

"I think Elsa has assumed I am mediating some sort of disagreement, so I may as well start things off," said Lydia in a businesslike manner.

She proposed a plan for Ursula to enter the cafe, order loudly, be disagreeable and then to quibble about the food. Velvet looked a little uncomfortable.

"I don't want to put people off coming in," she said, with some concern.

"If we don't catch the perpetrator there won't be anyone left to come in," snapped Lydia, then she softened. "What I mean to say is, we must look at the bigger picture Velvet."

"It's alright, pet," said Ursula patting Velvet's knee, "I can always get uppity about the tableware rather than the food if that helps - you have all that vintage old stuff don't you?" Velvet nodded. "I can make a big old scene about health and safety?" They looked at Lydia who was starting to feel a little exasperated.

"Yes, fine, whatever you think will look authentic, and, Faye, you keep your eyes on the other customers, see who is watching. Ursula can be rude and unreasonable to you both, get as many people looking. Then after she's gone, one of you can have a few tears and make a bit of a meal of it - get some sympathy. Get people talking in the village.

Does this sound reasonable ladies?" They looked at each other, and nodded.

"The next one can be at the Church, at the concert. Ursula has agreed to take Stella's place on the committee and do the seating and refreshments. Ursula, I'd like you to really try and rub people up the wrong way, get a bit personal, rush people, you know, get their backs up," Lydia grimaced in mock annoyance and Ursula's eyes shone in the delight of her forthcoming performance.

"Obviously, Faye, you'll be in the orchestra, you can spread a bit of gossip, 'back stage' as it were." Faye pictured the vestry full of instrument cases, the only theatrical element in there was the vicar's fancy robes which hung on the back of the door. Once more, her tummy turned somersaults, and last nights dream broke: Sergei Rachmaninov looming on the podium instead of their conductor, all six foot of him holding the sheet music out to her, the cello part underlined in red. His large hand dwarfed the baton as he tapped the music and shouted at her, his mouth expanding into a huge black darkness. She shook herself free of the dream, and tried to focus. The wooden stool was numbing her bottom and she shifted her weight.

They talked it through for another half

an hour, then rose to leave. Ursula bid them a flamboyant farewell, she surely was a character, but certainly no battle axe. Velvet looked forward to when it was all over and she could get to know her better.

Elsa appeared, as if by magic. "All ok ladies? Everyone happy?"

Lydia thanked her. "Yes, wonderful, we erm, straightened everything out, thank you." Elsa handed them all a fragment of rose quartz.

"For peace and harmony," she said, "I've blessed them." They thanked her profusely and herded Lydia out before she could ask what the hell she'd just been handed.

Back in the draughty Beetle, Faye shivered. They drove past Lydia getting into her black VW Golf. A sensible, powerful car representing its owner perfectly, thought Faye. She didn't even own a car until the other day, and now she had a beauty.

"Oh my God Velvet, I haven't updated you on what happened!" she gasped, and she recounted the weekend's events. When they got back to the cottage, Velvet came in for a cup of tea, and Holly and Faye showed her the photos. They sent a picture of the car to Joe.

He sent back a row of heart emojis. Faye and Holly looked at eachother conspiratorially, then Faye tapped Velvet's hand.

"Velve, Holly and I were wondering if you would like to use it for the wedding?"

Velvet beamed.

"Although I don't know who can drive it, neither of us have passed our tests!" Faye added.

None of that mattered for now - Velvet was sure one of the lads from Joe's garage would oblige them by playing chauffeur for the day.

She clapped her hands in delight. "Joe is going to be ecstatic, thank you so much! I'm so happy for you both, what an amazing windfall, he must really have thought a lot of you. God I wish I had an uncle like that!"

She left them, full of excitement and drove straight to the garage to tell Joe the news. He scooped her up in his big arms. "I told you something would come up. I don't suppose they've got another uncle with a big hotel have they?"

Chapter 23 - The King and Eye

It was Sunday. The Decadia was busy, and Nancy was helping out in the kitchen. The clock was clunking its big retro hand around to one thirty. Every booth was full, except one where they had plonked Holly and a hot chocolate to keep it occupied until Ursula arrived. Every time the bell above the door jangled, they jumped. A group of lads got up from their table and ambled over to the counter to pay.

As they left, Ursula wedged herself in, on the verge of greatness, by the edge of the doormat. She surveyed the room - any one of them could be the murderer. The man in the overalls, his slim fingers wrapped around his cup, his stained teeth, tufts of nostril hair hanging over his coffee - it could be him! She felt slightly queasy at the prospect. The trim little lady in her sixties, spreading jam on her crumpet - she looked handy with a knife; or the large man sitting opposite her who barely fitted behind the table - he may be more nimble than he looked.

Holly clocked her in the doorway, and was relieved to vacate her table - the third hot chocolate dumped in front of her was beginning to give her a sugar rush. She closed her laptop and quietly went out to the kitchen. Without eye contact, Ursula sashayed through the cafe and slid into the booth, setting her large handbag beside her. She studied the menu for a few minutes.

Meanwhile, in the kitchen, Holly was cramming the contents of a bag of crisps into her mouth in a bid to balance out her blood sugars, all the while pacing up and down, whilst Nancy, oblivious to the plan was slapping bacon onto the griddle and scrambling eggs in a large pan.

"Oh my god, we're up," hissed Velvet into Faye's ear. Their tummies lurched in unison.

Faye put a hand on her arm, "It's OK, stay calm, just go and take her order - she'll probably be an arse about it, but don't worry, we can do this!"

Velvet strode past the tables and stood before her, pen and pad poised.

"Good morning, what can I get for you today? Eventually Ursula looked up from her menu with a scowl.

"Hmmm, I'm not really a cooked breakfast sort of person, do you have anything other than greasy fry-ups?" She asked, her nose wrinkling with disapproval.

"Well, on the next page, you'll find some other traditional breakfasts, such as porridge, crumpets, coddled eggs, kippers, eggy bread or potato cakes. We are happy to do any combination," said Velvet, helpfully.

Ursula pursed her lips and ordered eggy bread with crispy bacon on the top and a pot of tea for one. She was actually quite hungry now at the sound of all that and made a mental note to come again and sample more of the menu, but for effect she added:

"You clearly have no concept of the 'continental breakfast', which is what one is used to, having travelled extensively, but I suppose it will do. Please make sure the bacon is crispy. I don't want that flabby stuff you put on builders' breakfasts."

Velvet winced inwardly, her bacon was never flabby, but she nodded and headed towards the kitchen rolling her eyes in mock irritation.

"God if she wasn't putting it on, I'd

have told her to shove her breakfast where the continental sun don't shine," whispered Velvet to Faye inside the kitchen door.

She called the order through to Nancy, and pegged the paper copy to the board. Faye went behind the counter and quickly made a list of who was in the cafe at that time, and hid it under a pile of napkins.

Out in the hallway, a camera had been installed within the damaged Elvis bust, his missing eye languishing on a shelf in the cupboard below. Carefully angled towards the door, the King monitored the comings and goings. Holly came out to clean the empty table and tried not to look at Ursula who was tutting and sighing loudly as she inspected the condiments. Faye walked hesitantly towards the booth with her tea and set it down on the table with a clank.

"Careful! I don't want it in my lap, thank you," she exclaimed, and a few heads turned. Faye blushed and mumbled an apology. A few more minutes ticked agonisingly by, and her food was ready.

"You take it," Velvet pushed the tray towards Faye, "I can't do it, I'm going to blow it, I know," she added nervously.

"Fine," said Faye, determined to get it over with. She walked towards the booth.

"About time! I was about to call the manager," barked Ursula. Faye repeated the order to her as she set it down on the table.

"I know what I ordered, thank you, I'm not a simpleton!" she snapped at Faye, who backed away and turned towards the kitchen.

People were starting to notice, watching her face as she walked by, and she obligingly crumpled her brow.

Velvet set about clearing another table, and before too long, Ursula called over to her. "Excuse me, young lady? Can you bring me another pot of English Breakfast, and this time with a cup that doesn't dribble scalding tea down my sleeve, this one has a crack in it!" - she held the little damaged Shelley teacup aloft for inspection by the entire cafe.

"You do know that cracked china can breed Legionnaires' disease don't you?"

Velvet looked appalled and took it from her, apologising profusely. "I'll be right back madam," she added, clasping the little cup to her bosom for protection. She knew it would come into its own one day.

Meanwhile, Elvis kept watch over the doorway with his bionic eye, recording every customer that came and went.

The girls jumped - "Excuse me? Is anybody actually going to bring me my tea or do I have to go to India to pick it myself?" Ursula bellowed from her booth. They actually wanted to giggle this time.

"God, she's over doing it a bit now, who does she think she is, Dame Maggie Smith?" said Velvet. Nancy looked around from the hot end of the kitchen.

"What is going on out there? Who is that, making such a fuss?" The girls decided it seemed a bit silly to keep Nancy in the dark, so as Velvet gathered the tea things, Faye, feeling a touch guilty for already breaking her promise to Lydia, relayed the plan to her in hushed tones.

"Blimey, just as well I didn't go out there and tear her off a strip!" said Nancy, rolling her shoulders and wiping her brow on her sleeve. Faye thought it unlikely, as Nancy wouldn't have said boo to a goose. She returned to the flames and cracked some eggs into a pan.

Out in the cafe, Velvet set another pot of tea and a perfect cup and saucer on the table before her faux customer. Ursula was in her element. "I do hope its not stewed," she said, with an irritated sigh. She noisily poured the pot from a height, and remarked on what a bad pourer it was, splattering tea in the process.

"I think if you pour a little more gently it should be ok," said Velvet, in an attempt to soften the situation.

"I was pouring tea before you were born young lady, and I do hope you aren't going to charge me for this after giving me near third degree burns?" she added, with a flourish.

Velvet was starting to blush as she stammered, "well yes, I suppose so"

"There's no suppose about it," barked Ursula, abruptly bringing the conversation to an end.

Velvet returned to the kitchen feeling very self conscious, tears brimming in her eyes. She couldn't believe how she was reacting - it was all pretend, but she hated making the cafe look so bad. Faye looked around at the customers. There were at least four people watching intently. She dipped behind the counter and made a few more notes.

Holly appeared by her side. "Mum, stop

bobbing up and down, you're making it really obvious you're up to something". She whispered.

"Oh right, good point," Faye replied, and slowly rose from behind the counter.

"OK, now you look like you're in a lift, Mum, just act natural forgodsake!" Holly whispered hoarsely.

Ursula had made a spectacle of herself, as promised, and she strutted up to the counter and insisted she not be charged a penny. The girls stood red faced and embarrassed as they reluctantly agreed, and she finally left. Exit, stage right. The atmosphere immediately changed. Customers started to chatter again, quite a few commiserated with them about that 'awful woman' and things went back to normal. Velvet obligingly squeezed out a few tears, her genuine upset bubbling under the surface.

Breakfasts and brunches came to an end and Velvet flipped the door sign to 'closed' for a well earned break before light lunches and the afternoon tea menu started.

From up the stairs, Lydia strode down with one of her officers who unceremoniously stuck his hand into Elvis' head to retrieve his little camera widget and plug it into his laptop. Velvet rummaged in the cupboard and slid the King's missing eye back in, and secured it with a new piece of sellotape. One day she'd get around to glueing it properly. She thought about the little cup, Legionnaires' disease indeed. She turned the lights off at the front of the cafe, and they sat down in the very back booth.

"Well done everyone. One of my officers is following Ursula home now, as a precaution. Her husband is at home, so she won't be on her own. I think it went very well. You all looked pretty convincing."

Lydia debriefed them efficiently, in full Inspector mode. Velvet and Faye were exhausted from the strain of the morning, and sat like a couple of sacks of flour, their feet buzzing under the table. The officer tapped rapidly on his keyboard, didn't share anything with them, and then suddenly packed it all up and headed back to the police station via the back door.

Lydia, seeing their disappointment, said "the footage will go back to the station for analysis, ladies, for face recognition and comparison to other footage we have in the area, for the nights in question. You did well. I'm confident we'll flush him out."

"Him?" said Velvet.

"My instincts are that we are dealing with a male perpetrator, yes. There are certain factors, measurements and height of individual, strength involved and a partial footprint. Of course, murder in a public place is fraught with contamination but, yes, I believe we're looking for a man."

Faye thought of the list she'd made under the counter and hauled herself up to go and retrieve it.

"That's half of these we can cross off then," she said, plonking it on the table. They briefly went through the list and Lydia gratefully popped it straight into her black rucksack, then she was off.

Faye looked at Velvet and blew out a relieved sigh. "I feel a bit used and abused do you?"

"Oh God, me too. But I suppose if it catches the killer...," the word stuck in her throat. To think he may have actually been sitting in her establishment, sipping tea.

"Oh Faye, I wish we hadn't started this. It's like poking the dragon," she looked sickened. Faye put her arm around her. They comforted each other and before too long, the cafe was open once more, the musical booths were switched on, the decades slipped into each other. Memories were jogged and nostalgia tweaked for the customers looking for afternoon tea with a difference. An elderly couple sat in the 1940s booth, crooning quietly to Vera Lynn, honeyed memories of a very different era spread thick as clotted cream on their scones.

Velvet turned the sign around on the door, as the last customer left. Joe had a Sunday roast on the go upstairs, and as much as the smell drifting through the floorboards was enticing, Faye and Holly needed to get back to the cottage for the dogs. They made their way over the road and up to the edge of the common linking arms and breathing in the fresh afternoon air.

"Mum, we've hardly had a minute to ourselves since we got back from Hastings. Let's stay in our pjs tomorrow morning and chill out."

"That sounds like heaven, love," Faye replied. She knew at some point she must practise her cello, but it could wait until the afternoon.

When they returned, the dogs were fast asleep in their usual spots; Rollo on the back of the sofa, and Margaux curled in a tiny ball under the blanket. They both jumped up and danced about the girls' feet yelping. Faye groaned, her feet were killing her as it was.

"I'll pop them over the common, they need to get out," she said. "Not on your own, Mum," said Holly, putting her shoes back on. Faye smiled at her daughter gratefully. "We'll stick to the grass, I don't feel much like venturing into the woods anyway."

On the common, there were still a few people out and about. A family strolling after a big lunch, a boy lagging behind, bashing everything in his path with a large stick. A couple strolling arm in arm, a small white West Highland Terrier prancing around their feet.

Faye bent down to tie the lace on her boot, and on the way up she winced, as the weight of the week, hours of cello practise and standing all day. caught up with her back.

"Let's find a bench Holly, and we can sit whilst the dogs have a run around," she groaned. They passed a few benches taken up by families and as they approached another Faye recognised the occupant. The man with the ancient Pekingese. Faye stopped to say hello, as she had promised she would do the next time she saw him. The elderly man with the watery blue eyes looked up at her and smiled.

"Hello Fella," she said, to the snaggle toothed dog, his tongue lolling out to one side. "How are you today? Are you having a nice walk?" She addressed the man. He looked at her and smiled.

"All the better for seeing you my dear," he said, in a surprisingly strong deep voice. His face then changed, his brow furrowed and serious. "Your instincts are quite correct, do not stray into the woods - stay out in the open, Faye." His hand on top of his walking stick, strained and taut with age, gripped tightly as he pulled himself up to standing. "Good afternoon, ladies" he said, and walked away, Fella's audible raspy panting fading into the common beside him.

"Woah. Gandalf didn't want to chat then!" said Holly, as she took his seat on the bench. Faye sat down and watched curiously as the elderly duo made their way towards the high street. "I didn't expect him to sound like that, his voice is quite booming, and he looks so frail. I wonder what he did for a living, I wonder what his name is?"

"Well he knew yours Mum. Actually, how did he know yours?" Holly puzzled. Faye thought about it.

"I must have said it, or maybe he just knows me from somewhere, orchestra maybe? Actually, I don't know."

A slight pang of unease in her chest reminded her that they'd never actually been introduced. But that pang sank like a stone into her stomach as she accepted it was more likely that her notoriety as a widow, a bereft child, a sad lonely lady who lived in the cottage, was probably why he knew her. For the most part, these events had faded over time with locals, but of course he was old enough to have witnessed them all. Perhaps he had known her parents, or her teachers, or the Reverend. She sighed and looked at Holly. Such a beautiful creature, her daughter, golden red hair catching in the setting sun, trailing over her shoulders from out of a green knitted hat that brought out the colour of her eyes - jade, with flecks of gold and bronze that spilled onto her cheekbones as freckles. She marvelled at how she had produced such an exquisite human being. With renewed vigour, she rose from the bench and grabbed Holly's hand.

"Come on, we are going to walk these dogs, cook something scrumptious for dinner and get on with our lives. We have a flat to sell, a car to collect and some money to spend, girlie!" Holly whooped in agreement startling

Margaux, who had sneaked onto her lap for a rest.

They walked on, arm in arm, planning a shopping trip for a new suite for the lounge. The dogs trotted along beside them, oblivious to the fact they wouldn't be allowed up on it, at least for the first month anyway.

Later that night, Faye lay pinned to the old sofa by the dogs. Rollo sat, his fluffy triangular form heavy on her tummy, Margaux on her legs, upside down with her stubby paws in the air. The sofa lay sagging and unaware of its fate beneath them. She felt a ridiculous waft of guilt that she quickly dismissed. It had borne witness to so much over the years, but 'out with the old, in with the new' she mused. Then she patted its flattened arm, as she hauled herself out of its baggy leathery embrace, disgruntled dogs spilling onto the floor.

Chapter 24 - Six Foot of Russian Gloom

T he description of Rachmaninov by one of his peers mimicked the pianist as he practised for his concert on Saturday night. To him, it was indeed a gloomy prospect, playing this most beloved concerto with an orchestra of amateurs in some suburban church on the outskirts of London, but his tour manager couldn't secure him a gig in the capital.

He gloomily went through the runs and chords over and over methodically, and awaited the orchestra to do an entire run through of the piece. The piano was acceptable he hoped, and the church actually had very good acoustics. The orchestra had welcomed him, he'd smiled at everyone, they had shaken his hand and complimented his playing. He couldn't really complain, but the nagging perfectionist inside him would never truly be satisfied with what they had to offer. Granted, there were some exceptional musicians here, the cellos weren't bad, a good wind section but there were a couple of violinists who should have hung up their instruments years ago. But a gig was a gig. The pub was comfortable, clean and the bar well stocked. His spirits raised at the prospect of a drink afterwards.

"He's not as handsome as his photo," whispered Jenny, wetting a reed and attaching it to the mouthpiece of her clarinet.

"Nor as young!' a flautist whispered back. Indeed, the photograph in the programme was of his younger, slimmer self, taken a few years ago when he had a thicker head of hair, no bags under his eyes and midriff that wasn't protruding uncomfortably over his trousers.

During the rehearsal, Reverend Fields was pottering in the church. He had taken to arranging the flowers himself since the untimely demise of Stella. With the Saturday night concert, Sunday morning services and a double christening in the afternoon it was going to be a busy weekend. He gathered the empty containers from around the church and the floristry snips and foam from the cupboard. He looked down at the scissors in his hand and felt a small pang of guilt at relishing the prospect of doing the flowers himself. Stella was the last person to handle them, albeit clumsily. His thoughts were broken by a particularly dramatic part of the concerto, the pianist thundering down the keyboard, his long nimble fingers clawing and stretching as he reached for the notes. It truly was awe-inspiring to see such talent - he himself could just about fumble through All Things Bright and Beautiful. Clutching his floristry tools to his chest, he held his breath, and when the cacophony of the orchestra chimed back in, he breathed out and headed to the kitchen. Placing everything on the counter, he slipped out the side door and off to the greengrocers to see Pam, to get a good deal on the flowers. The foliage would be free of charge. The local woods were most obliging on that score.

On the high street, shoppers were out in force. People buzzed about the shop doorways, the cafe was busy, and the card shop had re-opened with Cheryl Mayhew at the helm. He made a mental note to drop in to visit her and see how things were going. The poor girl was making the best of things since her mother's funeral. She had taken on another part-time girl from the village who drifted about the shop with as much enthusiasm as the first.

A little waft of excitement grew as he approached the greengrocers. Just as it had been in his mothers day, the side of the shop that Pam Cox inhabited with her flowers was bursting out onto the pavement with colour. He knew exactly what he wanted and pointed out the large pink peonies, clutches of tiny star like chrysanthemum, and some pale blue shards of delphiniums. Blue for a boy and pink for a girl, the twins' christening being his inspiration. He felt like an artist choosing his paints, and politely asked Pam if there was any discount for the church.

"Oh, go on then Reverend, I'll do them at cost and throw in some ribbon," she said kindly.

Ted tutted loudly on the other side of the shop. He didn't like giving discounts, especially not to snooping vicars who stuck their noses in other people's business. Reverend Fields had been very supportive of Pam when she had a car accident years ago. She had been in a neck brace for weeks, and he had kindly assisted her in the shop, much to Ted's irritation. She clearly had a soft spot for him, but Ted felt he outstayed his welcome. Of course, the Reverend himself hadn't quite realised the real reason he was there. The smell, the feel of the flowers, and the memories of his mother. It was all so familiar and comforting. Poor Pam had never been the best driver. Her florist van had more scrapes and scuffs than she'd care to mention, especially to her husband. The old Morris Minor van with hand painted flowery logo on one side, 'Pippins Flowers and Pippins Fruit & Veg' the other, was known all over the village - partly because it had been there for years, sold on with the business - but mainly because of her precarious parking when out delivering. However, she was a nice enough person and very obliging when it came to supplying St Val's with flowers.

As the Reverend strode back to the church with armfuls of pink heady blooms, Ted Cox picked a fight with Pam, and the air around Pippins was blue. The air inside the church wasn't much better as a disagreement had broken out between the guest pianist and the first violin. The conductor, his hair dishevelled, was trying in vain to interject and calm things down, but seemed to lack authority in his casual slacks and jumper.

The Reverend asked Ursula, who had popped in to count the ticket sales, what had happened. She recanted the altercation with glee.

"Well, the orchestra were starting to pack up, when the first violin muttered something about his tempo - the Russian chappy heard him and, well, talk about light the blue touch paper, he went up quicker than a roman catholic... candle! I mean, Roman Candle!" She looked embarrassed, but the Reverend didn't batt an eyelid. He was used to people slipping in the odd religious gaff in front of him, such as "I swear on the bible, Reverend" - it frankly amused him watching them squirm. His all time favourite was during a baptism, a very earnest god parent who, when asked to approach the font, stepped forward and stood on the fancy italic writing on a floor plaque. When realising her error, emitted "oh Jesus, what am I like?" to a bemused congregation.

Ursula returned to her tickets, and went off to count the seats and label up the rows alphabetically with laminated slips of paper.

Faye couldn't get out of there quick enough. She'd had enough confrontation for one week. She battled down the aisle with her cello case bashing into her shins.

"Allow me," said a voice beside her. It was Jim, the trombone player. He took the cello out of her hand before she could say a word, and strolled down the aisle balancing it out with his own heavy case in the other hand. She scuttled on behind, thanking him shyly, wondering if he was planning to walk her all the way home. However, when they reached the door, he put it down and walked off up the road. She smiled to herself at the absurd gesture. Just then, Velvet called out to her from the pub doorway and she changed her mind about dropping the beast home and crossed the road with it. The gang were inside, having a celebratory drink for Max and

Howie's engagement. Holly was behind the bar serving, and she took the cello and put it out the back. Faye sank into the padded booth - she hadn't realised how much she needed a drink after the drama of rehearsals. The ice cold gin and tonic slid down very nicely indeed.

"I was watching out the window waiting for you to finish," said Velvet loudly into her face. "Can you believe it, two weddings! But we aren't doing the double wedding thing," she bellowed, "I don't want to hog the limelight with my dress," she carried on, "not that I've bought one yet, but everyone just looks at the bride, don't they."

She had a point - the bride did tend to be the focus of a wedding. "Very thoughtful of you Velvet," Faye said, with genuine admiration, but actually she wasn't really in the mood for wedding chatter, she wasn't even sure why. Maybe it was tiredness, being last to the party, and the only one sober. Friday night was always busy down at the Kings Head and the noise of the pub seemed to rattle in her ears.

"Are you alright Faye, you look a little.... over stimulated?" Said Max putting his arm around her.

"Yes, it's been a long day, I think I just need my bed," she smiled.

"Hey, congratulations again, Max, I'm so happy for you both," she added.

This was the first time she'd seen them since their announcement on the group chat. Gradually, Faye started to unwind a little. Max had a fatherly way about him that she found reassuring.

Over on the other side of the bar, in the quieter side of the pub, Alexei was nursing a pint of lager and a vodka shot. His head felt heavy and his back was sore from sitting on the hard piano stool. Any shift in height from his set up at home made his long back ache, despite adjusting the seat up and down. He longed to go back to his own bed, but this was his life now, touring, earning, getting his name out there. If he could secure a couple of big recitals and a recording contract, he might be able to take a break in the summer.

He looked over at the merry throng in the other bar, with no wish to join them, looking away before anyone caught his eye. He drained his pint, knocked back the vodka and headed up to bed. The old pub floors creaked and groaned as he made his way up to his room. He unlocked the door, and walked over to the window to close the heavy brocade curtains. The lamp posts were casting a glow onto the street below. Reverend Fields was locking up the church opposite and a few people were outside the pub talking and laughing. Further up the road, a tall figure coming out of a doorway caught his eye. He recognised him as the lanky trombone player, striding haphazardly towards the common with his long case.

These English people led such small provincial lives, he thought. Imagine living across the road from the only concert venue you played in! He rolled his eyes and shut the curtains. Within minutes he'd showered, climbed into the old oak four poster bed and fallen into a deep boozy sleep.

In a parked car across the road, was a young policeman. He was watching the activity on the high street. He sent a text to Lydia, who was quietly sipping a glass of wine in the corner of the pub. She replied, her heart thumped in her throat suddenly. She took a slug of the wine and headed to the ladies toilet. There, she texted Faye to meet her. A minute later, the two ladies were standing side by side, pretending to preen themselves in the mirror. Finally a woman who was in one of the cubicles left, and Faye nervously turned to Lydia.

"What's happened, what is it?" Lydia quickly filled her in. "We have a suspect, we've been following him all week, his name is James Brown."

"The soul singer?" said Faye, wide eyed.

Lydia paused in disbelief, and said slowly "No Faye.... he's dead. James Brown the trombonist - I think he calls himself Jim?"

The penny dropped and Faye stifled a giggle. "Oh 'Jim Bones' we call him, Jim Bones" and she mimed his lanky walk. "Oh no, I can't imagine he'd hurt a fly, he's a bit of a, well, a wally really," she added guiltily.

"Well wally or not, he's been acting very suspiciously, going up to the woods at night, wandering about the streets after dark. Murderers tend to revisit their crime scenes, you know. Anyway I have an officer following him now. I'm going to head up there and join him, and I've called for backup" whispered Lydia, her eyes darting towards the door as it started to open.

It was Velvet. "Everything ok Faye? Oh Lydia, I didn't know you were in tonight!"

They updated her, and she was appalled at the thought of Jim, one of her best customers as a suspect. "He comes in most mornings for a bit of breakfast - he doesn't cook much since his mother died. Oh my word, he's always up so early, he's first in some mornings, unless he comes in on his way home from murdering people that is...." Velvet said, putting her hand about her throat, trying to make sense of it.

"Either way, he's definitely up to something with that trombone case, and I intend to get to the bottom of it," said Lydia.

Jim 'Bones' Brown reached the edge of the woods. He took a small torch out of his pocket and shone it through the trees. The creatures of the night scattered silently away from the feeble beam of light as he entered. Once out of sight of the high street, he set his case down by a large tree, unclipped the large brass clips and opened it on the forest floor. He crouched down, his long legs folding up like a deckchair, reached in and pulled out the large metal instrument. But this was no trombone. He popped the torch into his mouth so he could use both hands, cursing himself for not buying the head torch he'd seen in the camping store in town. He turned levers, extended the length, unflipped flaps, as his father had shown him, and finally pressed the on button.

The metal detector sprang to life with a beep, lights flashing softly in the gloom. He rose, unfolding his long form and swept it back and forth over the grass and leaves, walking slowly as he went. It was five minutes at least before the first beep. Nothing but a section of umbrella. He put it in his pocket out of the way, and on he went, deeper into the woods. This nightly ritual never bored him. If he could find a few decent things he could sell them in the vintage and collectables shop in Swanbridge, where he worked, three days a week. He had his own shelf in one of the cabinets, mostly consisting of historic coins, the oldest being Tudor, Henry VIII's squashed face adorning one side; a roman clasp, and part of a hair comb. But the real treasure he had yet to find - his mother's wedding ring, the reason he started this whole escapade, lost on a Sunday walk years ago. She was heartbroken, and her tearful face stayed with him from that moment on. He vowed to find it, had retraced her steps many times, but in doing so, had started to find all sorts of interesting pieces. It led him to his job, in the aptly named 'Time Warp' shop. The only drawback to his secret hobby, was just that. He didn't have permission, or indeed a licence, to use a metal detector on the common or anywhere for that matter. It was expensive, and what if they said no? It would be 'game over'. This, and his desire for privacy, resulted in the clandestine nature of his nocturnal outings.

Sometimes in the early hours of the morning, before daybreak, he would fit a few hours detecting in and then head for breakfast at the Decadia, stamping his telltale muddy boots down the high street, removing the clumps of earth on the way.

He heard a series of beeps from the detector. Crouching down, he dug a small hole with a little trowel he kept on a string attached to his zip pocket. He unearthed a coin. A large Victorian penny. The images on both sides flattened and matt with age, he rubbed it between his fingers and slipped it into another zipped pocket. As he stood up a huge torch light flooded his eyes, and a voice told him to stand still and raise his hands. He let go of the detector and torch, and two police officers strode forward and brought his hands down behind his back. They put hand cuffs on him and Lydia read him his rights.

Apparently he was being arrested in relation to a series of crimes and they wished to talk to him at the police station. He hung his head, knowing the gig was up, he'd have to cough up for a licence now and he wondered if they'd seize all his finds, and his equipment. He didn't protest as they led to him to a waiting police car parked on the verge, and helped him into the back seat. He noticed his trombone case on the ground next to the car being searched by another officer. The lights were flashing, a few Friday night stragglers were standing watching, shivering in the night air. He recognised Faye and Velvet, who had marched up the road after Lydia, protesting. The car pulled away and tears stung his eyes, plopped onto his cheekbones and ran down his thin face. The inability to wipe them was almost as unbearable as the hand cuffs digging in his wrists behind him.

"May I have these taken off please," he begged quietly. "I promise I won't be any trouble." The officer in the back assessed the situation and asked Lydia, who nodded.

"Thank you, I'm so sorry. I'm not trying to be difficult, I'm just terribly uncomfortable." He rubbed his wrists, wiped his face and sniffed back the tears.

Lydia frowned in the front seat. He was awfully polite and mild mannered, and she wondered if the girls had been right. Still, it's always the quiet ones, she thought to herself, as they turned into the station carpark. It would be interesting to see what his alibis were for the times of the murders.

Velvet and Faye turned back towards the high street and walked, huddled together, back down to the pub. "It can't be him Faye, he's harmless, a bit gormless at times, but very sweet," Velvet sighed.

"I know! It's ridiculous, I can't imagine him attacking anyone! What the hell was he doing in the woods? Was that a metal detector I saw? Maybe he's a treasure hunter?" Faye wondered, her eyes widening. "Maybe he knows about some lost hoard? There are royal connections to the area, aren't there?"

Velvet shook her head. "I think you're getting carried away Faye, he works in that vintage shop, you know, the one we were going to visit, and still haven't been. Maybe he finds bits of historic crap in the woods to sell in there? I mean, hats off to him for being enterprising, I'm not sure I could be bothered with that, just for a few old coins and a bunch of beer cans. I wonder if they have any wedding dresses in there?"

Up ahead, the pleasing glow of the pub spilled out onto the pavement, and they were glad to get back inside and rejoin the group.

"Where the hell have you two been?" said Joe, "you went to the loo about forty five minutes ago! I thought Faye was having one of her meltdowns or something." Velvet jabbed him in the side.

"No, I'm fine thank you Joe," said Faye, slightly alarmed at his terminology. Was this how they saw her? As someone who had meltdowns? She hoped not, and she knew that Joe wasn't always the most tactful person.

Her grief had definitely changed her, but she assumed that her personality, although altered irrevocably, was not that of some horrendous drama queen. She took a deep breath and chose to push these thoughts aside for now, knowing they'd inevitably come back, on a night when she had to get up early the next day, replaying every woeful scene until her eyelids fell shut from the exhaustion of regurgitating her life on the 'Midnight Cinema' also known as her bedroom ceiling.

The publican, John, called time and rang the bell behind the bar. The group chattered on, picking apart poor Jim, and his predicament. They said their goodbyes and Holly came out from behind the bar, swinging her coat over her head and plunging her arms into the sleeves.

"Come on Mum, I'm shattered," she moaned into Faye's ear.

"Don't forget the beast," she motioned to the back room.

They carried the cello between them back up the road, and Todd caught up with them crossing to the Common, and carried it the rest of the way. He was a little bit tipsy as he weaved his way across the grass to the cottage.

"Steady Todd, I've got to play that thing

tomorrow," Faye cautioned.

"Are you sure there's a cello in here? It's not a machine gun is it?" he joked, as he put it down by the front door.

"Oh Todd, it's not funny, poor old Jim!" They said goodnight, settled in for the night in their side by side cottages, and went to bed wondering if they could be wrong about Jim and that stranger things had happened.

But, of course, it wasn't Jim. After a harrowing evening of questioning, and a sleepless night in a cell, he was allowed to go home very early the next morning. He let himself into his flat, downed a glass of water and unfurled on the bed like a crushed autumn leaf, a husk of his former self, his former self being not much more than a husk to begin with. He hadn't been given his equipment back, nor his trombone case. He would have to put his instrument in a bin liner to take to orchestra if it was raining, that's if he made it all. With all these thoughts swirling around his head, he fell into an exhausted sleep.

The friends' group chat was pinging back and forth all morning. Rumours were flying through the ether, over field and tree, around the church spire and back again, until finally Lydia texted an emotionless message to

Velvet.

"As you are aware, an arrest was made, and the suspect questioned. He has been released - no charges were brought."

Velvet announced the news to the group, trying not to let on where she'd heard it. The pinging ceased and everyone got on with their day.

It was late afternoon when Jim awoke. He sat upright, looked at his bedside clock, and groaned. He'd missed the final run through. But, determined not to let anyone down, and to quell any rumour that may be circulating, he got up, had something to eat, showered and changed into his old dress suit. The trousers were a little too short for his long legs, and he rethought his brown socks, rummaging for a black pair in the drawer. He hadn't done any washing for weeks, and it was slim pickings. Suddenly his groping hand fell upon something at the back of the drawer. He froze, his eyes widened and he pulled out a ring. A gold band! A wedding ring! His mother's lost ring! It must have come off when she was pairing up the socks, over a year ago. She had become quite thin with illness in her last months, it must have slipped off her finger the day she went for that last walk, so she naturally thought it was lying in some leaves somewhere on the forest floor. He sat on the edge of the bed and cried with relief. All this time it was here, all this time he'd been searching. He was overwhelmed with joy and disbelief. It was as if she'd been guiding him, to dig out his father's metal detector, to make a living, get a job. He sobbed loudly then laughed, pulled himself together, and changed his socks. He put the ring on the finger of his right hand, it fitted snugly. Now, where was that damn trombone? He had a concert to play!

Over in the church, a couple of early birds arrived. It was too early to show their tickets, so they wandered around the church, picking up leaflets at the back. The musicians had been there all afternoon for a final run through, and were drifting back into the vestry after a break. Most of them had been in the pub across the road, but Faye was so close by, she nipped home to change and let the dogs out. They were pleased to see her, barking noisily. She let them out into the garden, and sat on a garden chair, her face to the sun, soaking up the early evening rays. At last Spring was on the way, the nights were getting lighter, and March had lived up to its name, stomping in and knocking February to one side like it was old news. Faye sat thinking, how once a month had drawn to a close, it just became filed away in history. February two thousand, September two thousand and eleven, twelve and so on, just another month in another year, all passing so quickly, the older she became. When she was young, the winters seemed so long and the summers endless. Spring and autumn were just interludes sprinkled with calendar dates for Pancake day, Easter, Harvest and Halloween. She looked at her watch, twenty minutes to get something to eat, change and get back over to St Val's - but the sun was so nice on her wintered face, she stayed another five minutes while the dogs worked the perimeter of the garden. Margaux did her signature 'squwee' as Holly had nicknamed it, on the patio, a piddle that ran around the paving slab in a perfect square. Faye chuckled and headed into the kitchen to feed them, and herself.

Timed to perfection, she closed the front door and turned to the common. Todd was just going out of his front gate. "I'm just on my way to the church Faye, wouldn't miss this one, I love Rac. II, it's going to be a packed house! Everyone is talking about this famous pianist, what's he like?" he said, waiting for her by the road.

"He's fabulous, plays it beautifully - you won't be disappointed Todd. He's definitely a bit of a showman, and has the temperament to match, but these great talents are quite often a bit highly strung," she replied, feeling pleased that tonight's concert had caused such anticipation in the locals.

They walked back there together, their shadows long and lanky over the grass in the evening sunshine, which prompted Faye to say "I hope Jim makes it, he wasn't there at rehearsal."

Todd was right, the church was packed. Faye was a little alarmed but she wasn't late, everyone just seemed to be there early.

"See you later Todd," she gave him a nod.

"Good luck," he said and she went to find her cello.

Ursula sat just inside the door behind a little wooden table, laptop open and money tin beside it. She had dutifully checked tickets, sold tickets and pointed out seats to everyone in attendance. Having done it for the theatre troop many times, it wasn't new to her. She felt a little crestfallen that she was going to have to be quite horrible in the interval - they might not ask her to do it again, and she was quite enjoying herself.

In the pub, Alexei was downing vodka shots. It wasn't through nerves, but habit, and maybe a bit of boredom. These tours were getting so tedious. He reminded himself of what his tutor had once said - "nothing matters but the music," and once again the six feet of Russian Gloom that was Mr Rachmaninov was at his side, steering him towards the piano. But first he needed a pee. He nodded to the barman on exiting the pub, loped over the road tucking his dress shirt back into his cummerbund, and swung his tailcoat over his head and down onto his arms.

Faye looked nervously at the empty seat in the brass section. There was no sign of Jim. The conductor assumed he was a no show. She rosined her bow and adjusted the pegs on her cello, tuning up the strings and running through a few bars. The cacophony of the audience chattering, blended with the readying instruments. The main door opened, and in walked Jim. He looked jubilantly at Ursula, "Good evening," he said, striding past her, his naked trombone glinting under the church lighting. There was a hushed silence as he walked down the aisle and took his seat in the brass section. Faye noticed his transformation, she felt strangely proud of him for clearly rising above what had happened.

Glancing down at his mother's wedding ring, the golden hue mirroring that of his trombone, he smiled at the musicians around him, and nodded to Faye and to Velvet in the audience. He finally felt he had put something to rest, and could now move on with his life, start living instead of merely existing. But first, Rachmaninov.

The quietness erupted into applause as the conductor appeared, followed by the leader of the orchestra clutching his violin and bow in one hand, his lopsided glasses fastened with sellotape. Then, the maestro himself, Alexei, who despite having downed at least half a bottle of vodka, walked in a straight line to the piano and sat down with a flourish, flicking the tails of his suit behind him. A few moments passed, and Todd held his breath in the audience. The first ominous bars of the second piano concerto resounded through the ancient building. The orchestra swept in and then the piano, Alexei's hands trickling up and down the keys, the most beautiful melody drifting out of the wooden body of the instrument, hammers inside pumping up and down as the strings reverberated. It was magical. The audience were enraptured, not least the Reverend Fields, who stood at the back leaning on a pillar, his face flushed with joy, his eyes fixated on the pianist in wonder as he teetered on the edge of a crescendo, then dipped again into melancholy. The French horn came in, his poignant tones like no other in the orchestra, then, the delicate notes of the piano answered, the violins, the piano gaining pace and abruptly, the end of the first movement was upon them.

The orchestra tiptoed into the second movement - piano, then flute, clarinet with its soulful melody, winding around the piano, as the musicians swayed and moved like grasses by the sea, the ocean stiller than before, but ebbing and flowing, the piano tinkling over the waves like gulls dipping in and out of the water. Enraptured again, the Reverend closed his eyes, his brow knitted together in ecstasy, as if the hands of God had reached down and stuck a finger in each ear. Nervously, at the back of the church, Ursula was building her own little crescendo ready for the interval.

Velvet was utterly mesmerised, she'd never heard anything like it in her life. Joe was reading the programme, eager to know more about the extraordinary sounds he was hearing. Then, the most gorgeous melancholy melody floated out over the congregation, for that is what they were now, they were no longer an audience, they were witness to the extraordinary ethereal power of music. It swept through them, around them, engulfing and joining with their souls.

Shocking herself, Velvet stood up and clapped, unaware of the etiquette about saving applause until the end. But Alexei smiled, complimented by her exuberance and nodded his thanks, she sat down awkwardly, the third movement began.

Alexei swept his masterful hands over the keys once more, the crowd were silent, the orchestra rumbled quietly as he took the pace, then swept in around his notes like a stormy sea hugging a rocky coastline, waves crashing and ebbing around the passages.

Faye's hands were tiring, but she kept playing, up and down the fingerboard, her tense strong finger tips pressing down on the strings, her other arm bowing backward and forward, tilting and dragging as the rich woody notes soared out of her cello. She loved every minute of it, totally absorbed in her surroundings.

The pianist took the lead once more, his expert fingers shaping the music, his eyes closed, no printed music in front of him, he knew every inch of this piece - it no longer held the form of black and white notes on a page, it was embedded into his soul in shapes and colours, tones and emotions spilling through his hands and into the instrument before him.

The orchestra took the melody and he sat motionless, then reclaimed the melody once more.

Up and up Alexei soared, notes sparkling under his fingers, his concentration total. The effect was spellbinding, the worries and woes of everyone there were wiped clean in an instant, at the resolution of the movement, the piano giving in to the orchestra, they became as one, as wondrous peace enveloped every person in the room.

The conductor's arms finally dropped, the place erupted, and those who had never whooped in a concert did so.

"Bravo!" bellowed Max, in a sea of applause.

The Reverend had tears running down his cheeks. Velvet stood again and clapped, and quite a few people were moved to join her, the usual English reserve abandoned. After everything the town had gone through, the release of tension that night was palpable.

Alexei was a little taken aback at their response - he was used to a good applause, but the emotion in the room moved him too. He stood and bowed over and over. The leader, first violin, leaned forward and shook his hand, their tiff over the tempo long forgotten; the conductor, ecstatic, his hair all over the place, gestured to the orchestra, and exhausted, they stood and bowed. Ursula stepped forward with a gift for the pianist, a bottle of some kind in a bag and some flowers which seemed woefully inadequate for such a performance. She retreated to the side, clapping as she backed up to a pillar. The triumphant performance under his belt, Alexei pulled himself up again from a deep bow and headed to the vestry wiping a tear from his eye. His tutor had been right, it was all about the music, and nothing else mattered. This little town would stay in his heart forever. The applause continued for the orchestra as Ursula sidled down to the refreshments area. Nancy was already there, stoically unpacking the glasses from the sectioned boxes.

"Are you ready, Nancy? I'm going to

cause a rumpus, just go with it ok?"

Nancy replied, "go for it lovey, I'll just crack on with the washing up once they start ditching the glasses." Lydia was sitting at the back of the church, elegantly dressed in her civvies, her hair down, long and straight, and a soft black suede jacket over a dark green woollen dress and black suede boots. She looked so different, Velvet did a double take, then tried not to look again as they weren't supposed to know each other. Seeing Lydia reminded her there was a scene to play out in the interval, and she wasn't that keen to be anywhere near it.

"Joe, can you get me a glass of white wine, love?" she asked. He hauled his large frame off the pew, massaging his own sleepy buttock with a large hand. "Yeah, if I can wake my arse cheek up!" She giggled nervously. "Go on... hurry up!" she shooed him off with the programme.

Alexei had emerged from the vestry, and stood soaking up the adoration of his newly formed fan club. It mostly consisted of middle aged ladies telling him how wonderfully he had played. He smiled and nodded, thanked them, glancing past them at the wine with a slight lick of his lips. His agent stepped forward with a glass for him.

One sip and he longed to be over in the

251

pub. "What in God's name is this? he said, screwing up his face and turning the glass around as if he would find a label on it. "It tastes like it was fermented in a soldier's boot!" His entourage of ladies giggled. He carried on shaking hands with people and making polite conversation.

Ursula was fermenting her own brew over by the wine table. She was loudly demanding "Red or white?" barking "dirty glasses on the trays please," addressing the queue like a headmistress.

"Please make a donation for refreshments, there's a jug of water and paper cups if you don't have any money, dear." The alienated paupers turned away from the wine table and formed a queue of shame at the water jug.

"No, Madam, do not put your dirty glass back on the wine table, it could get mixed up with the clean ones I'm filling!" Pam the florist was taken aback, but Ursula carried on, "and then someone will get all of your germs!" The man next to Pam backed away from her possibly plague-ridden glass, much to her embarrassment.

"The orange juice table is in the corner for the tea totallers," she called loudly, accentuating the phrase with her fingers as speech marks. Everyone heading for the tepid juice now felt like a raging alcoholic. She really was being as offensive as possible. Nancy in the kitchen was cringing as she furiously washed and dried the glasses, plopping them back into the partitioned boxes.

The Reverend Fields was admiring his floristry when Pam approached him. "You did a marvellous job Reverend, they look beautiful!" He blushed with pride. "Thank you Pam, I have to say, it was very therapeutic. I think if I hadn't gone into the church, I should have followed in my mother's footsteps into floristry."

Pam faltered, "erm, Reverend, that lady doing the refreshments, I don't mean to be difficult, but, well, she's extremely rude. My Ted is not best pleased, he said he'd give her a bunch of fives, and I'm not talking about bananas, Reverend," she said, glancing back at Ted, who was sitting perched on a pew one eyebrow raised in irritation and the other brooding low over his other eye. In his chunky hands, he warmed a glass of white wine.

"Oh dear, oh dear me," said the Reverend, and hurried over to Nancy who was emerging from the kitchen, apron soaked with suds and brow perspiring.

"What's going on Nancy? I hear Ursula is upsetting our lovely audience," he looked fearfully at Ursula, who was now slamming the empty bottles into a recycling bin making as much noise as possible. Nancy felt sorry for the Reverend, it really was a bit off not telling him the plan. She beckoned him into the kitchen and spilled the beans.

"I'm not sure I like the sound of this Nancy, using my Church, a sacred place, to set up a 'sting' without my permission!" He was appalled, but Nancy begged him not to approach Lydia, or Ursula's performance would have been for nothing.

"Reverend, they couldn't tell you before, after all, you could be a suspect!" He looked aghast, so she softened the blow by adding,
"I mean, we all could be - nobody is above suspicion." Calming down, the Reverend leaned against the kitchen worktop, and peered through the kitchen hatch.

"She's marvellous, isn't she? I never realised what a good actress she was, I do hope nothing bad happens to her."

He looked past her to the crowds of people returning to their seats, every one a suspect now, a sinister picture, perfectly framed by the serving hatch.

The second half of the concert carried on without incident. The orchestra, free from the anxiety of the Rachmaninov, now relished the shorter modern pieces. The audience clapped appreciatively, and afterwards the usual crowd of orchestral supporters stacked the musicians' chairs and tidied away every trace of a concert.

The Kings Arms was packed following the triumph of the concert. Alexei was in his element, surrounded by his fan club and drinking copious amounts.

Jim was still smiling, telling anyone who wanted to listen about his recent adventures and their conclusion in the sock drawer.

The drinks flowed and John begged Holly to get behind the bar to help out. "Yeah sure, as long as I get paid," she said confidently.

"That's ma girl" said Faye, proud that she could stand up for herself and not be taken for granted.

"Absolutely," chimed in Velvet, "she's had the best role model!" - she huffed on her knuckles and polished an imaginary badge of honour. "Seriously though, good on her!" Then she caught sight of John, who was looking very harassed. "We can help him collect glasses later though, this village needs to pull together at the moment."

Chapter 25 - Sunday, Muddy Sunday

St Valentine's Church, no longer a concert venue, sat peaceful and empty throughout the night, awaiting the Sunday morning service and the twins' Christening. The Reverend, however, tossed and turned in his bed, random faces from the audience haunting his dreams.

His roomy vicarage apartment, above the church hall, seemed claustrophobic and stuffy when he abandoned his tangled duvet five thirty the next morning. He was glad to get out and go for an early morning walk to plan his sermon and start the day, breathing in the fresh air of the Common.

Daffodils were emerging from their succulent leafy clumps. A Sunday morning breeze was blowing through the silver birch trees and tiny buds were starting to form at last - no rustle of leaves yet, but it wouldn't be long. He looked up at the newly risen sun doing its best to warm the town, then said a prayer. He prayed that the violence would stop, that no more innocent women would die, that the murderer would cease these horrific crimes and turn himself in. Please God, let peace return to the village, to the land and to the world. He knew it was a lot to ask, but he prayed anyway, his eyes drifting across the layers of vanilla, white and honey in the sky. His stomach rumbled, he checked his watch and lastly prayed the Decadia would be open for breakfast.

Velvet was indeed down in the cafe already, and Todd was in early - the Reverend was surprised he wasn't the first customer of the day. A cup of tea and some scrambled eggs on toast, and he was revived.

Todd had walked Faye's dogs on the common - she deserved a lie in this morning. They lay beneath the table, snoozing after their walk, muddy little paws curled under them and a small dish of water nearby, put down by Velvet. She didn't mind dogs in there, if they behaved themselves and there were so many dog walkers about on the common at the weekends, she'd have been daft to exclude their hungry owners from her clientele. It was business as usual and both men took comfort from the normality of the day.

***

A few streets away, in a small detached house, Ursula sat propped up in bed, cooked breakfast on her lap, newspaper to the side of her. Her husband Charles was downstairs, eating his in front of last night's recording of Match of the Day. She mused to herself that she should find a critics review in the newspaper of last nights performance. "It went rather well," she muttered to herself. She recalled the look on the florist's face when she told her off about the glass - it made her appreciate the power of these women, the control they wielded over people, it was intoxicating and no doubt addictive. She was going to have to check herself, and ensure that being a battle axe didn't become a habit. The blade of her knife came down upon an unsuspecting sausage, she pierced the bite sized chunk with her fork, swiped it in tomato ketchup and loaded it into her mouth. She had to keep her wits about her, having made herself a target. Despite being aware of the police presence, a pang of fear arose out of nowhere and the tasty sausage turned to ash in her mouth. She pushed the breakfast aside and said out aloud, "well if a thing's worth doing, it's worth doing well." Swinging her legs off the bed, she sat up, looked in the dressing table mirror and exclaimed to herself, "Showtime!"

Not far away, Detective Inspector Appleby was downing a coffee before heading to the station, her bony fingers gripping the mug. She would be co-ordinating surveillance today. The focus would be Ursula, and her comings and goings; who interacted with her, and who appeared in her general vicinity.

The officers assigned to watch her were getting bored already. Watching a suspect engaging in shady dealings was one thing, but a middle aged woman going about her business in suburbia really was another. However, it had to be done - Lydia was wasn't willing to be responsible for another murder if the killer took the bait.

In her car, Lydia turned the music up and steadily drove across the common. The town was stirring its lazy Sunday bones; a few walkers were setting off for the woods, and people were already milling on the high street. She turned past Fox's Gallery to see the owner come outside with the swing-sign declaring the gallery open.

Max hated this task, he always smashed his shins with the heavy base. Sometimes the sign didn't get put out on the pavement until midday. Opening on a Sunday was frankly a bit of a pain, and usually the customers were tourists or afternoon strollers on their way from the antiques shop and the church. At closing time, he was usually sweeping crusty mud out of the door from walking boots, but every time he reconsidered opening up, he had made a sale in the week from someone who had seen something there on a Sunday afternoon. So, begrudgingly he struggled out with the flapping swing sign and flicked on the lights above the facia.

Howie was up in his studio, tea going

cold as he was immersed in some sketching. A new idea had begun to take shape in his head, and he needed to get something on paper before he sabotaged it with overthinking.

"Are you coming down Howie? I've made a fresh pot," called Max up the stairs. "Oh, and Faye texted to say don't forget dinner at the pub at four." Howie was looking forward to a late Sunday lunch this afternoon at the Kings Head, and stopped drawing momentarily, picturing the enormous Yorkshire puddings, crispy on the outside and soggy middles laden with gravy. He called back down "Got it! I'll be down in five, love." Creative spell broken, he tucked his pencils back into the cloth bag and tidied up the studio a little.

Carrying his cold cuppa down the attic stairs, he tipped it down the bathroom sink en-route to the kitchen, knowing he'd end up slopping it down the stairs if he didn't. Max was just pouring a fresh cup.

"We're open by the way, the great British public are ready to descend." And almost instantly, there he was - a lone man in full cycling gear, helmet perched at a ridiculous angle on top of his head like a high vis bishop, chinstrap welded across his forehead. Max's chin trembled as he controlled the urge to giggle at the spectacle before him. The man strode about the place, talking loudly on his phone, "Ciao, see you at supper babe," the words oozing like lava from his lips. He hung up. He stopped at one picture, hand on hip, leaning his weight on one leg and throwing a lycra clad buttock out to the side, with a wibble.

He spun around with a squeak of rubber shoes, and addressed Max.

"Hi there, are you the owner?" his nostrils flared confidently, as they sucked the air in from around Max. Before he could reply, the man carried on. "I'm liking what I'm seeing," he growled, his lip snarling over his large white teeth.

"Good," replied Max. I'm glad one of us is, he thought to himself.

"I'll call back in the week, and ah, do some business with you my friend, I need at least six statement pieces for my new offices in Docklands." Max handed him a business card, and a catalogue.

"Max Fox," he said, and extended his hand, trying to appear more friendly. "I hope you bring something a little larger to transport them," he quipped, gesturing to the spindly bicycle propped up outside the door. The man shook his hand limply, his cycling mitt clammy with sweat. He didn't appear to have much of a sense of humour.

"Cheers mate, coolio, I'll bring the Range Rover and some muscle." He thanked Max and strode out, tripping up slightly as his rubbery cycling shoes caught on the architrave. The door swung shut. Max instinctively screwed up his face and said ugh, childishly, wiping his hand on his jeans.

There was a chuckle behind him. It was Howie, who had been peeping through the gap in the door. "High vis lycra should be banned on a Sunday morning," he said, blinking into the stream of sunlight through the window.
Max grimaced "I'll speak to the Vicar!"
Howie laughed. "I think his nostrils have been burnt into my retinas, did you see them Max? I thought he was going to inhale you!"

Max let out a snort of laughter. "Seriously though, I hope he's good as his word, we could do with the sales." They watched, as the racing bike disappeared down the high street, its rider perched like a wasp on its wavering frame.
The day dragged as Howie tried to get back his creative streak - he sat behind the counter, keeping an eye on the gallery, his sketch book open, one pencil behind his ear

and one in his hand. A few people came in for a browse, but there were no sales.

Max got to grips with some book keeping. Things were a little tight, and not just financially. His trousers were digging in uncomfortably around the waist. He'd put on a few pounds and was starting to worry about looking fat for the wedding. Dieting all week, he had managed to resist the temptation of the fridge, but all he could think about was food. He threw himself into his paperwork while Howie worked on his new ideas.

At last the time ticked around to four o'clock, and Max tiptoed past him and went outside to bring in the dratted swing sign and turn the lights off. He turned the sign on the door to closed and thought of roast potatoes. Howie, engrossed, didn't even look up from behind the counter as he passed by again. Max knew better than to disturb him when he had an idea brewing, but his tummy was complaining loudly. Howie eventually sensed being watched and looked up, surprised at the gloomy gallery in front of him. "Max?"

"Yes, its dinner time Howard, move your arty farty arse I'm famished!"

Howie closed his sketch book and climbed off the chair he'd been curled up on for the past few hours. His leg had gone to sleep, and he limped across to Max, who was loading his feet into some loafers. Howie knew better than to come between Max and a roast dinner. He had considered going for a quick pee, but decided to hold it until they got to the pub. They made their way down the high street, a little wary of each other. The sun was waning now, and the temperature had dropped. As they arrived at the pub, Ursula and her husband barged past them at the door. Max was too tired and hungry to say anything, and they went in behind them and spotted the others already sitting at the table, drinks flowing.

Ursula found a table where she could get maximum attention. She sat herself down, arranged her handbag and scarf on the back of her chair, and her husband battled at the bar to order drinks and two roast dinners.

She had spent an age at her dressing table, trying out make up that made her look harsher than she really was. She'd settled on a dark plum lipstick, which made her lips look thin and mean, black eyeliner and dark brows. Her hair was curled, but not brushed out, and she looked every inch, the harridan. The two police officers tailing her, found themselves a corner table and sat down with their non alcoholic beers.

At last, Max tucked into his dinner and as the roast beef, Yorkshire puddings and roasties worked their way into his system, he started to feel less 'angry little shopkeeper' and more 'accomplished art gallery owner' as the gravy, and a glass of red oozed pleasantly into his bloodstream. "Better?" asked Howie, smiling at him.

"Much," he replied, piling a crispy roast parsnip into his mouth. "Howie, where do you want to get married?" he asked, parsnip demolished. "Do you want a church wedding? A big bash in a hotel somewhere? Or shall we elope and go on a cruise, and get married on the beach in our flip flops?"

Howie thought about it. "I think we might regret not sharing it with this lot, you know," he said, glancing at the merry table of friends, "...and would they ever forgive us if we just went off and got married on our own?"

Max looked up and down the table, Howie was right. There was plenty of time to be alone together, now was the time to make some memories.

"Let's put some feelers out next week, look at a few venues online, have a little drive out and see what we can come up with." They clinked their glasses together, and took a sip. "And Howie, I'm so fat, I need to lose weight or you're going to look minuscule next to me in the wedding photos. I think I need to join a gym," he confessed.

Howie looked across at him, "Max, you look fantastic, stop worrying, but yeah, join a gym if you want, or maybe start cycling, -you'd look great in lycra, I know a guy...." Max shot him a warning look then laughed.

Across a carpet of fleur-de-lys, beer stains and muddy footprints, Ursula screamed, stood up, and her chair fell backwards onto the floor.

"There is a maggot in my roast beef! Someone call the manager!" she shrieked, dramatically stumbling backwards, staring in horror at her plate. Her husband was so taken aback he knocked his wine clean off the table, the glass rolled in a dribbling spiral and came to rest against Howie's shoe. He leant down and picked it up, padded over to them and put it back on the table. Sure enough, there amongst the peas and meat was what appeared to be a maggot of some kind. He blanched and held his hand to his throat in revulsion. Max rose and set the chair back up behind her and guided a repulsed Howie back to his seat.

"It's probably nothing, it's fine Howie, I'm sure it's nothing." The staff stood frozen behind the bar, waiting for the manager to appear. One of the policemen was coughing loudly having inhaled a mouthful of his pint. His colleague simultaneously slapped his back, and fumbled with the button under his own jacket to activate his body cam to film. They hadn't been expecting this.

John the publican dashed out from the back room and was at the table in two large strides. He whisked the plate away from in front of her. "I'm so sorry Madam, let me investigate." He hurried the plate off to the kitchen for examination. Ursula sat back down with a thump, unaware her chair had even been lost, and found. Across the table, Charles hated that she was making a fuss. They exchanged angry whispers. The other diners began picking at their meals again, cautiously turning over the slices of meat and eating around it.

Ursula fidgeted in her seat, periodically craning her neck to look at the kitchen door. She tutted loudly and rolled her eyes, muttering about customer service and food hygiene. At last the door swung open and the surgeon came out with his patient, a new plate of roast beef and all the trimmings. He reached the table and exclaimed in a loud voice, "Madam, it was only a piece of pasta from the vegetarian option of macaroni cheese." There was an audible sigh of relief from the entire pub but the battle axe raised her blade.

"Well, that's as it may be, but I expect a full refund! Apart from giving me a flipping heart attack, I think it's a disgrace that my meal has been contaminated with the vegetarian option. I mean fortunately I'm an omnivore, otherwise it could have been another very different story!"

A stunned silence swept over the pub, apart from a snort from Max, who sat, his shoulders shaking with laughter, his face reddening. The others started sniggering too, all except Faye, Velvet and Nancy who looked at each other helplessly, wanting to support Ursula who was doing such a grand job.

Max could hold it in no longer. The knife and fork still in his hands, he doubled over and howled into his elbow, knitwear muffling his laughter. The publican, at this point was struggling to keep a straight face. Ursula knew she had to change tactics a little. She got out of her seat, hauled poor Charles out of his, mid potato, and crossly said to whoever was listening, "I don't intend to eat another mouthful of this second rate food, and I'll be phoning the food hygiene inspectors in the morning. We'll see who's laughing then!"

She marched towards the bar and demanded her money back. The young barman looked at John, who nodded, and waved his hand above his head in defeat. She snatched the cash out of his hand and they left. There was a loud "oooohooooo" from the drunker clientele, and a round of applause. The two police officers in the corner began downing their pints whilst scanning the room to see if anyone was following Ursula. They surreptitiously slid away and out of the door.

"What the hell has got into you, woman?" demanded Charles, when they got outside.

"The concert debacle and now this?" She stopped marching and took a large deep breath and burst out laughing with relief. "Oh darling, you poor thing, I didn't even let you finish did I?" and she leaned forward, and brushed a bit of potato off his chin. "I'll explain everything when we get home." She glanced over her shoulder at her fan club of two who were getting into their unmarked police car.

Someone else had been watching. His disdain for dragon ladies once again, triggered. Some, he had tricked then killed; others he had lain in wait, ambushed and slain in cold blood. It had begun with keeping a secret, with hiding the truth. He didn't even feel it had got out of hand, more that it had awakened a calling. He'd put up with women like them long enough. His mother was one. She had ruled the roost at home, his father, a mild mannered man who had crumbled under her torment. As a teenager he had despised his Dad for being so weak, and he had dealt with his mother by charming her, learning her weaknesses, and rounding on his own father to gain her favour. When the poor man died at forty six from a massive stroke, the absence of this steady gentle soul left a terrible void and he realised his mistake. This man, this kind simple soul had done nothing wrong - his father had been trapped. The guilt had washed over him like the inky black sea on a dark night. He left home as soon as he could, sleeping rough on a London street. He found work, made a life for himself, met a sweet girl, married her, and broke the chain. He raised two sons with strength and compassion, his wife by his side. He was, in his eyes, a success because he had not become either of his parents - but circumstances changed, something happened and he became something else entirely. Perhaps it was the irrational fear of the life he had made, crumbling around him, or an antidote for the guilt that had weighed on him all these years, but something had solemnly flicked a switch in his mind, a clunk of bakelite that lit a wire that shot through his brain, igniting a notion that grew into an obsession.

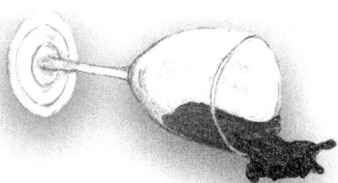

Chapter 26 - Spring has Sprung

April pushed its way in, daffodils finally bloomed, and buds were emerging on dormant grey twigs. The sunshine gained strength, warming patios and washing lines, then with only the darkened sky as a warning, hail pummelled the common. The sun came out again, and then the rain showered a light, damp covering on the grass and flowers. Cardigans went on, came off, and went back on again. Walkers took no chances with the weather, and thin rain coats made an appearance as thick winter overcoats were pushed to the back of closets. At last, spring had sprung.

Todd was in the garden, doing the first mow of the season. Up and down the lawn he strolled, pushing the petrol-fuelled beast that looked more insect than machine, fumes billowing over the fence into Faye's kitchen. She shut the window and returned to the kitchen table where her laptop was open, cursor blinking in expectation of the next sentence.

Composing a thank you letter to her uncle was proving a heart wrenching, but cathartic task. Holly had suggested it, she'd seen the idea online somewhere. Since the phone call on Valentine's day with Aunty Anne, Faye's mind had been like a ferris wheel, each revelation about her uncle a swinging chair rising into the light then sinking back down without stopping to gain any sort of resolution, round and round in her head. Holly was right, it was time to pull on the big brake, stop the wheel and examine each one in turn.

She took a deep breath, exhaled, sipped her coffee and sat forward to type.

She thanked him for paying for Ben's funeral - she told him how she now understood his reticence in explaining his reasons, how, strangely, she felt closer to him since his death. She was sad that he had stayed so separate from them all these years, as, in fact, she was sure she would have understood him a lot better than he could have imagined. She thanked him for loving them, albeit from a distance, and for leaving everything to her and Holly in his will. She went through everything, listed all of the wonderful things about his apartment, the car, the books. She explained what she intended to do, and what it meant to them financially and personally. All of this tumbled out of her mind, through her fingers and onto the keyboard. She came to the end, and signed off with her name and a kiss. She shed a few tears, swigged down the last of her coffee, and closed the laptop. The morning had gone. She felt her focus   returning, her mind gradually starting to quieten. She called Holly down to the kitchen.

"How about a bit of sofa shopping?" she suggested. "Oooh nice, do we get lunch out too?" Holly asked, cheekily. "Yes, come on then, lets make a day of it, I'll ask Todd if he can watch the dogs."

She waited for a pause in the hedge trimming - he'd moved on to the topiary now - and popped her head over the fence.
"Todd, would it be alright if the dogs came over for a few hours? Holly and I want to go shopping for a new sofa."

He looked at his beautifully mown lawn and sighed inwardly. "I tell you what Faye, why don't I drop you down to the retail park with the dogs and I'll take them to the far end of the woods, then bring them back here for a play? That way, you won't have to walk them later." (And they won't carve up my lawn, he thought to himself.)

She was delighted, "Oh Todd, you're wonderful, we can jump on the bus back, and we'll bring you a present!"

Todd didn't drive very much, he didn't

really need to - but, he still kept his car, his road tax and insurance going.

The car was under a carport at the side of his cottage. He revved it up to 'clear the pipes' and reversed out onto the road.

"Your chariot awaits, ladies!" he called through the open window.

Holly giggled and climbed into the back with the dogs. Faye sat in the front and did up her seatbelt. The old Ford Cortina was long and old fashioned. It reminded Faye of her childhood, in particular going home with a girl from school for tea and marvelling at her mother's new car. Faye's parents never owned one, being right on the high street and not far from the bus stop it seemed pointless. Todd's Cortina was somewhere between brown and bronze with chrome trim. The PVC seats had a smell about them that reminded her of drinking tea out of a polystyrene cup, and they made no attempt to look like leather, there was no faux about it - these were plastic and proud with little dimpled sections that reminded her of the top of a crumpet. Todd drove like a little old man, adjusting his mirrors and seat over and over before putting it into gear and pulling away. They wound through the country lanes and out onto the main road. Twenty minutes later they reached a large sign "Welcome to Fairview Retail

Park". To Holly, it might as well have been Disneyland, she rarely went to these places and was keen to get a burger and a milkshake from a new outlet there that everyone had been talking about at college.

They pulled into a space, and the girls got out. The dogs went to follow but Todd managed to grab both leads before they escaped into the carpark. "Close one!" he exclaimed.

"Sorry Todd, they are little buggers, I hope they behave for you, thanks so much for this!" Faye stood back from the car and waved as he pulled away. It was nice to get away from the High Street and all of the locals. They turned and strolled, arm in arm into the large furniture shop. Their quest to replace the old saggy sofa had begun.

Todd steadily drove back along the main road and turned off into a lane and then to a car park cut into the woodland. He let the eager little dogs out. Margaux walked alongside him, long nose into everything; Rollo took the lead today, standing on three legs, front paw aloft, sniffing the air ahead for danger. He had taken a chance letting them off their leads, but there was little danger of them reaching the road from here and they would get a much better run. He strolled purposefully along the brown mulch paths, the drone of a large bee caught his attention, the first he'd seen this year, its large fluffy form hovering over a patch of newly opened wood anemones. The woodland was awakening at last. He turned a corner and a large black rook landed on the path in front of them. Rollo launched forward barking. The rook backed up but refused to take to the air, instead it squawked back at him and he stopped barking, just a small whelp erupted from his bearded face. Margaux was afraid, and she hid behind Todd's legs. Confused, Todd put them on the leads and tried to shoo it away, but it stood its ground, its head on one side eyeing him defiantly. Something inside Todd informed him politely that this was out of the ordinary. He edged around the path, avoiding the crow who remained facing him, turning around as Todd moved. Unnerved he picked up his pace. He turned his head, and realised to his astonishment that the crow was walking behind him, following them. Margaux's tail was between her legs, and Rollo's ears were flat against his head. They carried on through the woods and at some point, he looked back, and once again it was just the three of them. Within a few minutes, he had put the incident behind him and was once again marvelling at the beauty of an English woodland in spring. There were a few leaves forming on the more exposed branches of the trees, and the chirrup of birds was all around. The bluebells were peeping through last year's dead leaves with their bright green long foliage, and he looked forward to May when the forest would be covered in them. For now, only bright yellow buttercups dotted the grassy patches along the edges of the paths. He breathed deeply, and the dogs skipped and ran through the trees, in and out of the bracken and bushes.

He started to tire as the path turned slightly uphill, and the simple bench made from three pieces of wood up ahead became his target destination. He reached it, and sat down gingerly, hoping it would take his weight.

Sitting down on the tenth settee, the girls sank into sumptuous leather, only to be supported before it swallowed them whole into a set of perfectly tuned springs beneath the upholstery.

"So, what do we think, leather or fabric?" said Faye. "Things we need to consider are, comfort, practicality - the dogs for instance and colour. Oh, and probably price," she added, and pulled a face. Holly sat back and closed her eyes and inhaled. The smell of the leather was decadently pleasant.

"I think leather," her eyes snapping back open, "although... that one's so cute, Mum" she said, pointing over at a ditsy multicoloured patchwork sofa.

"Yes it is, but I think we'd get tired of it after a while," said Faye, who couldn't decide whether it would match anything else in the living room. Holly's tummy growled audibly and Faye patted it and asked playfully, "What's that? You're hungry Mr Tummy? Why didn't you say so?" Holly squirmed.

"Get off Mum, someone will see, OMG I'm not five!" Holly pulled her mother out of the comfortable settee and they wandered back to the giant automatic doors and left.

They weaved their way across the parked cars to the other side of the park where the brand new burger place called Sammie's, stood, with its red and white facia, brightly tiled interior, fifties vibe and mocked up juke box at the front.

"Velvet and Joe would love this!" said Faye, delving into her handbag for her purse. Before too long they were tucking into a big juicy burger each, with hot crispy fries on the side. Faye laughed as she watched Holly, her cheeks hollowed as she sucked up the thick peanut butter milkshake through her straw.

"OMG Mum, this is divine!" Faye tried to slow her own eating down, realising that she was virtually inhaling the tasty meal. She could see how eating fast food could easily become a habit, and was glad Sammie's was tucked away on this retail estate.

***

Meanwhile, Todd found a Polo mint in his pocket, and popped it into his mouth. He rolled it around, releasing the cool flavour, and poked his tongue through the middle childishly before crunching it savagely with his back teeth.

The dogs had finished surveying the area around the bench, and had settled by his feet. Rollo put his head on Todd's shoe and Margaux sat lopsidedly leaning on his shin. They really were very sweet dogs, Todd thought to himself. He felt fortunate to have the chance to walk them, but not have the responsibility of owning them. He thought about the strange incident with the crow and didn't relish the thought of walking back down the same bit of path to the car. Maybe he could loop around. He got up, disturbing the dogs from their rest, put his hands on his hips and looked around at where the path split into three. Just as he embarked on a new route another walker appeared through the trees. It was Ted Cox, the greengrocer. He was striding purposely with a bag slung over his shoulders and a jacket in his hand. He looked irritated and hot, a few beads of sweat running down his temples. Todd attempted to say good afternoon, but the words never reached his lips. Ted practically pushed past him on the path, refusing to catch his eye. The dogs panted and watched him pass, unbothered. His large desert boots crunched the leaves and twigs underfoot as he strode on. Todd turned and headed back down the path he had come - rook or not, he didn't fancy the path that Ted was going down. In fact, he felt distinctly uncomfortable now, the woods seemed to take on a sinister remote feeling and he decided it was time to head home, feed the dogs and have a good strong cup of tea in the garden.

***

The girls, having finished their lunch, were heading to the other large furniture outlet on the park.   They passed beneath the large illuminated sign that read "Sofa So Good" above the door.   "Good grief, that's a lot of three piece suites!" exclaimed Faye, "we could be here all afternoon!"

They made a start, following the sparkling granite paths around the store. A prowling sales assistant clocked them within seconds, and followed at a distance, ready to pounce.

On the mulchy pathways of the woods, Todd reached the car without any further encounters, and after loading in his canine neighbours he felt a waft of relief as the door reassuringly clunked shut, pushing down the little locks for good measure. He started the engine, and rumbled slowly out of the car park towards the main road, the rough surface crunching under his wheels. Tucked under some dark fir trees, to the side of the entrance was Ted Cox's greengrocers van.

"I wonder what he's up to," Todd muttered to himself, putting his foot on the accelerator. Glad to be on his way, he reached for the radio, turning the little metal dial until the car was filled with the soothing sounds of Radio Three, John Denver crooning about walking through a forest, with no mention of confrontational crows and grumpy greengrocers.

***

Faye finally finished filling in the sales slip and delivery details, and made a payment for the sofa of their dreams. In fact she'd bought a three seater and a two seater for the little lounge at home. They had gone for leather, a sort of ranch leather finish, or so it was called, a little scuffed but in a good way. It was as if she couldn't quite bear to go with something that looked totally pristine in case it showed the rest of the house up. The prowling sales assistant had actually been very helpful. Holly had got bored, and was wandering around looking at the other furnishings on offer - pictures and lamps, big trendy clocks, and thick piled rugs that smelt of newness. It made her want to go home and throw everything in her bedroom away and start again. She looked over at her mum, chatting away with the shop assistant. He was taller than her, in a smart suit, with a nice face, a beard and dark hair. It felt strange seeing her mum with a man, and she made a viewfinder with her fingers, watching them interacting inside the little square. She briefly entertained the fantasy that he was her Dad; that he was padding down the stairs in his pyjamas, sitting on their new settee with Rollo and Margaux curled up watching the telly. That she would call "Dad, do you want a cuppa?" and he would answer, "yes please love, careful with the hot kettle!"

Her little vision was interrupted by another shopper who barged past her to look at a rug. When she looked back, her mother had finished the transaction, and was waiting for her on the shimmering granite tiles, alone, happy with her new purchase. Holly stepped away from her daydream and back towards Faye. Outside they linked arms again.

"Come on Missy, let's find the bus stop.

Time to rescue Todd from the dogs," said Faye. "No wait, we promised him a present," reminded Holly. They wheeled back around and headed for the chocolate shop.

Todd was back at home, the dogs lazing in a sun spot on the patio, and he sat on his lounger with a mug of tea reading the local paper. The murders were never off the front cover these days. This time, it was an article about how Stella Mayhew's daughter was replacing the bench where she died with a new one, dedicated to her with a brass plaque. Todd raised an eyebrow, wasn't the bench already dedicated to someone? A young RAF pilot he recalled, Stanley something or other. It seemed Stella was managing to elbow people out of the way even in the afterlife. He turned the page and started reading an article about the concert the other night, topped with a photograph of the Russian pianist shaking hands with the conductor in front of the orchestra. He looked at the cellos, Faye's banana smile, her eyes darting to the side, no doubt looking at Holly in the audience. He was absurdly proud of her, as if she was his little sister. She had coped so well over the years with everything life had thrown at her. Rollo got up and stretched, padded over to him and jumped into his lap, ignoring the fact that there was a newspaper in situ. Todd eased it out from under him and pointed at

Faye, "look Rollo, there's your clever mummy!" The little dog looked everywhere except where he was pointing, and drooled on the violin section.

Todd was about to give up trying to read the now crumpled heap that was his newspaper, when another small article caught his eye. It was about the conservation group who looked after the common. There were to be areas cordoned off in May whilst they worked on the drainage leading to the main pond - apparently it was blocked with debris, and this was preventing the swamp area from draining. It would last for about a week, and walkers were encouraged to stick to the outer paths until works were complete.

The dogs started barking, Rollo shredding what was left of the newspaper in a bid to get to the front door. They had heard the girls before the doorbell had even sounded.

"Hello, hello, come on in, shall I pop the kettle on?" Holly produced a box of chocolate florentines, Todd's favourite, from behind her back.

"For me? Oh how lovely, I'll definitely get that kettle on now!" And he made for the kitchen.

"Nice walk?" Faye enquired.

"Yes, erm yes, a bit odd though," he hesitated, wondering whether his episode with the rook was worth telling. "The dogs got a bit spooked, a big crow, a rook I think, it had a go at Rollo - and then the greengrocer, you know, Ted, nearly ploughed into me walking through the woods."

"Oh really, do they have a dog?" she asked.

"Well, he didn't have one today, he had a face like thunder, that's what he had. Oh, did you choose a new suite?" he added.

Faye told him all about it while they enjoyed the last of the afternoon sunshine. She glanced at the dishevelled Kingshurst Record on the table.

"Oh dear, Rollo I assume? Sorry, he loves to interrupt a newspaper, you're welcome to my copy." He declined, and said he'd read it now, and when they had finished their tea, they gathered the dogs and went next door in a flurry of chatter. Todd was a sociable man, but he had limits. He was ready for a bit of quiet time now. Too much chit chat exhausted him. He pottered in the garden until a chill in the air sent him indoors, and once inside, he closed the kitchen door, removed the bags from the hook and stood staring at the items on his notice board. He flattened out the newspaper, cut out the little piece about the work on the common, and pinned it to the board. Anything relating to the area could be the missing piece in the puzzle.

Finding resolutions to problems was something Todd's accountancy background had afforded him. He was no sleuth and didn't hanker for the spotlight, to be the man who solved the crime, but, he craved the truth.

The sun sank away at the end of the garden, yet Todd still stood in his kitchen, staring at the cork board. When he finally looked up, the kitchen was in darkness. He tore a small piece of paper from the edge of the newspaper and reached for a pencil. Upon it he wrote a name with the question mark next to it and pinned it to the board.

Chapter 27 - A Sign of the Times

Jim Bones had popped into the Decadia. He wasn't ordering anything, but asked to speak to Velvet. Nancy called her from the kitchen, and she appeared, drying her hands on a tea towel.

"Hi Jim, how are you?" she asked, puzzled, by his request to see her.

"Velvet, hello, listen - Faye said you were on the look out for a vintage wedding dress? Well, they've just made a whole vintage bridal section at Time Warp, upstairs."

Velvet squealed in delight. "I knew something would turn up" she said, clasping his hands and squeezing them.

"Anyway, some of the dresses look brand new apparently, I haven't actually looked. They aren't cheap, mind you, but I thought I'd better let you know," he added, extracting his hands from her grasp.

"Thank you so much Jim, I'll get over there as soon as I can. She turned and gave

Nancy a pleading look. "Go on then, I'll hold the fort, and Holly is in later.

Approximately six minutes passed before she was in the car and rumbling across the common to Faye's house.

Faye stood by the garden gate, looking out across the common for Velvet. Swathes of cow parsley were now adorning it, lining the paths down to the pond and around the edges of the clearings, its honeyed scent hanging in the air. Every year when she saw it blossom, she was catapulted back to childhood, remembering the day she picked huge armfuls of it, took it home to her mother who put it in a large pitcher in the hall. Within the hour they regretted doing so, as the sweet scent turned to an acrid pong filling the house with a smell that could only be described as that of a public loo. They'd hastily carried it outside into the garden, laughing as they went, tiny petals and pollen floating to the ground on the way, Faye holding her nose.
Velvet stopped outside, and was about to beep her horn, but Faye was already hurrying down the garden path, handbag flailing, keys jangling in her hand. She clambered into the Beetle and gingerly shut the door, not wanting to give Ethel a shock, she was a dear old girl.
Swanbridge was a fifteen minute drive -

fifteen blissful minutes of singing along to old songs on the radio. Velvet parked outside the shop   pulling up the handbrake with a ratcheting groan.

They pushed open the door, and the old rusty bell above clattered dully. The first thing to hit them was the smell - a violet waft of old perfume, a touch of mildew, some sort of vanilla room spray mingled with musty cardboard boxes. Faye lingered with the door open, in a vain attempt to let a bit of fresh air in. Her eyes everywhere, Velvet scanned the shop which went back miles. The front section was dedicated to collectibles, coins and china. Velvet's gaze stopped on a shelf of teacups, and Faye had to remind her what they had come for.

"Yes, I must focus!" she agreed, although her eyes told a different story, popping out on stalks at the retro furniture and homewares.

They reached the back of the shop, and climbed up a spiral wrought iron staircase to the clothing section. Someone had made a lovely job of dressing the back wall of the shop like a bridal salon. They had decorated it with flock ivory wallpaper, hung some long drapes and a large gilt mirror. Faye smiled, at least her friend would be getting some sort of bridal boutique experience, which is more than she had. They approached the racks in trepidation. One by one, they scraped the hangers along the rail, pulling out dresses. Most of them were second hand wedding dresses from the eighties, shiny yellowing satin and lace with huge puffed sleeves and a mass of pearl embellishments; a few slightly worrying seventies offerings, the decade that fashion forgot, which went from white silky kaftans, hippy cheesecloth to an alarming high necked bo peep with fur cuffs. Velvet was starting to become a little crestfallen. Then, towards the end of the rail were a number of dresses in crispy vinyl zip up covers.

"Jackpot!" exclaimed Velvet. "These must be the ones Jim was talking about, look at the logo!" and there, printed on the slightly discoloured bags, was a line drawing in fifties style of a perky bride in a knee length dress. "Marjorie Joyce Bridal," it read diagonally under the lady with a slogan below that read "Modern Styles for Today's Bride." Faye read it out in a mock posh BBC English accent.

"They look fantastic," said Velvet, her hands shaking, as she unzipped the cover of the first one and slid it out from its pungent vinyl cover. It was strapless, tea length with a full circular skirt. It lacked the net petticoats to make it stand out but it was the perfect style for Velvet. The workmanship on the gowns was far superior to anything she had seen on modern dresses, they were beautifully lined, and finished with hand stitched beading.   One by one, they unzipped the covers and looked through the gowns. They were of varying length, with no size labels inside them, but they looked tiny.

"They must be sample dresses Velve, they are teeny weeny." Each one had a silk tag attached to the satin covered hangers with a girl's name embroidered on it.

"Oh how adorable Faye, they've got names!" Velvet clutched one named Barbara to her chest, and headed for the fitting room, a calico curtained off corner with a chair and a small mirror.   She needed Faye's help to do the tiny crystal buttons up on the back. One after another, she worked her way through them. Audrey, Pamela, Maureen - all fabulous. Each time she appeared, Faye would melt, she looked stunning in all of them, as if they had been modelled on her.

"Which one do you like best?" Velvet looked helplessly up and down the rack. "I don't know, I want them all Faye," she whined.

A cut glass English voice behind them spoke, "I think you look beautiful in all of them my dear, but if you want my advice, you'll consider Shirley. She was always my favourite, and has everything the modern bride dreams of, style, grace, and a touch of allure."

The owner of the voice was an elderly lady - her face was lined, but with exquisite bone structure, high cheekbones and a small upturned nose. Her hair was fine, backcombed and hair-sprayed into a perfectly quaffed cloud of golden blonde with a single curl on her forehead. She was immaculately dressed in black, a leopard print swing coat with gold buttons over her shoulders, her bony arms and long delicate hands protruding through slits in the poncho style jacket. Gold bracelets jangled as she spoke, gesticulating with her hands. This is where the smell of violets had originated clearly, her perfume was heady and strong, Velvet wanted to pinch the bridge of her nose as the aching scent drifted up it. The girls were momentarily mesmerised with her.

"Thank you, I'll take another look at, erm Shirley." Dragging their gaze away, they turned back to the dresses and checked the labels. Velvet found it and pulled it back out of the bag. The woman was right. It had everything - the tea-length full circular skirt in heavy slipper satin, embroidered sweetheart neckline, satin covered buttons and tiny seed pearls and crystals highlighting the embroidered flowers. On the back was a large full bow with tails that ran down the back of the skirt. She decided to try it on, rushing to the fitting room in a flurry of satin and silk.

A man's voice asked, "everything alright ladies?"

"Yes, thank you," Faye said, poking her head out of the curtain. "Just trying to make a decision, they are all fantastic. The lady has recommended this one, so I'm going to try it on again," and she held 'Shirley' out of the gap in the curtain.

"The lady?" he asked.

"Yes, the lady with the blonde Marilyn hairdo - she said she liked this one best," said Velvet, stroking the skirt of the dress against her, the cool satin felt divine under her hand.

"Did she smell of violets, by any chance, this lady?" asked the sales assistant, with a faint smile on his face.

The girls looked at each other. "Yes, quite strongly actually," Faye said in a hushed tone.

"Oh that'll be Marge. She loves a bride

to be," he replied.

Velvet grinned, glad to have made the old lady happy. "Well, I'll give Shirley a whirl," and she pulled the curtain shut.

Marge had been right. Shirley was an absolute knock-out. How had she missed it the first time around? She re-appeared and Faye clapped her hands together.

"That's the one! All you need is a veil and some petticoats, and we can pop up to town for those, get some shoes too, and make a day of it - have brunch at Fortnum's! What do you think?" Velvet wasn't listening, she just couldn't stop smiling.

"What do I think?" she said at last, "I think I've found my dress!"

Deliriously happy, Velvet carried the vinyl encased dress down the spiral staircase and towards the counter. The sales assistant rung up 'Shirley' on the old till, and Velvet parted with her hard earned cash, saved up over the last few months. She looked about for Marge, to say thank you, but she must have left. Chattering excitedly, they made their way back to the car. They drove away from the vintage shop, making plans for their trip to London, failing to notice the old original, partially flaked off sign, painted many years ago on the brickwork side of the building "Marjorie Joyce Bridal" with a fifties bride swinging her full circular skirt below.

Chapter 28 - Season's Greetings

Faye made good on her promise to Velvet to take in the delights of the West End. They brunched in Fortnum's, where they sat, working out an inventory for the wedding day. They shopped and laughed, and worked their way around the large department stores, ending in Liberty. The beautiful old building housed a gorgeous bridal department, and here amongst all of the brand new lengthy voluminous gowns that would have drowned her tiny frame, she found a pretty veil, embellished with matching tiny seed pearls and some beautiful white satin sling-back fifties style shoes with pointed toes. Holly and Nancy had met them afterwards, and together they treated Velvet to a little hen party, with cocktails and dinner. At last Velvet felt her trousseau was complete. The plans were set and all they had to do now was pray that the weather held.

The residents of Kingshurst made the most of the sunshine. Gardens enjoyed a well overdue tidy up, and the sound of strimmers and mowers blended into the background noise of the village.

Easter weekend came and went, a relaxed time where families got together for roast dinners, and exchanged edible gifts mostly of the chocolate variety.

Faye was still giggling about Holly in the chocolate shop looking blankly at the chocolate bunnies and Easter eggs.

"You know, I didn't realise rabbits laid eggs," she stated, and immediately realised her ridiculous statement and fell into helpless laughter.

***

Reverend Fields was feeling particularly tired after Easter. He was even contemplating booking a trip abroad -North Macedonia to be precise, as apparently there were a great number of Byzantine churches to wander around with exquisite frescos.

Yes, some sunshine, culture and local cuisine seemed very appealing. However, there was far too much going on in the village - with parishioners being picked off one by one, he wondered if he could drop everything and go on holiday just yet. He walked down the aisle of the church and undid the large bolts on the main doors, swung them open and bent down to hook them back to the iron loops embedded in the walls. He felt the warmth of the sunshine absorb into his black clothes and the sensation was glorious. Maybe he did need a break. He would email the bishop later that day, and maybe pop into that travel agency on the high street. He was sure he could be spared for a week, before the weddings booked in for May began.

Easter had been busy in the Decadia. With the children off school, families had been enjoying the novelty of the different booths. The beginning of the year had been tough on all the businesses in the high street, but people seemed to be out and about now that the weather had picked up.

Papier D'Amour was doing well - Valentine's cards had helped, and possibly the notoriety of the previous owner. Cheryl was glad to have pulled the last of the Mother's Day cards and gifts out of the racks, followed by Easter greetings cards, but now it was officially wedding season and in the window she was crouching uncomfortably, changing the display.

"Mum would have loved these wedding bits," she said, with a little sniff, arranging the bridal trinkets on a white silk covered stand. Little lucky horseshoes and teddies in wedding attire, champagne flutes and mugs with Bride and Groom emblazoned on them. When it was finished, Velvet walked past and clapped her hands with delight. Stella's daughter smiled gratefully, and Velvet did a thumbs up with one hand and pressed flat the butterflies in her tummy with the other. The girl smiled back, and clambered out of the window and nipped out to speak to her. "I'm sorry I won't be around for the evening reception Velvet, I'm flying to Portugal to see Dad - I've been putting it off, especially as he didn't come back for Mum's funeral, but there are some things she left him in her will, I think she still had a soft spot for him, despite all his affairs."

Velvet felt sorry for her, the traits she had of her mother seemed to have died with Stella, Velvet wondered, if perhaps, she never was like her at all, that she'd just been 'fighting fire with fire' all this time. She seemed a very nice person.

Velvet replied "that's alright, never mind, maybe we can get together when you're home lovey, I hope you straighten things out with your Dad - at least you'll be getting some sun sand and sea while you're there!" They parted company and Velvet carried on her way.

She had one month to finalise

everything. At least the reception was sorted. They had booked the function room at the Kings Head. John had given her a special rate as she was a fellow business owner on the High Street.

It seemed ludicrous that now they had a wedding car, she could walk to the church if she wanted to, then across the road to the wedding breakfast, but it completed the look of the wedding. Her mother had made noises about staying the night at home before the big day. It could be fun, and maybe we could drive around the block a couple of times after the ceremony, she thought to herself, as she crossed the road to Pippins for some lemons.

Pam, whom she had asked to do the flowers, was busy making up a birthday bouquet when she walked in. Another little waft of excitement swept over her. She had chosen a posy of pink roses, white freesias and rosy pink berries as a start, leaving the rest up to Pam. Ted was sitting in the corner reading the newspaper and slurping on a cup of tea from a dingy looking mug.

"Alright treacle?" he asked, with a grin that stopped short of his eyes. "What can I do you for?"

Velvet looked about the shop. "I need six lemons Ted; four big cooking apples, a pound of tomatoes, a large box of eggs, a lettuce, and oh, and a couple of cucumbers, please.".

He licked a grubby finger and peeled a carrier bag from the pile. He began weighing out the produce into paper bags, toppling them smoothly into each from the scales and twirling them closed with a flick of the wrist. He expertly packed them into the carrier, finishing with the eggs on top and the cucumbers slid down the sides of the single plastic bag. He totted it all up on the till, his hands dwarfing the buttons as he prodded them. Velvet paid him in cash and he stabbed his chunky fingers into the drawer to grasp the tiny coins for her change.

"Cheers love, you take care now," he growled into his mug of tea, his eyes darting this way and that to check for customers before settling back into his newspaper.

Velvet tottered back across the road with the bulging bag, the handles growing longer with every step. She cursed herself for not taking one of her many 'bags for eternity' from her stash in the car.

Chapter 29 - Bishop's Move

Over at the Vicarage apartment, Reverend Fields clicked send on his email to the Bishop. Emailing was one thing, but booking a holiday online was quite another - so earlier he had ventured down to the high street, where the two ladies in Seas the Day had been most kind, offering up brochures of fancy hotel holidays, but he knew where he wanted to go.

When they realised he wasn't after an all -inclusive to the Maldives, they scaled down their attack and started looking up flights and accommodation for North Macedonia. It was all but booked, just one long finger nailed mouse click away, but he had to await confirmation from the Bishop.

"Leave it with us, Reverend. When you hear from your boss," and she looked above as if the Almighty would be scrawling a signature on the leave request himself, "pop back and we'll finalise your booking my love."

Excited, he went home to check his email, only to be disappointed - there was no response from the Bishop.

The next morning he was awoken by a knock at the apartment door. Assuming it was the postman, he went to answer in his dressing gown and slippers. On the step though, was another vicar. A small man with curly dark hair, young, possibly in his late twenties or early thirties.

"Good morning! Reverend Fields?" he asked brightly.

"Erm, yes, and you are?" he asked politely, looking the young man up and down.

"Reverend Jasper, Carl Jasper," he replied, affably.

"Erm, do come in," Reverend Fields smiled awkwardly, unsure what this man was doing on his doorstep at a quarter to seven in the morning.

"The Bishop sent me, to cover for you - you requested leave?" Reverend Fields was dumbfounded.

"I didn't even know he'd read my email, erm, I haven't actually booked my trip yet! I can't think why he sent you straight away, but please do take a seat and excuse me while I wash and dress."

He dashed into the bathroom and showered as fast as he could, wrapped himself in a towel and stood dazed, as the early morning caught up with him. He shook himself awake, dived into the bedroom and rummaged in the wardrobe for some clean clothes. Pulling on some socks he leaned across to his laptop on the desk and opened up his email. There was still no reply from the Bishop. Maybe this fellow was coming a few days early, to get to know the place? Feeling somewhat railroaded, he sat on the edge of the bed and took a deep breath. He could show this Jasper chap around, go through a few things, get packed and get going! Excitement replaced the odd feeling. He returned to the lounge to find the young vicar leafing through The Kew Gardens Guide to Growing Roses.

"Do you grow roses, Carl?"

Reverend Carl Jasper looked up from the book, and laughed. "Not anymore, I'm afraid! The thorns quite finished me off!"

"Yes, one must be properly attired for gardening, they play havoc with ones cassock."

The conversation stalled. "Breakfast!"

said Reverend Fields, "let's head down to the cafe on the high street, they do a marvellous breakfast, and we can have a sort of, handover chat, if you will," he suggested. Reverend Jasper nodded and stood up.

In the Decadia, Velvet and Nancy were washing up between customers. The two vicars came in, the little bell announcing their arrival. Velvet ducked out of the kitchen and seated them.

"Ooh, two for the price of one!" she said brightly, then regretted the silly remark.

"Yes, quite! We are the Men in Black!" chirped Reverend Fields, with a snort, also instantly regretting it when he noticed Revered Jasper's face had neither acknowledged nor enjoyed his quip. This was going to be a long day. He coughed and introduced them.

"Velvet, just so you know, I'm taking a short sabbatical, a week away, but I will be back in plenty of time for the wedding. This is my temporary replacement, Reverend Jasper, and if you need anything he will of course, be at your disposal."

"Pleased to meet you, Reverend Jasper," she said, resisting the urge to curtsey, and wondering to herself where the urge had even come from.

"Welcome to Kingshurst, to my little cafe, I hope you enjoy your week here."

He smiled and replied. "Thank you, I have quite a task in front of me."

Reverend Fields felt a punch to his gut. "Well I wouldn't like to think of my parish as quite that onerous-" he peppered the statement with small nervous laughs, trying to make sense of Jasper's meaning, but the young man had already taken his seat at the table and was looking at the menu. Velvet and the Reverend Fields exchanged glances, - she felt a little sorry for him, this guy seemed like a bit of a jerk. She suddenly had an unpleasant thought, what if this Jasper chappy was after the Reverend's job, and he ended up marrying her and Joe? She turned her nose up at the thought and took their order, two coffees and one poached eggs on toast.

Nancy was washing a teapot in the kitchen sink. She was not in a very good mood. After a restless night, she had woken from a disturbing dream about being chased across the common by some unknown assailant. The fact that she had been wearing a ridiculous pair of high heeled platform boots in the dream hadn't alleviated the feeling of unease. She had taken so long to fall asleep, too, fretting about the card she had posted for Valentine's day. She hadn't been very lucky in love, and had never had a serious boyfriend. She was mortified at the prospect of finding one in today's world of online dating, and felt it had been her last chance. The only thing that had sent her to sleep in the end, was the resolution that if it didn't pan out, she would give up on the idea entirely and re-home a cat. So distracted was she, that when Velvet came in, prattling about the double act out front, she didn't even look up. Instead she thought of Todd and his gentle ways; his attention to detail in everything he did, his soft smile and kind eyes. She wondered if it was true love she felt, having never experienced it. She wondered how he felt about her, and whether there might even be the slightest chance that he felt something for her? Then, ashamed at her silly crush, she felt miserable again.

Velvet stopped talking and looked at her, washing the same teapot she'd been washing before she'd left the kitchen, lost in a soapy sea of emotion.

"I think that one's clean Nance," she said, gently knowing Nancy wasn't quite herself.

Over the common, the object of Nancy's unrequited affection was busy working on tax returns. Every year, as well as working for his clients, he helped his friends with their accounts. Fox's Gallery, The Decadia, a couple of the musicians from the orchestra to mention but a few. He was very professional, thorough and never missed a deadline. He'd been especially busy this year with some new clients, and was looking forward to a break after the end of the financial year. Sun was streaming through the window of his little study. Fixating, for a few moments, on the dust particles as they danced and turned in the shafts of light, he lost his concentration from the tax returns, and went to make a cup of tea. He put the kettle on and stepped out onto the patio for some fresh air.

Todd took a deep breath in, then exhaled, trying to rid himself of whatever it was, deep in his ribcage, that was niggling. He couldn't pinpoint the origin of this feeling - a kind of dread or expectation, but of what, he did not know. The kettle reached a crescendo of boiling bubbles, and he returned to the kitchen to make the tea, hoping the steamy brew would drown whatever it was. He grabbed a couple of fig rolls for good measure, padded back to his study, and looked out of the window towards Hunters Wood.

By the edge of the trees, a van was parked up on the grass, and workmen in dark green overalls with high vis tabards were busy unloading equipment. They rolled out a large industrial hose and a pump. Clearly work on the blocked subterranean stream that connected the ponds of the common and beyond had begun. Armed with long rakes, shovels and drain rods, they headed into the woods with strict instructions not to disturb the wildlife on the pond, as there were a number of goslings already this year and the ducks had started to pair off. They decided to begin by clearing the culvert by the swamp area, deep in the woods.

Faye was out walking the dogs. There had been so much rain over the past few months, the 'magic swamp' as they had named it, was very high and the gnarled trees created all sorts of wiggly reflections that danced on the surface of the water.

She heard the men start up the pump, and they stood in their chest waders in the water, raking out large clumps of sodden leaves, rubbish and fallen branches. A shower of stale boggy water spewed out of the hose, pumped from the swamp. Hopefully they would be finished soon, and the levels would be better on the main pond. With all the new ducklings on the way, they needed to sort it out - there was hardly any water by the reed beds, and the geese and ducks needed hiding places to make nests and lay their eggs. Faye left them to it and walked back across the clearing. Buttercups dotted the grass with their yellow glossy petals, The only splash of colour to grace the tufty coarse grass. She drank in the minute explosions of colour, determined to treasure them. The tiniest of golden moments.

***

The next day, Reverend Fields was at the airport. He checked his passport and wallet for the umpteenth time and made his way to the departure gate, boarding pass in hand. In his rush to leave, he'd forgotten to check his emails, but surely the Bishop had replied by now! He thought of the ladies in Seas the Day - they had been delighted to see him again, and they had excitedly finalised the details of his trip. He had returned to the flat and packed his bag - carry on luggage was all he needed, it was only for five days. Good sturdy walking shoes, linen trousers, black of course, and a matching black shirt. His white dog collar was the finishing touch. He had this set of clothes left over from when he was a missionary briefly, a few years ago. The lifestyle hadn't really suited him, he decided he wasn't at his best on shifting sands, although he tried, prayed and did his best to fit into the lifestyle of a missionary, he wasn't in the right place. He knew it, and the Bishop knew it. He was mightily relieved to be given a parish of his own upon his return, and being in the town where he grew up was an added bonus. Hanging onto his position here, was another thing altogether, and leaving Reverend Jasper in charge was unnerving. There was something about the man that left him uncomfortable. He didn't appear to be that interested in the parish accounts, or the admin that had to be done - the practical things, including which key fit which lock, where the light switches were, the church timetable and parish meetings. He groaned inwardly at the impending pile of paperwork that would await his return. Perhaps Reverend Jasper was only interested in saving the flock, guiding the lost and keeping the found? Fair enough. He boarded the plane, found his seat and left the ground.

Back at St Valentine's Church, the night was drawing in and the temperature had dropped. The Reverend Carl Jasper was standing in the pulpit. Although no service was scheduled for that evening, a small congregation gathered in the front pews and he spoke quietly to them, answered questions and made plans. His deep blue eyes flitted from face to face. The lights flickered inside the small church while outside, the lampposts down the high street flickered, too. There was a storm brewing, and the last April shower of the year turned into a heavy downpour which swept over the grateful spring growth of the

common as the page of the calendar turned to
May.

Chapter 30 - Love Me Tender

Velvet stayed the night at her mother's house. She hadn't lived there for years, but her mum had insisted she travel from home on her big day. Asleep in the spare room, once her own bedroom, she was boxed in by an exercise bike, a yoga ball and a wall of cardboard boxes that contained all of her Dad's records.

She was awoken by her mother hovering about outside the door, whispering to her younger brother. He still lived at home and appeared to have no intention of ever leaving. A quiet knock on the door and a pair of fluffy slippers appeared, further up a mug with the word "Bride" on the side, before her flowery dressing gown wrapped mother shuffled into the room. Velvet had barely slept, too excited to drop off, she'd tried the old tea cup inventory trick, but eventually she fell into a sickly dream fuelled sleep. She was glad of the mug of tea, its reviving properties flooded her veins and settled her tummy, and she started feeling a little better.

"Thanks Mum, did you get any sleep?"

Her mother, tiny in stature like her, shook her head.

"No love, I was tossing and turning all night, I'm so excited! Your Dad slept like a log though, snoring like a blooming power saw, he was!"

A voice from the landing boomed, "they don't call me the lumberjack for nothing!" Her father, who was in fact a fencing contractor and landscape gardener, stuck his head around the door.

"Morning baby girl!" His ruddy face, round and shiny, and his sandy quiffed hair hadn't changed in the last twenty years.

"Morning Dad", answered Velvet. "Don't forget we have a bathroom rota today guys," she called after him, and a collective groan from the boys confirmed they had heard her.

Over at the pub, Ursula was putting the finishing touches to the tables. The function rooms at the Kings Head were upstairs, at the back of the pub. With a long row of bright multi-paned Tudor style windows and a grand fireplace, it resembled the great hall of an old manor house.

Ursula was under strict instructions to get the flowers over from the church after the service, and place them in the reception room. She had offered to co-ordinate the wedding with the promise that she wouldn't make an impromptu scene, (this wasn't the time!) and if asked, she would say she was helping out the Reverend, but in all honesty, she and Velvet had struck up quite a nice little friendship behind the scenes.

The church looked beautiful, the heady aroma of roses and freesias filled Reverend Field's nostrils pleasantly. He heartily approved of the arrangements, then again, Pam could do no wrong in his eyes. Marvellous woman, he thought to himself. He had been home for a week, had caught up on his admin duties, and had been busy writing the wedding sermon for Velvet and Joe.

Upon his return to the Vicarage apartment, the Reverend Jasper had already left. He was either a very tidy house guest or he'd not stayed there. The spare bed was not slept in, as far as he could tell. Perhaps he'd preferred to stay at the pub. It was of little importance to him, but all the same, he expected to find a note, at the very least. The spare key was perched on the rim of the plant pot on the hall table, the exact position he had left it and nobody had anything to say about his temporary replacement at all. The church wardens hadn't even seen him, although they reported the lights were on in the chapel every evening. Reverend Fields didn't have time to pursue his queries and soon found himself immersed in parish duties.

On the mantlepiece of the sitting room in Velvet's parents' house, was an Elvis Presley clock. It had just rung out twelve perfect little dings. Her three bridesmaids were ready and waiting in the square hallway at the foot of the stairs. Hair and make-up had been done, with thankfully no tantrums or mishaps. The morning had gone without a hitch, thanks to the meticulous timetable that Velvet and Faye had drawn up in Fortnums cafe over brunch. Holly stood a little awkwardly, her pale complexion, fine wistful features and slender frame were markedly different from Joe's curvaceous sisters, their tanned limbs and inches of cleavage. The make up artist, Gemma, a family friend, had applied false eyelashes, false nails and half a gallon of hairspray to each of them. Holly declined the nails at first, but they persuaded her to have them, and she opted for the slightly shorter ones. They felt heavy and thick on the ends of her fingers, but she decided if it made Velvet happy, she'd go along with it.

Her hair was piled high on her head, with curls of reddish gold strategically selected to frame her face. The sisters had thick dark curly hair like Joe's, when it wasn't slicked back and sculpted into a quiff. Holly nervously checked her buttons and the buckles on her mary jane style satin shoes. She hadn't worn pale pink since she was tiny girl, but even she had to admit, the dresses were very pretty - the same pale pink as the shoes, with net petticoats and piping, they were very 1950s style, with satin covered buttons all the way up the back. They each held a small posy to match the bridal bouquet, and all wore the same perfume as Velvet who was determined her entourage would be a feast for the senses.

At last, the mother of the bride appeared at the top of the stairs, dressed head to toe in flamingo pink, with what appeared to be a whole wingspan of the salmon coloured bird pinned to her head at a startling angle.

"Gorgeous, Pat!" the girls called up. The words of appreciation stuck in Holly's mouth, so instead she nodded and grinned, eyes round, taking in the full horror of the clash of flamingo and baby pink.

Then Velvet came out of the bedroom, held her bouquet aloft and struck a pose at the top of the stairs calling "Ta Da!" She looked beautiful, like a little retro starlet ready for her leading role. The dress was perfection, and when she stepped into it earlier, and slid it dreamily up her body, the cool silk lining gliding over her skin, she felt like a goddess. Her mother took forever to do up the buttons at the back, but she stayed calm, they had plenty of time.

As she came down the stairs, her bridesmaids gasped and whispered. A few air kisses later, they were out into the May sunshine. It was blissfully warm, but not hot enough to make them perspire uncomfortably - the weather couldn't have been more perfect.

Her father's eyes filled as she came towards him. "Baby girl, you look a million dollars, I'm so proud of you!"

His ruddy face, that matched his wife's hat, had a single fat tear running down it. He took a handkerchief out of the breast pocket of his frock coat, and dabbed his cheek. The photographer stepped forward and posed the family in front of the house.

There was a honk of a horn, they turned around to see Joe's mechanic, Tom, a slim young man, somewhere under a large chauffeurs hat, driving the blue Mustang up to the house. "Oh my god he looks about twelve" laughed Velvet.

Following strict instructions from Joe, he parked up, jumped out and walked around the front of the car stiffly in his suit, and opened the door of the car. "Your chariot awaits," he announced, in his best posh accent. Joe's sisters piled in first, squashed into the back seat with the father of the bride, not concerning themselves with seatbelts, mainly because there were none. Velvet stepped into the beautiful car, and Tom closed the door and nipped back around.

The Flamingo was left on the pavement, standing on one leg waving off the bride. A few minutes passed and her and Holly were sat in the back of a taxi together with Velvet's brother Jay who, like his father, filled his suit to bursting point in the small front seat. His aftershave was strong and mingled sickeningly with the mother of the bride's lily scent. Holly felt queasy, but didn't want to open the window for fear of messing up her hair. At last, they caught up with the bride. Velvet was getting out of the car as they pulled up at the church. The photographer snapped away at each tranche of her journey to marital bliss.

Inside St Valentine's Church, everyone waited excitedly. The organist was playing an endless loop of Jesu, Joy of Man's Desiring. The notes floated out across the congregation, and circled back to him - he appeared to be stuck on the same few bars, and there was a frustrated growl from the organ loft as he broke free into the next part of the melody.

Joe's nerves were starting to show. As he shifted from foot to foot, the best man, Joe's other mechanic, Alfie, turned to face him and leaned forward to remove a smear of his mother's lipstick from his ear. "Lets get you cleaned up for the Mrs," he said.

Just then, the fanfare of notes from the Bridal Chorus began, Joe gulped and his face, like that of a naughty schoolboy outside the headmasters office, melted into a soppy grin when he saw his beloved Velvet.

Faye dissolved into happy tears watching Velvet coming down the aisle on her father's arm. The waist length veil they'd chosen in Liberty's suited the dress beautifully, which was puffed gorgeously by the tulle petticoats. Faye could just make out the biggest false eyelashes fanning out from her gleaming eyes beneath the veil. The Priscilla Presley vibe channeled to perfection. But then she clapped eyes on Holly bringing up the rear, looking as girly as it was possible for a goth girl to be, and she was utterly floored. Joe's gorgeous sisters walked behind her, the picture of glamour, but her ethereal grace was utterly unsurpassed in her mother's eyes. Faye fumbled for a tissue in her clutch bag and dried her tears.

The ceremony was joyful. It was Faye's turn to sit in the hard pews and watch her friend in the limelight. Max and Howie sat next to her, heads on one side, smiling at the couple. Behind them, Todd sat beside Nancy who could feel the palpable electricity between them, even if he couldn't. She longed to hold his hand. He turned and smiled at her, fishing a clean handkerchief out of his breast pocket for the glimmer of a tear on her lower eyelashes. He'd never noticed the colour of her eyes before, they were palest blue, with flecks of copper and green, made all the more glossy with happy tears. He decided, with a small flip in his tummy, that they were indeed a very beautiful pair of eyes.

The formal vows over, the Reverend Fields declared them husband and wife, and Joe, almost afraid to break his beautiful doll of a wife, tenderly leaned in and kissed her. The Reverend congratulated himself on a fine little personalised piece about the happy couple. Velvet's vintage china cup of emotions runneth over as he talked of their love so publicly, the congregation witness to their inner most feelings. She stared into her pink roses, unable to make eye contact for a few moments, also not wishing to cry and risk her eyelashes. Joe too, felt the weight of people behind him, and he looked down at his shoes. Then, holding hands, they walked to the vestry to sign the registers, and a relaxed chatter rose amongst the guests. It was a little chilly in the church, and a few cardigans and jackets subtly made their way onto the congregation while the organist struck up again with a slightly clumsy rendition of Elvis' "Love Me Tender". Max decided that singing along a little too audibly, with the wrong lyrics was now appropriate. Howie rolled his eyes and smiled.

Wedding guests turned to look at them, Todd leaned forward and whispered the correct words in his ear, being unable to bear it a moment longer.

"Stop it, both of you," sniggered Faye, "she'll be out in a minute and she won't like it if we are all messing about!" They behaved, Faye, the only mother amongst them holding sway.

Triumphant, the happy couple burst through the vestry door and the whole place erupted. The organist crashed into the Wedding March, taken by surprise. Out into the sunlight they walked as man and wife, the guests prising themselves out of the pews followed gratefully, a few numb buttocks were patted into life and frozen toes wiggled of the sandal wearing brave on this early tender summers day.

Across the road, Pam the florist stood and smiled at her handiwork. "Oh Ted, don't she look lovely? Ted, look, Ted!" The grocer looked up from his paper.

"Nice motor" he said referring to the gleaming Mustang. "Shame they had to put them bloomin' ribbons on it". He growled and returned to the racing section. Pam sighed and looked back at the wedding party.

"Remember our wedding love?"He softened and looked up again smiling.

"Yeah sweetheart, you was the belle of the ball." He winked at her and picked up his mug and tapped the side expectantly.

She scowled. "In a minute, Ted, I'm watching the wedding! How about you put the bleedin' kettle on for a change?" He grumbled and heaved himself off the stool and headed out to the kitchen.

After the photographer had finished posing the guests in different combinations, they waved the bride and groom off for a little drive around and crossed the high street to the pub. Ursula swung into action aided by Jay, who begrudgingly agreed to help her. They struggled out of the church with the pedestals of flowers and transferred them to the pub. Reverend Fields was sorry to see them go.

Joe took the wheel and they sped up over the common, alone at last.

"Hello Mrs Russo," Joe said, nudging her with his arm.

"Hello Mr Russo," she replied. Russo was Italian for red, and she liked the fact her new name translated to 'red Velvet'.

"Much as I'd love to drive off into the

sunset Joe, can we get back to our reception now?" she laughed.

"I could drive this car all day Velve, it's a banging ride!" They pulled around the roundabout, and headed back down to the village.

"Don't forget, later we are going to sneak out for some photos on the common, just you and me and the girls, before we lose the light."

A big cheer went up when they arrived back at the pub. John, the publican, had loudly announced their arrival, ringing the bell to call everyone to attention. They dispensed with a receiving line, opting for a more casual reception. The drinks flowed and the food laid out on platters was buffet style - there was no table plan or formal seating arrangement, apart from the top table. An enjoyable afternoon was had by all.

At four thirty, during a lull, the photographer suggested now might be a good time to take the romantic photos that Velvet had wanted. Joe was reluctant to leave the bar, but after rounding up the bridesmaids, prising one of Joe's sisters from the lips of his mechanic, a small party of them strolled in the summer sun up to the edge of the common. Faye joined them, walking arm in arm with her pretty-in-pink baby girl. The high street was now quiet and they crossed over to the grass. The photographer started working through his list of poses. Joe behaved himself, actually quite enjoying the attention. Faye took the opportunity of nipping over to the cottage to let the dogs out in the garden for five minutes. There was nobody about and she marched over the grass, her small heeled shoes coping admirably with the the turf underfoot. She let herself into the house and called them. Ecstatic to see her they danced around her taking it in turns to roll onto their backs and show her their fat little tummies. She popped them into the garden and turned back to the kitchen to get their feeding bowls, filled them with their favourite dinner and placed them on their mat to find after she'd gone.

She nipped to the bathroom and tidied up her hair and face, came back and called them in from the back door. "Margaux, Rollo, dinner, come on, dinnertime!" They failed to appear. "Oh come on pooches, dinnertime!" Still they didn't appear.

She stepped outside to look for them and to her absolute horror she noticed the side gate was wide open. "Oh no no no, oh shit, shit shit, who opened the bloody gate?" she cursed and went out to look for them.

Across the road, on the grass, the pair of them were pelting across the common towards the wedding party on the opposite side of the main road. Waiting to see if they got across safely, heart in her mouth, Faye then nipped indoors and grabbed both leads and crossed over after them.

"Why today? Really! Margaux, Rollo!" She muttered as she ran, stumbling in her kitten heels over what seemed to be a very different landscape from the one she'd crossed earlier. Holly saw them coming and realised what had happened. She frantically called them but they sensed freedom, having been shut in all day. Margaux was the ring leader, and always had one eye on an open door. They barked and circled the group, tails wagging and tongues lolling. Velvet and Joe were laughing, but as an owner Faye was all to aware of the roads crossing the common and her heart was in her mouth.

Todd and Nancy had wandered up the road to see how the photos were going. Max and Howie had come out for a vape, and wandered up with them, all fuelled with Prosecco from an afternoon of toasts. Before too long, the whole group were converged on the common, the dogs dancing around them, and poor Faye struggling to keep composed while she darted in and out of the tipsy group trying to catch the furry escape artists.

Fortunately, the photographer and the happy couple had peeled off and were busy taking romantic shots next to a beautiful oak tree. Fay was relieved as she feared one of them would jump up at the bride and muddy the dress.

Then Margaux stopped dead in her tracks and sniffed hard at the air in front of her. Something had wafted up the old girl's long, lean nose, and a mix of curiosity and instinct got the better of her. Before Faye could reach her with the lead, she bolted for the woods, her stubby little legs pumping like pistons, her long ears flapping out behind her head. Rollo obligingly followed. At least it was away from the road, but Faye's heart abruptly moved from throat to the pit of her stomach. They'd never find her in there.

Faye froze, unable to follow, and lost all sense of what to do next. There was no way she was running through the woods in kitten heels and a floaty dress. Holly trotted over to her side. "Mum what shall we do, shall I go after them or do you think they'll come back?" Faye looked down at her feet "You can't go traipsing through the woods in those shoes Holly, and anyway, I don't want to spoil Velvet's day. You stay with the girls, let's just wait, they may just circle round and come back." She looked at her watch. "We'll give it five minutes."

Five minutes came and went. Just as they were about to go back to the cottage, Rollo pranced out of the trees and trotted towards them, wagging his tail. "Oh thank God" said Faye, and lunged at him, snapping the lead expertly through the ring on his collar. "She won't be far behind." Todd strolled over.

"Everything ok girls, have you got them both?" he said, looking behind them.

"Erm, no just Rollo, but I'm sure she'll be back in a minute," said Faye brightly, not wanting to draw attention away from the newlyweds, but when Holly was looking the other way she made a face at Todd that told him all he needed to know.

"Right, well, I'm popping home to charge my phone and I'll be back," he said conspiratorially, dragging Nancy by the arm towards the cottages.

"I'll, erm, drop Rollo home - Holly you stay here and try and catch Margaux if she turns up."

Max and Howie clocked that there was a problem, and strolled away from photo shoot, gathering pace to catch up with the others.

"What's going on, has she made a break

for it?" said Howie breathlessly.

"Yes, she's in the woods somewhere. The little cow has done this before, she was gone for two nights last time - we were frantic," said Faye, marching over the grass.

They entered the house, and Faye quickly changed into some trainers. Nancy borrowed a pair of wellies, and they took fleeces from the coat hooks at the bottom of the stairs, a torch, some treats and a dog blanket from Margaux's bed. She shut Rollo in the kitchen with his dinner, grabbed her keys and they left the house. Mildly confused, he twitched his white eyebrows back and forth, then curled up in his bed next to Margaux's and went to sleep. Regrouping at the front gate, they went back over to the common. Holly, watching from afar, shivered. Trust Margaux to pick today to go feral, she thought, poor Mum.

Velvet was blissfully unaware of what was going on, and she and Joe had finished with their photos and were giggling and drinking the champagne that the photographer had brought up as a prop. Reluctantly, Holly had re-joined the other bridesmaids and watched as her mother, the boys and Nancy started their search and rescue mission.

"Where are they off to?" called Velvet.

"Oh they are just going for a stroll, I think, they've drunk a bit too much," said Holly, who knew exactly what was happening.

"Don't be too long, Faye! The disco starts at seven thirty!" she called after her friend.

Out of earshot, they began to talk frankly. "OK, firstly, I'm SO sorry about this guys," said Faye. "Someone had opened my side gate, I don't know who, or how, as it's locked from the inside, but it was wide open. Secondly, I know what this dog is like, she'll go for miles following a scent and get stuck in the undergrowth and just stand there like a lemon until we find her. She's such a little weirdo. Last time we found her stuck in a load of brambles, remember that Todd?"

He nodded, "yes, I certainly do. She just didn't understand why she couldn't move. She's a funny one."

They carried on walking, calling her name, whistling, shouting "dinner", "treat" and hissing the usual clincher, "what's this?", that usually got her running towards a clenched hand to find out what indeed this was.

"What's that?" said Max, referring to a noise coming from deep in the woods.

"It's the Common Conservators, they are unblocking the culvert to drain the swamp. It usually drains by itself this time of year, to fill the main pond.

"Oh, working on a Saturday, that's commitment for you," he replied, thinking of his own business that was shut for the day.

They carried on down the usual paths, following the way that Faye took on most of her walks, hoping that Margaux would return back to a familiar route.

A voice startled them all, it was Rick and Hendrix walking from the opposite direction. "Are you looking for your sausage?" He asked playfully.

"Yes, have you seen her?" Faye answered desperately.

"Yeah sure, she zipped past us about ten minutes ago, going like the clappers, didn't even stop for a sniff - thatterway," he gestured lazily with his arm to the right, and she thanked him.

Max was last to follow, staring back at Rick with a question on his lips. "Howie, that guy, wasn't he, oh never mind, you're too young to remember," and he caught them up.

"Faye, we'll loop around this way, and meet you at the top, in case she turned off," said Todd steering Nancy towards a path even further to the right.

"Good idea, see you in a bit then," she replied. Nancy followed, her eyes everywhere, looking for the dog. Half way up the path they reached a bench where an old man was sitting. "Stop a minute Todd, let's ask this chap, and I just need to sort my sock out," she said, and sat down, bending down rescue Faye's walking sock that had made its way under her foot.

She noticed the little dog under the bench. It was Fella. She addressed the gentleman. "Afternoon, I don't suppose you have seen a sausage dog running loose have you?" He turned his watery-blue penetrating eyes to hers. "I have indeed, she looked to be on a most important mission."

Todd, slightly irritated at his omission of her whereabouts, asked "Did you happen to see which way she went?"

He turned his fluid gaze to Todd and replied, "towards the bog, dear boy, towards the bog".

They thanked him, and now that Nancy had the woollen socks pulled firmly over her calves once more, they set off to join the others. As the two paths began to converge, Faye caught sight of them through the thinning trees and called.

"Any luck Nance?"

"No sign of her, but some old boy we met saw her running up towards the bog."
"Great, that's not far now, I bet she's schmoozing the workmen for a snack, wait till I get my hands on her!" Faye said, crossly, but her apparent anger only masked the horrible fear of losing her beloved troublemaker. She had been such a comfort to her over the years. Every night she would start off in her basket next to Rollo's, but by morning she was indubitably under the duvet, head on the pillow, snoring away next to Faye as the sun rose. The notion of losing her little bedfellow prematurely was unthinkable.

The sun was starting its descent, dropping a stunning backdrop of orange and yellow light through the trees. As they reached the clearing, the sound of the pump suddenly stopped, leaving only the bird noise. The swamp was draining nicely, only a small area was still languishing under the murky water.

The men appeared to be packing up their equipment. "Excuse me, have you seen a dachshund dog anywhere up here?" Faye called over.

"No love, sorry," one of them replied, looking the strangely attired group up and down. Crestfallen, she turned to look back at the way they'd come. "Maybe she didn't make it this far, Margaux! Margaux!" She called and tears of frustration brimmed her eyes.

Howie, who had sobered up considerably turned to Max and grumbled. "Bloody dog, she's really taking the piss now!"

"Ooh talking of which, all that Prosecco," said Max, and headed for one of the larger trees, in what was, until yesterday, part of the swamp. Mid flow, and regretting his choice of tree, with the ground sinking below his brogues, something to his right flickered into his field of vision.

"Sausage!" he shouted. Hastily doing up his flies, and ignoring the startled look from one of the workmen, he stumbled out from the mud, the black silt oozing over his shoes. "I saw her, I think I saw her". The others turned back.

"Over there, the other side of the

water!" he pointed frantically to the far side of the swamp. There was a chorus of "Margaux, here girl!" and then Todd spoke loudly.

"Right everyone, stop shouting her name. I'll go around and try and coax her out. Nancy, walk behind me with the treats, and Faye, stay over there, she'll think you're going to tell her off and bolt again."

He was right, this needed careful handling, but Faye was a little wounded by the presumption. Max was scraping the black gunk off his shoes and Howie took his turn to have a piddle in the bushes. There was now a chill in the late afternoon air, and they were all glad of the fleece jackets from Faye's hallway. Todd and Nancy crept around the waters edge, the dog treats warming to a gooey lump in Nancy's hands. Todd reached behind to take them from her, but she misread the gesture and took his hand in hers. He didn't let go, but turned and looked at the joined hands, she felt a wave of electricity pass through her and she squeezed his hand tight.

He looked into her face, pulled her closer and whispered, "dog treats?"

"Oh, yes, of course," she handed over the squidgy, meaty lump.

There was Margaux, nose down, following the trail of some long gone fox. She was filthy, with mud and something else that looked revolting caked on her backside. She knew they were there, she smelled them fifty feet away, but her instinct to carry on her mission was too great. A small misshapen dog treat landed in front of her. She lunged forward and gobbled it down in one. The spell broken, she looked up. There were Todd and Nancy poised in the bushes. Another treat dropped, she edged forward and took it. Another and another - she hadn't realised how hungry she was. She sniffed the air wondering how many more there were.

Todd turned to Nancy and whispered, "let's sit down, pretend we're on a picnic," and they sank slowly to the forest floor.

"Act nonchalant," said Todd, faking a laugh and smiling at her.

She shivered, bemused, and tried her best to look like she was picnicking in green wellingtons and a pale blue chiffon dress at sunset. He noticed her teeth chattering and put his arm around her shoulders to warm her up. It felt so nice that she didn't care that she was cold, that one of her socks had once again gone south and her dress had a large bramble stuck to it that would inevitably leave loops and runs when she removed it.

Margaux continued to sample the air, her little cheeks flapping like gills, as the scent of meat wafted up her long snout. Todd continued to launch the morsels ever closer to the impromptu picnic site. He turned to Nancy and grinned hopefully.

"Yum yum, these treats are delicious," he said, pretending to eat one. She copied him smacking her lips, feeling utterly ridiculous, "nom nom nom I love dog treats!"

Margaux gave them the side eye, like only a dachshund could do, and doing some nonchalant acting of her own, she pawed the ground, raked up a few leaves and sniffed them thoroughly. Another treat landed, another foot closer.

Meanwhile, the others stood shifting from foot to foot, shivering in the clearing. "Where have they gone, they've disappeared?" wondered Faye.

Howie was in a sulk now, he longed to return to the cosy pub, down a few more glasses of bubbly and wait for the disco. Max sensing his shift in mood pulled him to one side.

"Howie, I know this is annoying, I know you're cold, but Todd is great with dogs, he'll catch her in no time, just be patient, I'm sure we'll be back at the pub soon. Trust me, ok?"

Howie felt bad now. "I know, I know, I'm a terrible friend, sorry." They shuffled back over to Faye and huddled together. Max broke into a hushed rendition of 'We'll Meet Again" and the three of them swayed along to his crooning, the last of the sun shimmering over the water.

Something caught Howie's eye as he gazed over Max's shoulder. Something edged with orange light from the sunset, something that looked for all the world like a hand. He blinked his eyes hard and looked again, backing off from the huddle.

"Max, Max...."
"I know, my singing is terrible" replied Max during what would be the instrumental part, had there been any musicians willing to accompany him.

"No, Max, its not the voice, its the, erm, hand," Howie whispered hoarsely.

Max, puzzled looked down at his hands, then up at Howie's face, then turned to follow his unwavering gaze to the bog.

"Holy shit, is that what I think it is?" Max whispered in reply.

"Faye, Faye, come here love." he said quietly, she was still humming the song and dancing around in circles.

Max caught Howie's eye and nodded his head towards the workmen who were now the other side of the clearing, heading back to their van. Howie briskly started after them, breaking into a run. He caught Faye's arm and pulled her in close.

"Sweetheart, let's go and stand in the last bit of sunshine, shall we?" and he pulled her across so that the big tree was in front of the grisly silhouette.

"Do you think they've found her?"

"Who?", said Max jumpily.

"Margaux, of course, who else?" she said.

Nancy's nose was starting to run, the cold air made her eyes smart and in turn, her nose drip. She fumbled for Todd's handkerchief, still in her pocket. This picnic on the ground was turning into a hell on earth, and she could feel the damp of the forest floor rising through her dress. Todd's plan was working, however, and with every throw, the little dog was getting closer. He took a chance, he threw another treat and when she looked directly at him, he smiled a broad grin and said gently "hello darling, who's a good girl, come and see Uncle Toddy, come on sweetheart," and held out the last remaining crumbs. She went for it. She wagged her tail, rolled her head in delight and trotted towards his open hands. He grabbed her, her warm little vital body wriggling in his arms. She licked his face and made little mewling noises.

"Who's a good girl? Who's a sodding little cow of a good girl?" he said, through gritted teeth, slipping his thumb through her collar so she couldn't get away. He hauled himself up off the forest floor, Nancy helping him as he had no hands free.

"Oh my god, we've got her! Oh thank God, Todd, you were amazing, you did it! she said, giddy with excitement. She leaned in to kiss Margaux's dear little head just as Todd turned to her. Their lips didn't quite meet, in fact her nose briefly entered his mouth, and mortified she started to apologise, but he stopped her. With a kiss. He kissed her firmly, unmistakably, on the lips, joined by Margaux who smuggled her long tongue briefly up one nostril and licked her cheeks, her taste of freedom replaced by a taste of salty tears.

The dynamic duo returned with the runaway. Faye, whooped with joy. "Margaux, my love, my love! Thank you guys, I can't believe you caught her, you caught her!"

"It was Todd, he was like the dog whisperer, he was incredible!" Nancy said proudly, as Faye clicked the lead onto Margaux's collar. Still in Todd's arms, Faye pulled out the smelly dog blanket from inside her fleece, and he passed her over and Faye wrapped her up like a baby. She nestled in, the whites of her eyes showing as she peeped up at her mummy apologetically.

"Oh my darling Margaux, you scared me," she crooned affectionately, and bent to kiss her head, "and oh dear God, you absolutely stink you little moo," she added, curling her face to one side trying to avoid the nasty niff that emanated from the swaddling child.

"She's rolled in something disgusting" said Todd.

"Bath time for baby" said Max rubbing the bridge of her furry nose with a single finger.

"Where's Howie?" asked Todd.

"Just, erm, talking to the conservator chappies," said Max.

Todd looked behind him and saw them all trotting back across the clearing. Howie was on his phone, Max presumed calling the police. Any thoughts of the cosy pub far from his mind.

Todd frowned, "what's going on Max?" The girls looked at him for an answer.

"Um, I think, well, there's been, shall we say, a development. It appears that there is something, well, someone, how can I put this, erm, a person of the deceased variety, that is to say, a body, or at the very least a part of one..... in the erm, bog."

He pushed Todd to the right of the tree and pointed.

"Oh, dear God."

Chapter 31 - The Tollund Man

Back in primary school, Faye remembered vividly learning about a man found in a bog, back in the nineteen fifties. A large television on a tall trolley was wheeled into the classroom, a rare treat back then. The teacher popped a clunky VHS video in the slot and the fuzzy zig zag lines on the screen turned into a programme, made in the 1970s. A yellow title bounced onto the screen - 'The Tollund Man'.

The bespectacled presenter, wearing a flared brown suit, explained how early one morning, local farmers stumbled across what they thought was a recent murder. They called the police, but in fact, what they had found, was a man who had lain beneath the peat bog for many centuries, preserved by the very soil that entombed him. They were able, due to advances in forensic medicine, to determine that he was garrotted, possibly sacrificed and buried ceremoniously.

The grim photographs on the screen were of the leathery brown man, flattened from the heavy peat, but still with teeth and some internal organs. The presenter announced with enthusiasm, that because of this, they could even tell that his last meal had been a 'mix of cereals'. Of course, the six year old Faye immediately pictured a bowl of Sugar Puffs, mixed with Rice Krispies and Frosties in an old wooden bowl being served by his equally leathery looking mother. Faye never mixed her cereals, it was a horrid thing to do, the jarring sensation of different shapes of cereal on one spoon with the cold milk she found abhorrent. Sat in her school uniform, cross legged on the floor, she earnestly hoped her last meal would not be that. And so, with these memories triggered, she couldn't help but announce to the horrified group in the woods, "an ancient burial?" and then felt silly.

The workmen, still in their waders, had rushed into the water, and pulled the bloated, stiffened remains of a person to the side of the bog.

"With a Primark coat?" said Max, inspecting the label of the macintosh that lay open on the ground.

Nancy didn't dare look, she stood burying her head in Todd's chest. Faye managed to drag her eyes down for a quick glance. The coat was indeed from Primark. As for the rest of the person, whatever it was they had eaten for breakfast, certainly wasn't recent. The face was dark green in colour, the hair black and spidery, the hands bloated and black. It was a grisly spectacle and her eyes only lingered for a moment, which was enough to confirm that although her first thought in the clearing that moment was of the poor old Tollund Man and his horrible final breakfast, it wasn't he that they had found in the 'magic' swamp.

The police had arrived, a forensic team and DI Lydia Appleby. She questioned the group, and agreed that they could return to the wedding, but the party mood had left them. Especially Todd. He had pulled away from Nancy and gone very quiet. He insisted in taking Margaux home - Faye needed to go back to Holly and Velvet, he said. Nancy stood with her hands behind her back, now a little mortified that she had somehow thrown herself at him. They all thought of Velvet and agreed not to say anything tonight, it was her big day, so as night fell, back down the high street they went.

At the reception, Joe and Velvet were entwined on the dance floor, the DJ was spinning some love songs, and they obligingly swayed back and forth around the floor, guests dancing around them. The intrepid search and rescue team entered the pub. Velvet looked across at them waving furiously.

"Where the bloody hell have you lot been? You missed us cutting the cake!" she said in mock anger, hand on hip. The look on their faces stopped her in her tracks. "What's the matter, what's happened?"

Faye, feigned a smile. "Sorry lovey, Margaux bolted into the woods, we've all been looking for her - I couldn't leave her all night out there. Anyway all's well that ends well, she's home now, and we are back - as you can see!" she added, clumsily. "And I need a gin and tonic!" They all nodded in unison.

"Okay.... well go and get some drinks, you lot, and there's loads of food left," Velvet said, looking from one dirty startled face to another. Something was definitely up and it was nothing to do with the dog.

A few drinks later, and a plate of party food, the group felt a little better. The shock was wearing off. They even managed a dance. Faye danced with Holly who was having a wonderful day. "Mum I'm so glad you found Margaux, is she ok?" Faye assured her she was, relieved that she'd made the right decision sending Holly back to the wedding. However, after a few G&Ts, she felt a little maudlin, and she dived off to the ladies loo and sat miserably on the toilet, wishing it had been the Tollund man and not the Primark one, the gin working its way around her bloodstream.

She rested her head on the cubicle wall, almost falling asleep, when she heard Nancy come into the ladies cloakroom with Velvet. They were talking about Todd. Nancy was confessing her crush on him, and that he'd kissed her in the woods, but then he got all distant, and Velvet was saying she had guessed. Afraid that Nancy was close to spilling the beans about the body, she finished up in the loo, fumbled with the lock, and burst out of the cubicle. Nancy looked startled. Faye glared at her behind Velvet's back and raised a finger to her lips. Nancy mouthed the words "I wasn't gonna say anything!"

They changed the subject, and talked of the ceremony, of the Reverend and how lovely he was, of the dress and how fabulous it was, and of the car and how gorgeous it was. Anything but the green faced body in the bog on the common, and how grim it was.

Velvet touched up her make up in the mirror, and gave the dress a gentle tug up under the armpits. It fitted her like a glove, but with all the dancing, it had worked its way down revealing a little more of her cleavage than she would like.

"Nancy what on earth happened to your dress?" she asked, looking in the reflection at the blue chiffon rumpled pulls that used to be a skirt.

Nancy tried to smooth it back down,

"oh, I got caught in the brambles on the common," she said.

Velvet laughed teasingly, "oh and I know how!" Nancy blushed furiously, glancing at Faye.

"I heard, Nancy! You dark horse!" Faye said, nudging her with her shoulder.

Nancy burst into tears, "but I've blown it, I think he's changed his mind, he went all funny on me," she said miserably. They rallied around, as girls do in ladies' toilets.

"Sorry Velvet, sorry, I'm just being silly, it's the Prosecco," Nancy said, pulling herself together and remembering the vow they'd made, not to spoil her day.

"Come on, let's get back on the dance floor girls," she said, and pulled them both towards the door.

Outside, the soft pulsing flash of police vehicles lit up the trees above the common. The team of men and women worked through the night, sealing off the area, searching through the remaining water for any other items that could offer up identification. "DI Appleby, you might want to take a look at this," a young officer called to Lydia. She lifted the police tape and ducked underneath, picked her way through the mud to the find. She flicked on her own torch, and ran it over the object. It was a pull along suitcase, the sort you see at airports and stations, with an extendable handle. She gingerly pulled the zip with a gloved hand and it moved across the teeth more easily than she expected. She flipped it open. Inside were sodden clothes, shoes, a thick novel, the wet pages welded together, and a sponge bag containing toiletries and medicines, one of which was a prescription.

On the side of the plastic tub, was a label. She could just about make out the name printed there, frowned, and reached for her work phone.

"This is DI Appleby, can you run a name through missing persons for me? Yes, female, Mrs Moira Castle, yes Castle 'C' for Charlie, as in palace."

Todd sat in the dark, in Faye's kitchen. He had bathed Margaux in the butler sink, and sat on the floor by the radiator with her, rubbing her dry with a towel. The kitchen was nice and warm, and she soon curled up in her basket next to Rollo. The schnauzer had been so glad to see her, and they had stood nose to nose, apparently passing telepathic, conspiratorial messages to each other. Now she was settled, Todd pulled himself up and sat on a kitchen chair. He should have gone home, but he needed to think. He had two options: wait for the police to come knocking at the door, or phone them, and tell them what he knew.

After a little while, sitting in the dark he decided he couldn't face the empty house next door. At least here there were the dogs. His tummy churned unpleasantly, and suddenly a third option came to mind. He made the decision to go back to the wedding reception and find Max.

The pub was throbbing with the sound of the disco. Velvet and Joe were loving every minute of it. The 50s rock and roll had started, and Velvet's entire family took to the dance floor to jive with varying degrees of ability. It was fun to watch. Holly was dancing with Velvet's brother who was in total awe of the willowy bridesmaid, at least a head shorter than her, he knew all the moves and she was doing her best to keep up.

Faye and the others sat around a large circular table hardly speaking to each other, knowing any conversation would lead to the inevitable subject that none of them wanted to even think about.

When Todd walked in, they looked relieved, except Nancy, who looked anywhere but at him. She slunk away from the table and headed to the toilets. She stood looking in the mirror, the harsh lighting not doing her pallor any favours. She felt so ashamed, ridiculous and unattractive. She wished she could slink off to the kitchen and help with the washing up, that's where she was most comfortable, doing something useful, hiding away behind a kitchen door.

Todd sat down and tried to blend in with the others so that Velvet didn't notice how long he'd been missing. Faye stood up and put her arms around him from behind, and thanked him for rescuing Margaux, taking her home and being such a sweetheart. He patted her hand and said it was his pleasure. Howie got him a whiskey from the bar, and he downed it, slamming the glass on the table with more force than he intended. Max zoomed in on him. "Todd, are you alright mate, it's been quite a day," his dark eyes penetrating Todd's troubled expression.

Todd's eyes finally met his, then looked down at the glass. "Max. I know who it is, up there," Max moved his chair closer to Todd's.

"It's her, it's Moira," he whispered.

Max curled a clenched fist in front of his mouth and inhaled sharply through his nose. "You don't know that Todd, it could have been anyone, isn't she in the Algarve with a rich fella or something?"

Todd looked at him miserably. "The truth is Max, I don't know exactly where she is. She left me, she took her stuff, and sent me a text saying she was going to Portugal with someone, that it was over and I wasn't to contact her. I haven't heard from her since, I've been living in limbo all this time, waiting, waiting for her to come back and pick up where she left off," Todd lamented.

Max put his hand on Todd's arm. "Todd, I'm so sorry it didn't work out, that she hurt you," but Todd shook his head.

"No Max, you don't understand. I don't want her to come back, she was a narcissistic, manipulative gold digger, and everything I have built up over the past couple of years would be ruined if she came back and staked her claim! We are still technically married. The worst part is, and I'm ashamed to say, I... I, hope it is her. That makes me a terrible person and not to mention, a prime suspect!"

He clapped a hand over his mouth and whimpered, a few tears popped out over his fingers. Max darted a few nervous looks around them and pulled even closer.

"Todd, it's ok, it's ok, we can sort this,

we're all here for you, don't panic." He hated seeing Todd upset like this. Howie was dispatched once more to the bar for more whiskies. Faye was taking photos of Holly dancing, and hadn't noticed Todd unravelling a the table.

Nancy composed herself in the ladies' loos, and walked back to the buffet, planning to compress some food down her throat to muffle the agony she'd put herself through.

She took her fully laden plate out to the bar area to eat as she needed to be alone. Howie spotted her staring into space, forlornly shovelling mini sausage rolls into her mouth, one after another. Whiskies in hand he made it back to the table. He let Max continue his conversation with Todd, they looked seriously engrossed.

Faye sat back down. "Don't they all look adorable?" she said, looking at the happy couple and Holly still jiving with Jay.

Howie nodded. "Very cute, indeed. Do you want a drink Faye?" he asked.

"Oh yes please actually, another gin and tonic, thanks." The self appointed drinks monitor went back out to the main bar and ordered.

He tapped Nancy on the shoulder. "Drink, Nance?" She gave a pathetic nod, "yes please Howie, I'll have a vodka, neat."

He looked surprised. "Not your usual tipple my love, are you still in shock? It was absolutely horrible up there, but don't worry, I'm sure the police are dealing with it all now."

He put his arm around her shoulders, and gave her a squeeze. "It'll be alright Nancy, come on, come back to the table, love."

What he didn't know was that she couldn't give a monkey's arse who was in the bog, that it could have been Lord Lucan himself, for all she cared. All she could think about was what a fool she was, and how poor Todd must be so embarrassed, and that now she had to go to the Cats Protection League tomorrow and choose a bloody cat. She didn't even like cats, if she was honest.

Realising her need for space, he ordered her drink, asked the barman to put an orange juice in with it, and left it on the table in front of her.

"You know where we are, sweetheart," he said, and backed off with Faye's gin and tonic.

The DJ announced the last song. The

friends made a grand effort to get on the dance floor. They sang along to All you Need is Love, by the Beatles, and Velvet and Joe stood at the front singing back at them. Velvet turned her back and threw her bouquet high into the air. Joe's sisters launched themselves in the direction it sailed in, just as Nancy returned to the room, and it plopped straight onto her head. She shrugged it off, repulsed, as if it were the head of a recently axed traitor. One of the bridesmaids scooped it out from in front of her and clutched it to her bosom. Nancy shrank into the crowd of well wishers, wondering if today's excruciating humiliations would ever cease.

Guests spilled out onto the high street, and Velvet and Joe left in a flurry of confetti and blown kisses. They were driven to a small hotel in the countryside to enjoy their wedding night. They couldn't afford a honeymoon but Faye planned a little surprise, the keys to Uncle David's flat in Hastings, and use of the car for a week. They could use it as a base to explore the south coast in style. It wasn't a fancy holiday, but at least they could have some time away. The keys and the note explaining were back at the Decadia where she, Holly and Nancy were going to hold the fort while she was away. Holly had even phoned the nice neighbour, Alice, in Hastings, who agreed to leave a romantic hamper of goodies in the flat for them. Holly had ordered everything online, so all she had to do was let herself in and pop it on the hall table.

Faye smiled to herself as they left. Despite everything that had happened today, Velvet had had her dream wedding, and that was all that mattered. They would deal with everything else tomorrow.

Chapter 32 - Planes, Trains, and Automobiles

Alice did more than her word. She opened the door to David's flat, threw open a window and aired the place; put clean sheets on the bed, strung rose fairy lights over the headboard, put milk, eggs and butter in the fridge, a crusty loaf of sour dough on the kitchen side, with a pot of her home made strawberry jam. She placed Holly's hamper on the hall table and scribbled a note on the pad with her telephone number on it, should they have any queries. She was a romantic at heart, and as she left the flat, she fished a congratulations card out of her pocket that she'd written earlier and left it on the doormat.

When the newlyweds arrived, having packed in a hurry, touched by the note from Faye and Holly, they were delighted with the effort everyone had made. Joe especially. The car was his absolute dream motor. A wonderful week away began; they strolled along the seafront, they sat on the beach, ate fish and chips in the old town, played in the penny arcades, went on a couple of funfair rides, drove through the countryside, visited a stately home, attended a vintage car show and laughed, loved and lived in the moment.

Back at 'murder central', Lydia was sitting opposite a very weary looking Todd. The inevitable knock at the door had come and he was prepared. He stood in the hall, his noticeboard under his arm. He even had a small holdall with him full of essentials. He had a diary with dates scribbled in from two years ago, along with receipts he had kept, meticulously stapled together, as was his habit. Max was waiting for him, out by the front desk. He had followed the police car and was now pacing about, texting Howie. He recognised one of the undercover officers from the pub, the night of the 'macaronigate scandal' as named by Howie. He was walking towards him.

"Excuse me, Mr Fox, I have a message from Todd Castle. He may be some time, he has everything he needs thank you, and that there is no need to wait for him."

Max nodded at each point, and breathed a big sigh. Todd appeared to have everything under control. The officer continued. "In the meantime, would you be so kind as to leave us with your number sir, in case we need to contact you."

"Yes of course," he replied, ignoring the biro offered by the officer, and taking out his own stylish Mont Blanc pen, he scribbled his name and number on the policeman's pad with a flourish.

When Nancy and Faye heard the news that the Primark Man was in fact a Primark Woman, formerly known as Moira, they were appalled. "No wonder he went a bit funny Nancy, he must have been absolutely devastated!"

Her words did little to ease the shame Nancy now added to her layers of self loathing.

"Oh Faye, I made it all about me when poor Todd was traumatised that night. I was so self absorbed!"

Faye comforted her, "Nancy, don't be so hard on yourself, it was an extraordinary set of events - one minute we were happy at the wedding, then frantic about the dog, then elated, then utterly horrified, and on top of all that we had to pretend like nothing had happened in front of the bride! No wonder emotions spilled over."

"I s'pose so," said Nancy gloomily. She shuffled back to the washing up, and felt the comfort of the bubbly warm water on her hands as she plunged them into the sink.

At the end of a busy week in the Decadia, the three girls were shattered. The May bank holiday had brought extra people to the village, walkers and browsers, cars and nosey armchair detectives, determined to solve the recent crimes. Faye was amazed how ghoulish people could be.

The whole swamp area was cordoned off, and the conservators had been back, assisting police with draining the remaining water. More clues had been found, a shoulder bag containing a passport, purse and phone which had been sent to the forensic team for examination. A post mortem had taken place, and everyone was awaiting the results, desperately wanting to know if this was the work of the murderer or a stand alone case, an accident, or suicide. Rumours around the village were rife. In the small supermarket, Nancy had leapt to Todd's defence when she overheard two women gossiping about him, naming him as the murderer. She had felt a rage like never before and tore them off a strip about spreading malicious gossip.

At the card shop, Cheryl had returned from her father's villa. He had accompanied her home, but not to spend time with his daughter - to speak to the police. While they were away, she had seen an English newspaper, albeit a day later than publication. The name 'Kingshurst Village' had caught her eye, it was a piece about Moira. She had read it aloud, and her father had paled significantly under his leathery tan and sat down with a bump on the sun lounger, tearing off his sunglasses and looking at her in alarm. It turned out that Moira had had her sights set on him. He was the mysterious Algarve man. He was to meet her at Faro Airport, but she never showed. He had stood there in arrivals, with a bunch of cheap flowers for his new lady friend, but she never got off the plane, didn't answer any of his texts and he had left the airport empty handed, having handed the bouquet to a pretty blonde flight attendant. In a matter of days he had taken a shine to someone else and Moira was yesterday's news.

"And you never even thought to tell anyone?" his daughter asked, incredulous at her father's shallowness.
.
"Well, babe, I thought she'd just changed her mind, and deep down I was quite relieved I s'pose, she was a bit of a feisty one was Moira."

"Oh my God, Dad, you must tell the police. Come back with me for a week, you can help me go through Mum's things too, I've been putting it off."

Reluctantly, he had agreed, and a few days later, they were on the Gatwick Express train with their suitcases and duty free, bound for the village.

A picture was beginning to take shape of Moira's last days on the planet. None of it included Rice Krispies of course, but the garrotting part was definitely up for debate. The post mortem results were back and Lydia sat poring over them, her team waiting expectantly for the next set of instructions. Moira had died from strangulation. She, and all her belongings, had been thrown into what was at the time, a lake, by persons unknown. The murderer would therefore have to have been ignorant of the fact that the lake rose and fell with the seasons. An outsider perhaps. She groaned. Far from shedding light on the other crimes this one just added to the already confusing bundle of clues.

Twenty four hours was up, and they couldn't hold Todd any longer without charging him. Everything he said so far seemed reasonable, except that he didn't report her disappearance with the police.

For this, he was apologetic and admitted it was something he should have done, but was so relieved she'd gone, he left it and left it, until, it seemed a bit ridiculous to then go marching into the police station. Lydia could have granted an extension on his detention, but she believed him. His noticeboard was also very interesting. He had claimed to be just a concerned resident of the town with a penchant for murder mysteries. But, had he wondered in the back of his mind that she had been murdered? Or was this coincidental? She would turn it over to her colleagues to pick apart.

Max picked Todd up and drove him home in silence, not wanting to pry. The car was luxurious and modern compared to his own, and he sat back in the comfortable seat and closed his eyes. The thick tyres of the navy blue Mercedes rolled effortlessly up his driveway and he wearily climbed out, telling Max not to get out, he was going to have a soak in the bath and go to bed. He didn't even make it to the bath and fell asleep fully clothed on the settee, shell shocked and shattered.

During their journey home from Hastings, Velvet phoned Faye. They talked about the wedding, the cafe, the apartment, the neighbour and then Velvet asked the question that had been on the tip of her tongue all week. She knew something had happened, she didn't want to burst her bubble of happiness, and realised none of the others did either, so she had left it. Neither of them had watched the news, picked up a paper or looked at their phones all week, but now, returning to real life, she needed to be forewarned. Faye, as delicately as she could, talked through what had happened. Velvet and Joe listened to the grim details on speaker phone, in the beautiful blue Mustang carrying them up the A21.

Joe was the first to speak, "not wanting to speak ill of the dead, but she was a bit of a cow!"

Velvet scowled at him, rolling her eyes and added "obviously that's beside the point, but poor Todd, he must be so shocked."

Faye, relieved she didn't have to pretend anymore, texted the others to let them know that the cat was finally out of the bag. Nancy winced at the mention of a cat, she still hadn't been to the cat rescue place, putting off her inevitable feline life partner for another day.

At the gallery, Howie made Max a brew and they sat down together behind the counter and talked shop. It was nice to get back to business after such a strange week. Howie went through some of his ideas to boost trade. The last one he revealed, making Max close his eyes, and presenting with a loud "Ta Da", was given hearty approval from Max. Howie had taken a number of candid, relaxed photographs of the wedding, come home and made a series of watercolour sketches of the day. Framed and presented to the happy couple they would make an absolutely wonderful gift.

"Genius, Howie, they are fabulous! So personal!" They picked out the mounts and frames together, excited to get them ready for Velvet and Joe.

"I've got an idea, let's put them in the window and see how long it takes them to notice, that way, we can advertise it as a new service, too."

And so they did, placing the finished pieces on a series of easels in the window, with a written explanation on a card below.

It took three whole days for Velvet to clock them, and when she did, she burst into the Gallery, tears in her eyes, and hugged Howie so tight he feared she'd break a rib. She agreed to leave them there for the time being, she was planning on redecorating the sitting room above the Decadia and they would be her inspiration.

"They are just my favourite wedding present Howie, just divine, you've captured everything perfectly, look at the bridesmaids in the background there, oh my goodness, Faye will love these, oh, and Joe of course." Howie was delighted at her reaction. Max felt sure this idea would build a bit of community into their business - he didn't want to remain an elite, expensive gallery, only catering to wealthy collectors. Yes, they made a lot of money out of these people, but it was becoming soulless. People could come in with their snaps and photos and Howie could get to work creating an artistic take on their big day. They could still charge a good price, and people would buy them as gifts. Most brides loved their wedding being immortalised in some way. That night, he slept better than he had done all week.

Holly on the other hand, was having nightmares again. Faye had been vaguely aware of her wailing quietly in her sleep. Margaux had gone in, snuggled up next to her head a couple of times. One night, Faye woke fully and shuffled across the landing to her room. Holly's eyes were wide open but she was asleep, calling some incoherent name and reaching out to something in front of her.

"Mummy's here, darling, its just a dream Holly, it's alright, Mum's here," she soothed, perching on the bed and stroking her daughter's worried brow. The dream catcher on her headboard glinted in the light from the landing.

All the talk of unearthing Moira from the swamp had unearthed some unpleasant memories for Holly, of finding poor Janice by the lake last year. Sitting in the dark with her,

Faye wondered when all this was going to end. The temptation to up sticks and move down to Hastings was becoming a tantalisingly easy option. She pictured them riding off into the sunset in the Mustang. She'd have to learn to drive first, of course.

Chapter 33 - Rotten Apples and Perfect Pairs

T he footie was on the telly, and an onlooker would say Todd was watching it, but in fact, the players strutted about the pitch, in a sea of legs and trendy haircuts, and his eyes weren't focusing on any of them. He was feeling nihilistic, isolated and very down.

He had given every scrap of information to the police. The revelation that Stella's ex-husband was the 'other man' had knocked him a little. He had assumed it was a new acquaintance, a faceless silhouette with a wallet full of money, but certainly not portly, liver spotted, philandering Frank Mayhew. He thought to himself, that with respect, it clarified her gold digging tendencies.

Thanks to Frank, the police had been able to confirm that it was her intention to fly to Faro that day. They had dragged Cheryl through the mill trying to connect her late mother with Moira, but the dalliance with her father was long after her parents' divorce.

Lydia, determined to shed more light on Moira, decided that this week, she would absorb herself into village life. She opened her fridge and viewed the empty shelves. It was time to go shopping.

The next morning, Lydia walked through the churchyard, towards the high street. She looked up at the large slabs of limestone interspersed with flint edging that stretched up towards the steeple. The stones that made the footpath, through the small cemetery, were of the same stone. There were only a few headstones in the yard itself. No public burials had taken place there for over a century. It was well kept, daffodils and forget-me-nots softened the edges and the grass was mown neatly, a few daisies dotted the green carpet giving way to a wild area of primulas, purple Vinca with its dark glossy leaves trailing around the graves and yellow pronged celandine. A lone bee droned amongst the flowers, gathering pollen. She wondered who did the gardening, turned a corner and found the answer.

The Reverend Fields was industriously, snapping the jaws of a garden shears back and forth along an overhanging hedge, muttering as he did so. He seemed agitated.

"Good morning Reverend, I didn't know gardening was in your job description," she said, and he wheeled around, brandishing the shears in her direction.

"Oh, goodness, you startled me Detective Inspector, yes, well, I like to keep busy, what can I do for you?"

"I was just on my way to the High Street to do some, erm, shopping," she said unconvincingly. DI Appleby looked like the sort of person who ordered her groceries online, didn't send birthday cards and seldom nosed around antique shops or galleries. One of his eyebrows rose and he replied. "Well, I hope you find what you're looking for, although, I have to say, if it's guidance you're after, I know a fella," and he smiled and raised both eyes skywards. "Our door is always open!"

She thought it unlikely she would take him up on the offer, but thanked him and carried on her way.

The high street was deserted. It was a warm, spring day, but recent events were obviously having an affect on foot fall. She crossed the road and walked up to the travel agents. Seas The Day was open, but there was no one in the front shop when she walked in. The door clanked shut, and two ladies sheepishly appeared from the back office. Lydia clocked that the older one had a small blob of jam above her top lip, and a smattering of sugar across her cheek. The other lady was brushing sugar off her large bosom. "Sorry, have I called in at a bad time?" she enquired, realising it was clearly doughnut o'clock.

"No, not at all, we were just, erm unpacking some new brochures," she said following Lydia's gaze to her own top lip and sending her tongue on a quick search and rescue mission there.

Jam retrieved, she added, "how may we help you, Madam?"

Lydia explained who she was, and as succinctly as possible, asked if Moira had ever been in to book her flight. It was a long shot as most people booked online nowadays, but her instinct to pop in paid off.

"Actually yes, I remember her," said Geraldine from the other desk. "She came in asking if we did currency exchange, she wanted Euros to use in Portugal. I told her we could order them for her. She said she would probably do it at the airport then as she had cash saved up. So I asked if I could help with anything else. She said she'd been looking at flights online, but it was so confusing, so I offered to help". She added proudly, looking at Melissa for acknowledgement of her sales prowess. "Anyway, she sat here" she pointed at the chair the other side of her desk "I booked her a single ticket to Faro, I remember it distinctly, because.... well, I don't like to speak ill of the departed, but she was quite, erm, unpleasant."

Lydia was not surprised. It appeared that Moira was not universally liked. Reports of her aloof nature and uncharitable remarks were on the tips of the tongues of most people she'd interviewed. "In what way, unpleasant?" she asked.

"Well, I was just making small talk while the computer was doing its thing, I asked her if it was a holiday or work trip, and she told me to mind my own damn business!" Geraldine's face flushed at the memory. Melissa tutted and sighed. "So unnecessary!"

"I see. Well, if you could email my office with the flight details, I would be grateful," replied Lydia, handing her a contact card with her name on.

"Thank you both for your time." She glanced at the racks of brochures on the wall on her way out. They did look inviting. Maybe when she had more time she'd pop back and take a look and the cruises.

Lydia spent the morning going from shop to shop, browsing, asking questions and soaking herself in semi rural village life. Feeling peckish she stood weighing up the delights of the Decadia against a glass of something cool in the Kings Head. A wood pigeon flew down and stopped in front of her. Still unable to decide, she had a ridiculous notion - 'I'll see which way it flies', she thought, and stepped forward to startle it. Taking off in a flurry of iridescent pink and grey feathers it flew straight over the pub and on over the common.

***

Behind the pub garden and across the grass, Todd sat in his garden, staring into space. The wood pigeon landed on the patio just as he heard a small "hello". Confused, he looked at the bird, but it was Holly from over the fence. "Hello love, everything alright?" he asked, forcing a smile. She was standing on an old garden chair that had lived by the fence ever since Moira had insisted on six foot panels being erected around the garden.

"Yeah I'm ok, but we are taking Margaux to the vet today, she's not been herself since her escape. We are wondering if she ate something nasty in the woods."

When Todd stood up and walked closer, she could see he was pale and unshaven, the skin around his eyes almost translucent, as if it were attempting to bare his soul without his permission.

"Oh I'm sorry to hear that, I suppose she could have eaten something, she's a bit of a scavenger, bless her." Holly spoke again, a little shyly.

"Thank you Todd, for getting her back, and for sending Mum back to the wedding. Velvet would've been heartbroken if we'd not been there."

Todd was touched, "you're very welcome love, it's the least I could do."

She jumped down off the chair, and called "bye for now, I'll let you know what the vet says," and she was gone.

He looked around the garden, and thought how much he hated the fence, how he hated the prison Moira had made for him, and left him in, and how he detested the horrible orange creosote he'd slopped over it every year with a large paintbrush, the pungent smell that remained in his nostrils for days after. He hated the fact that Holly had fallen off the chair last year while talking to him and skinned her shin. He strode into the house and pulled out the yellow pages, sat on the bottom step of the stairs and flicked through to the letter G, he ran a finger over the adverts until he found the one he wanted, a chap with quiff standing by a fence post doing a thumbs up. He rang the number.

"Hello, is that Grace-Land-Scaping?" smiling at the clumsy link to Elvis, "Oh good, I'd like to arrange a fencing quote please. Yes, I know exactly what I want, four foot larch lap, with a foot of scalloped trellis, in that, errrr pale moss green finish, yes, the whole garden. Half past one? yes, I'll look forward to seeing you then, yes, the name's Castle, Number two, The Old Cottages, Kingshurst Common, yes that's right, Velvet's friend Todd, yes it was a lovely wedding."

He clicked the receiver back down on the old house phone, and instantly picked it up again, dialled a number and a voice answered. "Hello?"

He took a deep breath and spoke. "Nancy, it's Todd, would you like to go for a walk with me this afternoon? About three-ish? Great, ok, yes, I'll see you outside the pub then. We can have a drink on the way back if you like."

In the Kings Head, Lydia, having uncharacteristically handed her fate over to a pigeon, wished she was sipping a glass of Pinot Noir in her favourite booth and not a diet coke. She could have sat in the pub garden, most people were, but she'd had enough of people for one morning. The last shop before her liquid lunch had been Pippins, the green grocer. The proprietor served her, with a cheeky barrow boy banter. She remarked on how quiet it was today, saying it was probably because of the murder and casually asked the florist, who was apparently his wife, if she had known Moira. The woman became quite agitated and said she'd rather not talk about it. Lydia asked why, and she said she was superstitious. These two peaked her curiosity. He was shifty, eyes darting, one step ahead of the conversation, she seemed the nervous type and despite his banter, he had fixed her with dark brooding eyes and fired a warning shot across her bows.

"The lady doesn't want to talk about it, Detective Inspector." He knew exactly who she was. Lydia had an uneasy feeling about the pair of them and upon leaving, she used a trick she'd picked up from her father, also a detective in his day. She walked one way, out of sight, paused, and doubled back crossing the open front of the shop once more. It was a simple move, but a revealing one and, lo and behold, in middle of the shop there they were, arguing in hissed tones, with measured gestures. They were hiding some rotten apples somewhere, and she was determined to sniff them out.

Superstition was a funny thing, thought Lydia, it changed sage, rational people into blithering idiots and blithering idiots into self appointed wise sages. She reflected on the pigeon, maybe she was just trying it out for size, but she decided fate was not a good partner for a police officer. Picking up her bag of fruit and vegetables, she left the pub and crossed back over to the church.

The Reverend had finished clipping his hedge, and had moved on to weeding the paved area at the front of the church. "Still at it, Reverend?" she asked.

"Yes, it's like the Forth Bridge, Detective Inspector, have you finished your shopping?" he replied, eyeing her bag of produce.

"Yes, I think so, but may I ask you a few questions about some of the locals? There are a few things I'd like to clarify."

He frowned and stood up from his weeding. "Well, I'll happily give you any information that is deemed relevant, but as you know, I am bound by a certain amount of trust that my parishioners have with regards to my discretion," he said, earnestly.

"Yes of course, I wouldn't want to put that in jeopardy Reverend, it's just a little bit of background on a few folks I'm after. In particular, those who might not be familiar with the swamp, and it's tendency to rise and fall with the seasons. Not everyone is a walker, or a nature lover. Some people we've talked to didn't even know it existed."

He pondered her question and replied.

"Would you like a cup of tea, Lydia?" He tried her name out and she didn't flinch.

"Yes, I think I would," she replied.

***

At half past one, Velvet's father walked up the path to Todd's front door. Thirty minutes and a strong cup of tea with two sugars later, he had secured the job of removing and re-fencing Todd's garden to a more fitting style for a cottage Todd closed the door on the quiffed tradesman and uttered "thank youverymuch" with an Elvis style flourish.

The fact he had even dared to reimagine the perimeters of his garden, gave him the strength to do the same with his life. He hit the shower, shaved and dressed in clean clothes, and shoe horned his feet into his walking boots. He left the house and strode across the road, the common and down towards the pub with a renewed sense of confidence and freedom. Outside the pub, Nancy was shivering in the shade of the building. The day was only warm if one was standing in the sun. She saw Todd approach and her tummy did a small flip. She had postponed her outing to the Cat Rescue after Todd's call (she could always go tomorrow,) and then she'd rung Velvet in a panic.

"No doubt, he is going to apologise for the kiss and explain why he's not interested," she'd blathered.

Velvet had told her to stop being negative, and to keep an open mind. She sadly looked up at him as he reached her. He took her hand, and pulled her to the nearest picnic table to sit.

"Nancy, I'm so sorry I haven't seen you, I've not been myself since the night in the woods," he said. "It's just that I was rather in shock, and unable to focus, but now things are very clear to me, and...."

She interrupted."It's okay Todd, I

understand, you've been through a lot lately, I'm so sorry for your loss, and as for what happened when we found Margaux, please don't worry, I got carried away that's all, with the wedding and the romance."

He looked at her incredulously. "Oh, I see, it's just that, well, I was hoping that now I'm officially single, that I might start, erm, dating again," he said awkwardly.

Her mouth shaped a perfect circle which emitted the word "Oh" which hung in the air like a smoke ring. She emptily stared at her shoes. He continued, "...and that, well, you might consider being my first date?" he added shyly, dipping his head to try and engage her gaze.

A smile spread across her face, and she looked up at him, her pale blue eyes shining with golden flecks and tears. "Yes please," she answered, with a little laugh. Relieved, he dropped his shoulders and let out a deep breath.

"Well thank God for that, I thought you were going to say no!" She put
a hand to his face, and held it there.

"Todd, there's nothing I would like more than to go on a date with you, in fact, let's call this our first date!"

They stood up, and walked arm in arm into the sunshine across the road, through the churchyard to the far side of the common. From the Decadia, Nancy heard Velvet and Faye whooping with delight. She didn't turn around, but was sure they were doing a happy dance in the doorway to the cafe.

After Faye's shift, Holly met her outside, holding Margaux in her arms. They walked down the high street to the vet's, a small surgery down one of the alleyways. Inside, they sat in the tiny waiting room, stroking Margaux's head as she looked around nervously. She knew exactly where she was, and she wasn't happy about it. They were called through to a small consulting room with a table. The vet was new to the practice. He was tall, blonde, with muscular shoulders and a handsome, friendly face. He took Margaux from Holly, and she looked tiny in his arms. Faye was taken aback at how attractive she found him. She fumbled through her explanation for their visit and when he put the dog gently on the table for an examination, Margaux gazed up into his vivid blue eyes as if she'd fallen hopelessly in love. Holly rolled hers to heaven, both her mother and Margaux were behaving like a pair of soppy teenagers.

Faye pulled herself together and listed the sausage dog's symptoms. He agreed that

Margaux had a gastric upset, probably from scavenging and gave her anti sickness and antibiotic injections.

"Give her chicken and rice for a few days, maybe then add a little kibble, until her tummy settles," he said, in an antipodean accent.

"Kibble....." repeated Faye, mesmerised by his adam's apple.

"Mum!" Holly said, and nudged her with her elbow. "Yes, sorry, I was just, erm wondering, where your accent was from?"

He smiled, revealing a row of beautiful white teeth. "Australia, we moved out there when I was a nipper, but I've always wanted to come back, so here I am, in sunny Kingshurst Common."

Holly replied, as her mother appeared to be incoherent today. "Well, thank you, and welcome home! Come on Mum, let's get Margaux home."

She bundled her mother out into the waiting room to pay the bill, and steered her out of the surgery and into the alley. "Oh My God, Mother?" she said, "what the hell was that? Is that you flirting? No wonder you're still single!" Faye blushed and put her hands to her face. "I don't know what came over me

Hols, I'm so sorry, I, erm, just wasn't expecting to see a Demigod in there, just old Mr Quinn, who we usually see!" and she mimed the bent over old veterinary who owned the practice.

"I'm so embarrassed, do you think he noticed?" Holly laughed, "how could he not? You were practically fainting at his feet!"

Faye was mortified, "no, surely not, I'm far too old for him, oh dear, how embarrassing for him."

Holly put her arm around her mother, "Don't worry mum, he was pretty hot to be honest, and I'm sure he knows it. Nobody builds muscles like that without looking in a mirror!" They both laughed.

"How did you get so wise, missy?" asked Faye, grabbing her daughter's arm and entwining it with her own.

Margaux trotted along beside them, feeling much better already.
"Look at her Mum, her new boyfriend has cheered her right up!"

Chapter 34 - As One Door Closes

When the police were satisfied that they could glean no more information from her, Moria's family claimed her remains. There was a private cremation, thirty miles away from the village. Todd attended, and Max went with him. They stood outside the crematorium after the short service, and Todd nodded to her family grimly. They nodded back, and they parted ways - much like they had, at the wedding.

She was back where she'd begun. Poor deluded girl, never happy with her lot, never satisfied. For the second time - the first for her murder, Todd pitied her, but as he stepped back into Max's sleek navy blue car, he felt this chapter of his life was well and truly closed.

A few days later, everyone met in the Kings Head for a drink. It was the first time they'd all been together since the wedding and catching up had been long overdue.

Somewhere between pawing over the wedding photographs, reminiscing about the service, and talking openly about Moira and the drama in the woods, they managed to extract the two big events of that day from each other. It felt very healing. Velvet and Joe didn't feel at all as if their wedding day was marred, and Todd didn't feel his trauma was belittled. Despite their adulthood, there was a sense of maturity and mutual respect. It was friendship at its best, and everyone went home that night at peace with themselves and each other.

Todd and Nancy kept their budding relationship low key for now, but a few eyebrows were raised when they left holding hands.

"I bloody knew it," said Joe loudly after they'd gone, "I saw her buying a Valentine's card didn't I?"

***

Unfortunately, there was still the pesky matter of a murderer on the loose. Lydia and her team had been working tirelessly, processing all the information gathered. She was at the point where she was considering a curfew be put on the village. There was no trace of DNA on Moira, the swamp had seen to that. There was evidence however, that the murder was connected to the recent ones. She hadn't released this information yet, but according to the forensic team there were similarities, bruising to the left lower arm, indicating he had dragged her by the wrist. All of the other victims had bruising to the wrist. The only odd one out was Janice who had suffered a knife wound. Perhaps the murderer had struggled to finish her off? Whatever had happened, poor Janice hadn't deserved her fate. A regular person would have shuddered to think about it, but in Lydia's compartmentalised mind, she could feel empathy for the victim at the same time as solving the complex puzzle of her murder.

Her professionalism was as seasoned as her shop-bought shepherds pie. She opened the microwave and tipped the ready meal onto a plate, poured a glass of wine, and headed for the sofa.

The next morning, on a lorry, was another sofa, in fact, two. Wrapped in plastic, the new suite that Faye and Holly had ordered was on its way to the cottage. They had moved the existing sofa, 'Old Geronimo', as Todd had named it, rendering Faye weak with the giggles and unable to lift her end, out into the back garden, and wedged it against the side gate. The dogs immediately claimed it as their own, jumping up and sprawling out in the May sunshine. The lorry rumbled over the common, and Holly called from the front room window. "It's here Mum!" and they went to the front door to greet the new arrival.

Fifteen minutes later, after a little

pushing and shoving the new suite was in place. They were absolutely thrilled, moving from seat to seat trying out different angles. Todd took photos of them posing and posted them to the group chat. Holly went to the kitchen and put the kettle on, and Faye followed.

"Do you like it, Hols?" Holly nodded, "the only thing is Mum, the rest of the house looks a bit, well, how can I put this - shit!"

A little offended, Faye exclaimed "Holly! Don't be horrid, it's not that bad, is it?"

Feeling disappointed that her ploy to go for distressed ranch leather hadn't worked, she looked around with fresh eyes. It was a bit dated and tired. "Well, maybe in the summer we can throw all the windows and doors open, and do a bit of redecorating, spruce the place up a bit, how does that sound?" Holly grinned. "Sounds great! I'll borrow some of Velvet's home style magazines, she's got loads!"

"That's settled then," said Faye, looking around, but her smile faded at the prospect of erasing the choices her parents, then she and Ben had made, over the years in the little house. She knew in her heart that times must change and now that the flat in Hastings was on the market, the proceeds would at least enable them to make these changes comfortably.

The car was also put up for sale. It was a sad decision, because everyone loved it, but the ownership of such a vehicle just wasn't very practical. They had decided to buy a small car and to learn to drive. Joe had almost cried when he heard they were selling the it, and had then sulked for an entire evening in the flat above the Decadia when Velvet told him flat out that they couldn't afford to buy it. If it had been up to Faye, she'd have handed over the keys to Joe, but knowing it was partly Holly's legacy, she felt obliged to bank the proceeds for her daughter's future.

So, with a heavy heart, they sold it to a vintage car enthusiast who lived two villages away. He collected the Mustang half an hour after the new sofa arrived, and they waved it off over the common, the silver horse on the front gleaming in the sunshine.

Two hours later, Margaux began barking herself stupid on the windowsill. She'd spotted a horse that was loose on the common. The skittish animal had crossed the main road, and was cantering, bucking and kicking around on the green, not believing his luck being free - and then settled to grazing, tearing up mouthfuls of lush grass from under the trees. His tail swished sporadically, and his mane twitched in the late afternoon sunlight.

Margaux was beside herself with indignation, growling as she breathed in, staccato barking erupting from her little body. Faye ran to the window.

"What on earth are you barking at? Margaux, shhhhh, be quiet!" She grabbed the dog and tried to calm her, looking out to see what all the fuss was about.

"Holly, look out of the window! There is a blooming big brown horse on the common," she called behind her.

Rollo appeared and jumped up for a look. Unimpressed, the indifferent schnauzer twitched his eyebrows back and forth and jumped down. Margaux refused to give up her protest, and Faye had to shut her in the kitchen. She found her phone and looked up the number for the stables. It wasn't his first rodeo, she'd seen him out there once before.

Holly came down, and and they sat on the new sofa watching the drama unfold. Two young girls carrying a lead rope and a few carrots attempted to round up the beast, but he did his best to avoid capture. It went on for at least forty five minutes, and Faye felt their pain as she recalled similar episodes with Margaux on the Common. It was just that this naughty sausage was somewhat bigger, and with four hooves. Eventually, he gave in. He was tired, it was getting colder, and the thought of his nice warm stable and a bucket of mash was suddenly more enticing than a cold night on the common. The girls lead him away, his head low.

"Oh bless him, he just wants to go home now," said Faye, draining her cup of tea. They had taken it in turns going to the kitchen.

"Movie's over," joked Holly, "that's two horses gone off into the sunset today."

Faye smiled, thinking of Uncle David, maybe he was glad they'd set the Mustang free from under its tarpaulin, maybe this was a sign he approved of the new sofas!

One of the girls walked the horse back across the road, up a footpath to the rear of the yard, and into his stable. "No more escape attempts Geronimo, I'm double locking it this time," she said, drawing the bottom bolt across. He swung his big noble head over the door, and watched them preparing his dinner, the taste of freedom soon to be replaced with that of warm mashed oats and apples.

Chapter 35 - Flaming June

Max was buying a round of drinks. He carried the tray, loaded with alcohol and snacks, out to the pub garden. For the past couple of weeks, it had been warm enough to sit outside and getting cooler in the evenings, but approaching the weekend, the temperature had soared and Kingshurst and the surrounding area was enjoying a proper heatwave. The fine weather did everyone the world of good. Toes were on show, sandals and sliders, lightly tanned limbs, cotton dresses and linen trousers. It really was summer, and everyone crossed their fingers it would last.

The music playing was from a live band. The young guitarist strummed masterfully through a few covers of disco hits, crooning into the microphone that was set up in the corner of the garden. Howie was singing along, his reedy voice whining an octave above the music. Max groaned.

"Howie, sweetie, you'll attract the neighbourhood dogs!" Howie stuck a tongue out at him and carried on singing. For a moment Max was impressed with his harmonising, but alas the melody Howie was crooning soon departed company with the actual song, and he realised it was just a fluke.

Todd laughed, "Max, he's a lost cause! If you're tone deaf, you're tone deaf!"

Max shrugged and sat down. "I can dream, Todd!" Whenever they were at home he refrained from singing out loud because inevitably Howie would join in and ruin it. He patted him affectionately on the head, as he blasted a chorus of Abba into his ear.

"Lovely darling, now eat your crisps." Nancy smiled. She and Todd were sat so close together there was not a millimetre of light between them. Everyone was very pleased they had finally found each other. It was early days, but Todd was already picturing their future. She was so happy, that hiding in the kitchen at gatherings was becoming a thing of the past. They had been to Movie Night at Faye and Holly's, christening the sofas with popcorn; to the Gallery for an art event, drinks and nibbles at the vicarage to thank the church helpers, and not once had she felt the urge to pick up a tea towel. She half wondered whether she'd been invited to soirees in the past as the unpaid help, but none of that mattered now.

Velvet raised a glass "cheers everyone, here's to a long hot summer!"

They responded heartily, in agreement, except Joe, who hissed "don't Velve, you'll jinx it!"

She rolled her eyes and sipped her drink. Married life on the whole had been great so far, but even they were a little twitchy with each other in this heat.

Across the garden, in a quiet corner, sat Ursula and Charles, enjoying the evening and the balmy weather. Ursula was more than happy to retire from her role as the village harridan, but Lydia had begged her to give it another shot, to keep momentum in flushing out the killer. Reluctantly, she had agreed, and was picking her moment - but tonight wasn't it. She just wanted to enjoy herself and not spoil things for Charles. He was in awe of her bravery in taking part in this charade, but her safety concerned him. So she decided it was best if he wasn't around when she kicked off. She managed a few mutterings when heading for the ladies toilet, and some loud tutting on the way out, but that was it for tonight, besides, it was far too hot. John behind the bar was still wary of her and hid every time she came past. She longed to confess the truth to him, and apologise for her horrible outbursts, but for all she knew, he could be the guilty man.

At closing time, the group walked

slowly back up the high street, Velvet and Joe peeling off first, then Max and Howie, leaving Todd, Nancy, Faye and Holly walking over the common to the cottages. Holly was hot and tired after a long shift in the pub.

"We'll have a lie in tomorrow, sweetheart," said her mother, arm draped around her. "It's so hot mum, I hope I get some sleep," and she shrugged off her mother's arm and took off her denim jacket.

The air was very still, hanging around them closely like the breath of a clingy dog, damp and hot. Faye wondered if there was a storm brewing. He'll be riding tonight, she thought to herself, remembering the legend of Hunters Wood, and gave an involuntary shudder. They said goodnight, and went into their own homes. Nancy accompanied Todd into his cottage for 'a nightcap'. Faye smiled to herself, she doubted Nancy would be going home tonight. The tiniest pang of envy toyed with the idea of setting up camp in her mind, but she sent it on its way - no good came from envying the love of others. Maybe one day she would meet someone else, and with that, the handsome vet sprang into her head. Embarrassed by her own thought, she sang Abba out loud suddenly to cover up, as if Holly could read her mind.

"Young and Sweet only seventeen...."

"Whoa Mum, loud?" Holly said irritably. Faye blushed, but it made her realise that she was still a woman, with wants and needs of her own.

That night, the heat rose off the common, taking a winter's worth of rain up into the clouds as it went. Residents slept badly, with British reluctance to lie uncovered; duvets and sheets were on and off, legs protruded, vulnerable to the mystical dangers of dark bedrooms, and shrank back under the covers in fear. Alas, there had been no storm to clear the atmosphere, and windows of the airless houses were cast open all over Kingshurst Common.

Holly was grumpier than ever the next morning, and she stood in the shower, the luke warm water running over her. She didn't do well on broken sleep. Faye had got out of bed at five thirty in the morning, having given up on sleep herself. The kitchen floor was deliciously cool and her bare feet relished each step across to the kettle - despite the heat, a cup of tea was still the perfect start to the day. She went to the back door with her cup, picked up a book and padded out to the garden to curl up on the sun lounger to read a couple of chapters. The air was so still, only the birds disturbed it with their morning song and flutter of wings. Both of the dogs were still asleep, Rollo in his basket and Margaux under the duvet. Even in this heat she preferred to be covered at night, and had made sleeping even harder, her boiling hot little sausage body pressing up close to Faye.

It was probably going to be the nicest part of the day, thought Faye, and she relished the feeling of doing absolutely nothing for an hour or two, until Holly awoke. Eventually, when she heard the shower pump kick in from upstairs, she closed her book and went inside to make breakfast.

Over the common, an early morning mist was swirling on the clearing near to where Moira had been found. A single piece of police tape lay discarded on the ground. The conservators had filled most of the area back in, but there was still evidence of the swamp, the gnarly trees had strange plants growing around them, none of which grew elsewhere in the woods, their long green shards with tiny pink flowers clouding around the tips. At least they softened the landscape - the woods had very flew flowers in the summer, being mostly green with leaves and brown mulch pathways. The bluebells, wild garlic and wood anemones of spring were long gone. The heat had brought out a great number of insects too, and clouds of gnats gathered in the sun spots beneath the trees.

A fox trotted purposefully across the clearing, headed for a patch of sun and curled up next to a pile of logs, his busy night of hunting behind him.

As the morning wore on, the temperature rose again, and another sticky day lay ahead.

In her apartment, Lydia Appleby was getting ready for another day of investigating the Kingshurst murders. The incident room at the station was becoming unwieldy with notice boards. Grim photographs of the victims adorned them, maps, lists, suspects and witnesses. There were persons of interest and interesting persons. There were uninteresting persons who were interested in persons of interest, mostly of the nosy neighbour variety, who would phone the station with useless bits of information in a bid to wheedle out any titbits. Lydia knew another town meeting should be held, but she was putting it off as long as possible and groaned inwardly at the thought of addressing all those pudgy miserable faces, staring back at her with disdain as she tried to justify her inability to catch the killer. She swigged back the last of her black coffee, the bitterness triggering a wink in one eye. It was going to be a long hot day. If only the police station was fully air conditioned, but unfortunately the old wing, housing her office, was grade one listed. She grabbed a bottle of cold water from the fridge, ignoring the wilting fruit and vegetables she'd bought from the greengrocer. Her shopping trip for fresh ingredients had yielded no desire to cook with them. Lydia's vitamins came from a plastic tub on the window sill.

The grass on the Common was beginning to turn yellow and dry. It didn't take much for this transformation in the summer, and fortunately a few showers would return it to lush green, but for now the straw coloured patches were joining up with each other and soon the whole common would be dry as a bone.

The days rolled together in a humid haze, until one Friday afternoon, Ursula finally picked her moment. It was to be on the high street, and despite the fierce sun, there were quite a few people about, probably shopping for barbecues at the weekend.

Whilst eating her breakfast that morning, she made the decision to get it over with. She'd put on her best, worst garish dress - there was no point in making a scene if you weren't going to stick out like a sore thumb, she thought, therefore the shapeless, bright orange cotton dress with enormous daisies adorning the front made its way out of the wardrobe and onto her freshly showered body, having made its way from a market in Malaga fourteen years earlier.

A large floppy straw hat and enormous sunglasses completed the look, and she strode, despite the heat, down to the village with her pretentious open basket, towards Pippins.

Velvet and Faye were in on it after receiving a text and they hovered nearby, looking in the window of the Decadia, as if planning a new display. In fact, Velvet was thinking of changing the festoon blinds, and freshening up the window. She fancied a more punchy sixties look this summer, with vinyl records and sixties style Mary Quant flowers painted on the glass. She held a note pad, and pointed at the windows, noting things down and chatting with Faye.

On the other side of the road, Lydia was skulking in the shadows, pretending to talk on her phone. She had running clothes on, and her hair scraped back in a ponytail, big sporty sunglasses and the bottle of water she'd brought from home. She could have been anyone. Faye, who glanced over at her, was in awe of her physique. She was a woman nearing sixty, and her body looked decades younger, toned and lithe from hours in the gym.

"Blimey Velvet, Lydia looks amazing in that outfit, you'd never guess her age would you?" Velvet chanced a peek across the road and agreed. "I suppose, in her line of work, she has to stay super fit. She looks fabulous, look at her arms!"

Lydia caught them staring, and glared back at them from behind her sunglasses. She nodded her head to the side indicating that they should look the other way. They got the hint and styled out the stake-out faux-pas by pretending they were admiring the window displays opposite, in the travel agents and antique shop. Hands on hips, Velvet cocked her head on one side and then pointed animatedly up at her window. Faye obligingly got out a retractable tape measure and faked measuring the window sills. Lydia rolled her eyes behind her shades and wondered how she'd ended up with these two clowns on her watch.

Enter Ursula, stage left. She wafted into Pippins, in her sore thumb of a dress, the orange chiming perfectly with a display of clementines. Pam looked up. "Ted, customer!" she barked.

From the rear of the shop Ted, loped out, wiping his mouth, but missing most of the leaked ketchup that was smothering the bacon in his sandwich.

"Really babe?" he scowled to Pam, who was determined to keep to her side of the shop. If she gave in now, and started serving his customers, it would be the beginning of a very slippery slope, and before she knew it, she'd be running the whole shebang whilst he sat out the back putting bets on the horses, and listening to football on the radio, her absolute pet hate. It was bad enough on the television, but years of being trapped in the car while some overgrown schoolboy shouts commentary on a bunch of overpaid men in shorts spilling out over the airwaves, was her idea of torture.   She wasn't about to put up with it in the shop too.

Ursula stood, tapping her foot in the aisle.   "What can I do for you love?" he said flatly.

"Well, you can wash your hands for a start," she said tartly. Astonished, he looked down at his hands. They were indeed quite grubby from the unwashed produce, and now had the addition of smeared tomato ketchup and shiny bacon fat on his fingers.

"Right you are Mrs, be back in a mo," and he grumpily strode out the back. Pam sniggered.

"You told him love, dintcha!"

Ursula pursed her lips, picked up a grapefruit, and gave it a squeeze. Ted reappeared, hands marginally cleaner.   The dirt was so ingrained into his fingers from years of handling muddy potatoes, it would have taken some serious soaking to get them looking pristine again.

"I'll have two of these grapefruits please, firm ones though, and two punnets of strawberries, good ones mind - I don't want the sleepy squashy ones, I know what you people are like, hiding the over ripe ones underneath!"

Ted's heavy brow shot up and his eye twitched in irritation.

"I don't know where you usually go, Mrs, but we ain't in the habit of selling rotten fruit 'ere," Ted growled.

"Oh gawd, here she goes," hissed Faye to Velvet. Now Nancy had joined them outside, and was also playing at window dressing. She held the end of the tape measure whilst Faye ran it along the width of the window.

"I can't watch," said Nancy, and dropped the end of the tape measure. It shot back across the window and snapped back into the square casing, nipping Faye's hand as it went.

"Owwww, flipping Nora" exclaimed Faye shaking out the pain.

"Sorry Faye, I'm going in, I can't bear the suspense!"

Velvet tried not to laugh, "you wuss Nance," she said, as Nancy dived back into the cafe to safety.

"Oh don't be mean Velve, you know what she's like, she can't watch Dr Who without hiding behind the sofa!" They carried on measuring things for no apparent reason, trying to think of another activity that seemed plausible.

Ursula tutted and replied to Ted, "well, I usually have my fruit and vegetables delivered by the little man in Swanbridge, but he's on holiday and has closed for a month, they've gone to Australia. So, I suppose you'll have to do." Ted sighed and asked her if there was anything else she wanted. "Yes, I'll have a bag of new potatoes, I never know the weight, just a bag, and a bunch of bananas, no speckles mind you, I want them to last a few days, no brown bits, but not too green."

He went to grab a small bunch of greenish yellow bananas, and she shrieked, "not those! They are far too small! A small bunch of large bananas, not a large bunch of small ones!"

Ted could feel his irritation rising, but business had been a bit slow this week, and he needed the custom. He coolly submitted to her requests, however awkward, and banked every bit of her obnoxious behaviour for later.

Finally, after the other customers had borne witness to her performance, she paid Ted and sauntered out of Pippins muttering under her breath.

Out of sight, she relaxed, and pulled off the sunhat, fanned herself with it, caught her breath and popped it back on. Time for round two in the mini-market. Lydia tailed her at a distance and her apron clad associates went back into the cafe with a notebook full of useless scribbles.

Pam topped up the wilting buckets of flowers with a watering can. She was watching Ted. He had gone very quiet, tidying the pallets of fruit. She didn't like the look on his face. There was an ugly sneer that had taken over his mouth, his nostrils were flaring, and his eyebrows knitted in the centre, the outer arches raised until he looked crazed. She looked away, unnerved, leaned over, and turned the volume up on the small radio to lighten the atmosphere.

After battling her way around the mini supermarket, Ursula had managed to upset at least three members of staff, and a few shoppers. She emerged with her bags of groceries, and decided she'd had enough battling her axe for one day. Lydia used her mobile phone to contact one of her officers to follow Ursula home. She then jogged past her and up out of the high street leading the way. The officer, a young woman dressed casually, appeared from an alleyway and fell in behind her, chatting on her phone and carrying a bag of shopping. They watched her enter the house, turned and left the scene.

Once safely in her own kitchen, Ursula tore off the hat and glasses, flung the fridge door open and grabbed a jug of Pimm's she'd prepared earlier. Pouring herself a large glass, she kicked off her mules, tiptoed into the lounge and sat herself down on the sofa, the Draylon sticking to her sweaty legs. She didn't care, she flicked on the television and sat watching a cookery show, gulping her cold Pimm's. Soon, she'd fallen asleep, snoring loudly, empty glass resting on her bosom. She missed the end of the recipe for Plum and Pomegranate Pavlova, the wine pairing section, presenters sloshing the contents of glasses around their mouths, and now an episode of Poirot was playing into the gloomy lounge. She didn't hear the letterbox snap shut as something light fluttered down and landed on the mat.

Chapter 36 - Stormy Weather

At five o'clock, a cloak of darkness enveloped the sky around Kingshurst common. Before too long, a distant rumble of thunder was heard. The temperature had refused to budge, and the sweaty inhabitants of the village were desperate for the storm to break.

Faye was trudging wearily with the dogs, across the grass. Margaux stopped in front of her, and sniffed the air. She changed direction, and started to pull on her lead towards home. She could smell that rain was on the way, and didn't want to be caught in it. She hated most forms of water, even refusing to walk on the wet patio, so Faye resorted to pulling the garden table up to the back door in winter so she could relieve herself under it, on a wet day. Rollo didn't seem too bothered, and continued to move on, nose to the ground. Faye stood with the dogs pulling in opposite directions, rolling her eyes.

"Really guys, come on!" But she thanked her lucky stars they were only small dogs, and not great big German Shepherds.

Looking up at the sky she thought of her mother's words again,"He'll be riding tonight" - maybe Margaux was right, it was time to head back.

***

Ursula awoke, unsure of the time. It was so dark in the living room, the television had gone onto standby, and her head was pounding. Charles was away playing golf in Scotland, with two of his old pals. She had watched him packing the day before, relishing the prospect of having the house to herself for a couple of days, but now she was alone, she felt disorientated and out of routine. She rose from the sofa and shuffled out to the kitchen, her hair flattened on one side, and mascara under her eyes. She drank a large glass of water straight down, and blinked at the clock on the oven. It was only tea time! She could have sworn it was ten o'clock at night. Hunger rumbled in her stomach, but she didn't feel like cooking. She hadn't even put her shopping away from earlier, so standing in the kitchen in her bare feet, she unpacked her bags and filled the fridge, keeping out a bag of Caesar salad. She emptied it into a bowl and threw some left over cold chicken over the top, speared it with a fork, filled her glass with water and padded back towards the living room, crunching as she went. Crossing the hall, something on the doormat caught her eye. A piece of paper, folded in half. She stopped to pick it up, juggling her plate and glass and took it with her.

It was a handwritten note. Back on the sofa, she reached across to the side table, clicked on the Tiffany lamp and grabbed her reading glasses. Poking them over her ears with one hand she put them on, and balancing her bowl of salad on her knees, she opened the piece of paper. In very small neat writing it read:-

I know your secret.
If you want me to keep it come to the churchyard at midnight tonight.
Burn this note.
I am watching you.

Her blood ran cold for a moment. She looked about her, but then remembering that she didn't really have any big secrets, she smiled.

Bingo! she thought, someone has taken the bait at last! She surreptitiously tore the note in half down the side of the sofa, and took the blank half over to the mantlepiece, lit a candle and held it rolled up in the flame until it was burnt down, then threw it in the hearth. She doubted anyone was actually watching, but just in case, they would see her complying with their request. The next thing to do, would be to contact Lydia or the girls without being seen to do so. It was an uncomfortable feeling, thinking someone was watching you, but surely she'd be safe texting from the downstairs loo. She sat and ate her salad, and drank down the glass of water, then ten minutes later did an elaborate mime to let her watcher know she needed the toilet. She walked crossing her ankles and rubbing her tummy through the lounge and hallway to the loo, hooking her handbag over her wrist as she went. Once inside she pulled out her mobile phone snapped a picture of the note that she'd managed to tuck into her bra via the armhole of her dress. She hastily punched in a text to Velvet and attached the image.

In the kitchen, in the Decadia, Velvet's phone buzzed a couple of times. She felt the counter vibrate under her hands as she was wiping it down. The heat in the kitchen was oppressive, and she opened the small window on the way over, to check her messages. There was a text from Ursula. She zoomed in on the photograph, straining to read the writing. Her eyes widened and she uttered a whispery "oh my God," on an in breath. Ursula's text read: "Bingo, fish hooked, tell the big Apple, plan 2b there at 12, reply OK to proceed". Velvet quickly realised her code for DI Appleby and forwarded the message to Lydia. Within two minutes her phone rang.

"Velvet, its Lydia, please do exactly as I say, text Ursula back, just stating OK, nothing more than that. I'm assembling a team now."

Velvet agreed and with shaking hands she texted back OK to Ursula who was poised for action on the downstairs toilet. She snapped her phone closed and pulled up her knickers, washed her hands and looked out of the loo window at the darkening sky.

The message flagged up as 'read' on Velvet's phone, and she told Lydia.

"Right, I don't want you anywhere near this Velvet, you or Faye, understand?"

"Yes, of course," she replied, thinking about her promise to Joe to go to the pub tonight with the others.

"Let us handle things from here, alright?" reiterated Lydia.
"Absolutely, you handle it, just don't let anything happen to Ursula, she's such a lovely person," Velvet added. There was a pause.

"We'll do our best." The Inspector said

quietly.

Velvet raised an eyebrow, slightly perturbed by what she interpreted as an admission by Lydia, that things could potentially go horribly wrong. She decided that she and Faye would certainly not be staying away. The pub was on for tonight, and they wouldn't be going home until they knew Ursula was safe.

A flurry of texts crossed the common, wafted on the warm wind that snaked in and out of the trees, the ominous clouds building above them.

***

Ursula took a shower, modestly covering herself with a towel, just in case her 'watcher' was spying through the plughole at her.

She sat at her dressing table, feeling every inch the 'femme fatale', and not the 'dame victime'. However, she put on her nicest makeup, if she was going to be strangled, she wanted to look her best when Charles came to identify her corpse.

Getting out her favourite dress from the wardrobe, she caught sight of herself in the mirror and took a deep breath, wondering what on earth she was doing. In her best underwear, she stepped into the dark navy dress shot through with little silver stars, it fell about her shoulders and hips nicely, and she swung around checking her reflection, hoping that this wouldn't be the last opportunity she had to wear it. She brushed her hair and clipped it up at the back. She was about to put on a navy chiffon scarf, but hesitated. Why hand him the tools for the job? she thought, and pulled it off hastily.

Charles would be absolutely furious if he knew what she was doing, and suddenly her bravery left her, and she sat down on the pink velvet stool and started to shake. She looked back at herself in the mirror hissing

"Come on now, you can do this, you can make a difference, you can stop this bastard!" and she thought of all of those poor women, now under the ground or scattered to the wind. She pulled herself together, picked up her glittery navy pumps, and tiptoed out of the bedroom and down the stairs. The telephone in the hall rang shrilly, and she jumped out of her skin, dropping the shoes. "Yes?" she demanded, down the receiver.

It was Charles. "Hello love, everything alright? I got three birdies and an eagle today!"

She smiled. "Hello sweetheart, oh I am pleased for you! Stay off the red wine, and don't eat too much red meat, you know how it plays havoc with your digestion."

They exchanged chatter and before hanging up she said, "Charles, I love you". He paused the other end of the line, there was a crackle.

"I love you too, pumpkin. Are you sure you're alright?" She smiled a tearful smile.

"Yes, you know me, soppy old thing. Have a lovely evening with the boys, I'll see you tomorrow night."

"Goodnight darling" he murmured, and the line went dead. She replaced the receiver, her hand now steady as a rock.

***

That night, in the King's Head, the air was filled with tension, thick enough to scoop. Todd and Nancy were out of town on a date, and Faye and Velvet sat huddled at the end of the table indoors, by the window opposite the church. The boys had moaned about wanting to sit outside, but Faye and Velvet had insisted it was cooler indoors and there were too many bugs flying about in the pub garden. The men relented and sat sipping their pints, discussing the latest superhero blockbuster on at the cinema. It was ages since they'd been to the pictures, and there was a new cinema complex opening tonight at the retail park, where Todd and Nancy had ventured, but Velvet preferred the little old fashioned cinema in Swanbridge.

"When this is all over Faye, you, and Holly and I can go and see something fun at the Regal, much cuter than that new place, and there's a nice little bar that serves cocktails now."

"Sounds perfect, I can't stand these superhero movies, they are all the same," said Faye, guiltily remembering how much Ben loved them. Now of course, she would happily sit through War and Peace if it meant sitting with his arm around her for a few hours.

The minutes ticked by lethargically on the large clock in the pub, and equally slowly on the brass clock on the hall table at Ursula's house. At ten thirty, she decided to go to the pub and wait there, amongst people. She came out of the house, checking around, got in her car, hurriedly locking the doors and started the engine. She drove down to the village, and parked on the high street as close to the pub as possible. Mingling with some other pub goers, she slid in behind them and went to the bar and sat on a stool in the corner. "A double Pimm's and lemonade, please John," she said.

"No Charles tonight?" he asked, surprised to see her alone.

"No, he's golfing in the Highlands, I'm meeting some friends," she replied, never feeling so alone in her life. He handed over the sweet syrupy drink ,and she took a swig.

Relieved to move on to another customer, he left her, but something in her face bothered him, and she looked somehow vulnerable. He was a kind man, despite having a stern exterior, and he always looked out for his customers, even the difficult ones. He made a mental note to check back on her later.

Howie was chatting to Faye. He was telling her about the wedding plans so far, but in her peripheral vision she clocked Ursula on her lonely barstool. She budged her leg into Velvet's, and stabbed a finger under the table, towards the vision in sparkling navy at the bar. Velvet was on it. Trying not to stare, her eyes swept the room, taking in Ursula as they went. She nodded animatedly at Howie, appearing to join in the conversation.

"What is wrong with you two tonight?" he asked, looking at the pair of vacant nodders. "You're not listening to a word I'm saying," hurt that his description of wedding venues was apparently so uninteresting.

"Sorry, Howie, look, there's something going on. Faye, I'm going to tell him."

Faye looked unsure. "But Lydia said..."
"I know what she said," snapped Velvet, "but for godsake, this is our town, our people, and we've all been carrying on like nothing has happened and I, for one, am not going to sit around and let another person die..."

The last word came out slightly louder than she intended, and she tacked on hastily "...of thirst, waiting for another drink." Howie was utterly bemused.

"Okay, Velvet, I'll get you another drink then. Max, get Velvet another drink, will you?"
Max turned, saw the look on Howie's face and rose to get another round.

"What the bloody hell is going on?" Howie hissed at the two girls, now perched on the window seat. They huddled down and told him the truth. "Oh my God, I can't believe you kept this from us! Holy crap, Faye!"

Max returned. "What have I missed?" Before

too long, Faye and Velvet had shared the plan to catch the murderer with him, too.

"Swear on your lives you won't tell a soul," Velvet whispered to the group. "We could blow the whole thing if we're not careful."

Joe was suspicious after the stake out in the Decadia that day, and he put his arm around Velvet.

"I'm so proud of you treacle, but I'm also really annoyed with you - I do love you, but I'm not happy about it."

Howie rolled his eyes, then sensing they had all gone suspiciously quiet, gave a false laugh and lifted his glass

"Here's to planning the best stag night ever!" he said, and the hesitant group joined him in the impromptu toast.

"Looks like we've booked a murder mystery evening already," muttered Max, into his pint. The group huddled together deciding what to do. At the bar, Ursula turned and looked at them. A burst of affection swept over her, the girls were here for her, she felt it. The hands on the old station clock finally swung around to ten to eleven, and John rang the bell for last orders. Ursula's tummy churned.

John approached her, "did your friends not turn up, love?" he asked gently. She nodded, trying not to catch his eye.

"They texted, something came up." She slithered off the barstool, and headed out to the ladies loos ahead of Velvet and Faye, and a number of other ladies. When only the three girls remained, they turned to each other.

"Are you crazy?! You're not going through with this are you Ursula?" Velvet begged.

"Just let the police pick up whoever turns up there," Faye pleaded. Ursula turned back to the mirror.

"I have to, they have to catch him at it! Its no good picking up any Tom, Dick or Harry wandering through the churchyard at night."

"But what if he has a knife, Ursula?" , pleaded Velvet.

"No, I don't believe he will, he gave up on that method - that was only Moira, and they haven't proved it was the same killer,"

Ursula said, trying to placate them.

"It has to be done girls, we have to put an end to this - we've come this far." They nodded miserably.

"What are we going to do until midnight? The pub will be closing in a minute," Faye pointed out.

"Well, I was going to wait in my car," replied Ursula.

"I've got an idea, I'll talk to John. Maybe we can offer our services, he's short staffed tonight anyway, Holly is on a sleepover with her college friends." Faye left them in the toilets, and found John behind the bar.

"John, I can see you're struggling a bit, do you want me and Velve to stay and help you clear up? That lot out in the garden have made a right mess," she said, referring to the young women clumping through the bar in platform heels followed closely by a huddle of round shouldered boyfriends, hands in pockets. John's defensive look softened to desperation.

"Actually, that would be amazing, thanks Faye. Your lot can hang on in the other bar and finish up their drinks if they like."

But they all helped; taking their time, gathering glasses, sweeping the pub garden, turning off the string lights and illuminated signs. They sprayed and wiped down the tables, cleaned down the bar and the drip trays, collected the beer towels, and stacked the glass washing machine.

"Oh this is so great, thanks guys, I reckon I can have a lie in tomorrow!"

All the while, Ursula stayed sitting on a little chair in the vestibule underneath a sign that read:-

PLEASE BE CONSIDERATE OF OUR NEIGHBOURS WHEN LEAVING THE KINGS HEAD PUBLIC HOUSE. NO SHOUTING, LITTERING, SCREAMING OR FOUL LANGUAGE.

"Bugger that," muttered Ursula, "I'll be screaming my bloody head off in a minute."

Finally, it was ten minutes to midnight. The girls nipped to the loo, and found Ursula performing vocal exercises in front of the mirror, for what potentially could be her final performance. She took one last glance at her reflection. "Alright, Mr DeMille, I'm ready for my close up," she said, defiantly. The girls didn't have a clue what she was talking about, and herded her out.

"Let me go first," she said, "my car is

just outside," and she dipped out of the door, and quietly tiptoed to her car. Once inside, she locked the doors. The rest of them made a bit of noise, thanking John, saying good night and strolling arm in arm, up the road.

Once outside the Decadia, the five of them bundled into the doorway. Suddenly there was a terrible smell. "Sorry guys" said Joe guiltily. "Oh for goodnessake Joe!" Velvet whispered croakily. It didn't help that the night was stuffy and hot, the weather still refusing to break.

Lydia was in the Vicarage apartment. Reverend Fields was on pins, fumbling around in the pitch black. She sat, hunched at the window that overlooked the churchyard, glued to her radio, binoculars in front of her eyes. Her colleagues were in hiding, amongst the graves, and one above, sitting in a limb of the great cedar tree.

Ursula got out of the car and as she shut the door with a clunk, an enormous clap of thunder sounded above them, simultaneous lightning briefly lighting up the entire high street. The friends squeezed into the doorway even tighter to conceal themselves. The police officers shrunk themselves down as small as possible, to avoid detection. Lydia swore out loud, and the Reverend winced.

Then, as Ursula recovered from the thunderclap, and started to cross the road, the rain came down. Light at first, but by the time she'd reached the lychgate, it was streaming down in great rods of water which bounced off the pavements and filled her shoes. She paused under the lychgate, unsure whether to continue, her hand resting on the weathered wood beam. Then a low voice, just about audible, spoke near her ear.

"Evening, glad you came, we need a word." The owner of the voice grabbed her wrist, and she was too taken aback to turn around. He steered her roughly to the side of the church, and pushed her onto the bench by the wall. She managed to look up, and there, silhouetted by another flash of thunderous lightning, was Ted Cox, his distorted features snarling.

"Has my Mrs been talking to you? What do you know? Why are you always making a big 'hows yer father' everywhere you go?"

This wasn't the inquisition she'd been expecting.

"I don't know what you mean, talking to me about what?" she stammered back.

He bellowed at her.
"What did she tell you about that night, what did she say?" He came towards her,

pushed her down onto the bench, his hands around her throat.

"It was her, not me. It wasn't me what done it, and I've been paying the bleedin' price ever since," he yelled mournfully into the air above her face, and let go of her neck.

Confused, Ursula managed to wriggle free enough to reply.
"She done, erm did, what exactly? I don't know what you're talking about!"

He sat next to her, slumped, but hand firmly on her wrist, the rain pouring off his head and down his nose. "She ran him off the road, he hit a tree, she left him to die". He said miserably.

"Left who?" asked Ursula.

Ted continued to rage, "then years later, she goes and tells that bloody Moira! She tried to blackmail me, didn't she, crazy cow, thought she could squeeze a few grand out of me - but I saw her coming!"

He turned back to Ursula, his face changing again to a terrifying snarl.
"You bleedin' busy body women, think you can run the whole town, keeping everyone

in their place, telling us all what to do! Well you can't tell ME what to do, I make my own rules!"

He rose once more, dragging her behind him, and into the middle of the churchyard. As he pushed her down into the sodden grass, there was a thud of hooves and a great cry, and in the flash of the next bolt of lightening, a great horse reared up in front of them, its rider, clad in red and gold, glaring down at them, sword raised.

The apparition disappeared as suddenly as it had come. Ted shied away from the terrifying spectacle, and a flood of light from the massive police torches engulfed them. Officers appeared from all sides, and Lydia was down at Ted's side in seconds. The officers pulled him off Ursula, and pinned him to the ground, his face in the wet grass. It took three of them to hold the writhing muscular bulk of him down. Lydia shouted his rights to him through the pouring rain and thunder.

The group of friends were now weaving their way around the headstones, having pelted down the high street when they heard raised voices.

John was outside the pub in his dressing gown. "What the hell is going on?" he called into the filthy night. "Where did that horse go?". Faye closed her eyes, her mother had been telling the truth about the horseman all along. She staggered backwards in disbelief, her hands to her temples as if trying to press the information through to her reluctant mind.

Velvet was down with Ursula, kneeling in the wet grass. Lydia shot her a stern look for not having kept away. The Reverend, fumbling in fear, attempted to throw the large Bakelite switches inside the church porch way, his shaking hands unable to complete the task, until another pair closed over his, and aided him with the stiff heavy switches, flooding the area with harsh artificial light. He turned to see the Reverend Jasper, who smiled warmly.

Police were everywhere, their cars screeching to a halt in the road and carpark backing onto the church land. Ursula sat up, blinking into the light like a newborn lamb.

Her hands went to her throat, red welts were appearing there, and on her wrist, from Ted's big strong hands - grubby hands that were now firmly behind his back, in cuffs. He groaned and moaned and wailed, and the police officers pulled him to his feet. Lydia uttered the words she'd been longing to say for months

"Take him away, lads.". He went limp, and they jostled him towards the police car, and pushed his big head downwards into the back of it. Within minutes they pulled away up the high street.

"Lydia, I'm sorry...we couldn't keep away," said Velvet, but the Detective Inspector put a hand up to stop her. "Don't, it doesn't matter now."

Lydia looked at Faye, with pity in her eyes.

"What?" Faye said, "what is it?"

"Not here," said Ursula, taking command over the younger woman. "Help me up you two, before they dig a bloody great hole for me here."

Velvet and Faye helped her to her feet. The ambulance crew insisted on checking her over, despite her protests.

Lydia instructed two officers to bring Pam in for questioning. It was time to get to the bottom of their dirty little secret. She answered a call on her radio, apparently Todd wasn't at home. Velvet overheard and interjected, "Lydia, he's out on a date with Nancy, they went to the new cinema at the retail park, then they were going for dinner out in the countryside somewhere."

She looked at her watch. "I suppose

they could be at Nancy's by now, I'll text them both and tell him to come to the station. She smiled weakly at Lydia trying to get back in her good books.

"Thank you Velvet," was the curt reply.

At last the rain started to slow. Faye and Velvet huddled under the lychgate with Joe, his arms around them both. Max and Howie were looking after the Reverend, who appeared to have gone into shock.

"There was a horse, I saw a horse, did you see the horse?" He asked over and over. John nipped back over to the pub and returned with a bottle of brandy. He unscrewed the lid and handed it to the clergyman, who grasped it with shaking hands and took a generous glug, grimacing, but relishing its warming properties. Max sneaked a swig and handed it to Howie, then back to John who appeared to have a queue forming.

A fox appeared at the back of the churchyard, and stopped in his tracks, confused that his usual path to the pub bins was blocked by crowds of noisy people. His eyes glinted red and blue in the light of the emergency vehicles, and he ducked back into the undergrowth to find a different route.
Recovering a little with the aid of the

brandy, the Reverend opened the side door of the church for people to shelter.

Despite the air still being warm, they all shivered. It was much less humid and the smell of ozone hung in the air around them.

The ambulance crew released Ursula. She found the others inside the church, and Velvet and Faye moved apart and sat her between them. Velvet whispered to her "I'm sorry I didn't do anything to stop him Ursula, I wanted so much to help."

"You were here for me love, you both were, and that's all that matters." Ursula patted her hand. Velvet rubbed her back and Faye peeled the wet seaweed hair off her forehead, brushing the dead leaves out of it with her fingers. Howie smiled at them.

"Look how lovely they are, taking care of her like that," and Max looked over and smiled too.

"Howie, you're just as sweet, in fact, go and fetch that brandy, there's a good chap!"

Howie tutted at him. "For them Howie, not me," he said incredulously.
"Although I have to say, it definitely warmed my cockles".

Chapter 37 - The Bottom of It

According to Max, "the truth will set you free, but not before it's picked you up, shaken you, put you through a mangle, rolled you up like a pickled herring and fed you to the cat."

Faye smiled sadly at him. He'd been so kind. She felt a little embarrassed knowing they'd all been talking about her, deciding who was going to break the news, but her friends had chosen well. They sat on her new sofa, he held her hand and skilfully revealed the truth about what had happened to Ben. Lydia sat silently on another chair, a calming presence in the room.

Afterwards, she had thanked him, seen them to the hallway and they left, knowing that she was holding back her tears. She closed the door and sank to her knees and cried tears of anger, a strange mixture of relief and sorrow, years worth of misinformation, assumptions, revelations and darkest fears rose in her chest and spewed out like an old printing press slapping freshly printed pages onto the floor in front of her.

This was not the worst day of her life, but it was certainly one of the hardest. So much information to process, file and come to terms with. Where to begin, she didn't know, but something inside her changed. The sure knowledge that Ben had no power over what had happened, that he had been taken from her, he hadn't made a fateful error of judgement that night, and from this knowledge, she felt different. Not better, not grateful nor justified, but altered.

Max described to her what had come to light from the many hours of questioning in the police station. Lydia had agreed to him taking the lead in relaying the sorry tale to Faye. She sat, in awe of his command of language, manner and tenderness, thinking how this man had missed his calling in life.

The facts were given in event order, starting with Pam Cox, that in her usual haphazard fashion, she had been out making deliveries, had stopped to visit a friend, driven back, possibly after a few glasses of wine, and encountered Ben on his motorbike as he rounded the bend.

She was driving too far over, and he swerved to avoid her, and hit a tree. She failed to stop, she failed to report it, she left him there, alone and dying. She was filled with remorse, which turned to self pity as the years wore on. One evening, she confided in Moira during a boozy girls night out in the pub.

During questioning, Ted confirmed to Lydia with much disdain, that Moira saw an opportunity to blackmail him for a large sum of cash, presumably so she could exchange it at the airport en-route to Portugal.

She wrote a note to Ted, asking to meet her in the clearing. She had a taxi waiting on the main road. The cabbie had since come forward saying that he waited for fifteen minutes, then regrettably, drove away. Ted had intended to pay Moira off, but became enraged and strangled her, then dumped her body along with her belongings in what he thought was a lake. When work began to drain the swamp, he panicked and went to spy on the workmen, and this was the day that he'd been seen in the woods by Todd, who, upon hearing this, was appalled. He sat in silence, his hands to his face absorbing the closeness of his shave whilst observing his close shave with a murderer.

"I knew something wasn't right that day, I swear the forest was trying to tell me something, this bloody great rook was trying to see me off the path. It was very odd, then Ted comes lumbering past with a face like thunder. I suppose I was lucky he didn't finish me off as well," Todd lamented to the Lydia, at the police station, who, obligingly wrote down the words 'bloody great rook' in her notebook and raised an eyebrow. But, after what she'd witnessed in the church yard, she would no longer discount anything.

Janice had been the first unfortunate victim of Ted's slide into madness. Convinced she was trying to hint to him that she knew something, he became suspicious of her, coupled with her tendency for gossip, so he copied Moira's idea, and sent her a note saying he had information she may want to hear. She obligingly went to the lower pond, possibly thinking it was Stella she was meeting, but instead, met her grisly end. He strangled her, but unsure if she was dead, he stabbed her with a fruit knife for good measure.

And so the cycle began. Descending into lunacy and paranoia that Pam's dark secret had been disclosed to each of them, he took it upon himself to rid the neighbourhood of so called 'battle axes'. He truly felt he was doing the town a favour.

Poor grouchy Sheila was next, never to grace the refreshments table again, meeting her maker on the garden path, her lanyard finally wielding its power against her, in the hands of Ted Cox.

Finally, the mighty Stella, already missed for her legendary organisation skills, sadly lacking in the people ones. But, the people in question felt bad thinking it, which was one way of grieving, Lydia supposed, as she took notes of Ted's testimony.

The Reverend felt particularly guilty about her untimely death, his uncharitable thoughts on her floristry skills becoming a matter between him and the Almighty in numerous prayers since.

As for Pam Cox, she had had her suspicions about her husband, but was too frightened to face the truth. She had crumpled under police questioning, and Lydia charged her with Death by dangerous driving, failure to stop, and failure to report an accident. She was potentially facing a prison sentence, though somewhat shorter than her husband's. The sorry pair would never grace Pippins again, and their stunned offspring came to the village the following Sunday, and boarded up the shop. It went on the market a week later to pay for their legal bills.

To varying degrees, everyone had been affected by the events of that stormy night in the churchyard. Not all had seen the spectre, or admitted to seeing it, but John had already asked Howie to paint a new pub sign including the image of what they assumed was the legendary King on his horse, rearing in protest to the dastardly crime. It would be a fitting tribute to mysterious monarch to which no-one could put a name to.

The group of friends finally emerged

from a brief hibernation one late afternoon in the Decadia. They sat sipping coffee and talking it over. Faye arrived last, she hadn't been able to face anyone for a week. She and Holly had taken refuge at David's flat. They took the train to Hastings, set themselves the task of clearing the bookshelves and emptying the cupboards. Walks on the pebbled beach, the salty breeze whipping through her hair, had helped clear Faye's head from the dozens of tangled thoughts that were becoming miserably entwined within. Holly stayed close by her mother, her memories of her father were so few, but the impact of his death, loomed large in her life, despite Faye's attempts to put it behind them for her daughter's sake.

"Mum, I think it's time we went home," she said, appearing one morning in the bedroom with two cups of tea. Faye had sat up, looked out at the stunning view, the pier in the distance jutting out into the dark blue ocean, tipped with white frothing waves breaking on the stony bay.

"Yes," she said, with a sigh. That afternoon, they left the flat with two large suitcases full of trinkets, mementoes and books, leaving everything else packed up awaiting the house clearance people who Alice the neighbour would obligingly let in. Holly, with her uncle's guitar slung across her back, was determined to learn the instrument that summer. They struggled home on the train, and Todd picked them up at the station. A little strange with each other at first, Faye and Todd teetered around the subject of Mr and Mrs Cox, but as he saw them into the house, and Holly had taken her guitar upstairs, he took her hand.

"Faye, I don't know what to say, except, well, that I'm so sorry, and that I know Moira's death wasn't the same as you losing Ben...." he faltered, hands dropping to his sides, unable to express how he felt. She reached for his hand.

"Todd, it's ok, neither of us have the monopoly on trauma, the whole thing has been monstrous. I'll be alright, Holly and I have so much to look forward to, and so do you, Todd." She squeezed his hand. "By the way, I love the new fence, it looks so pretty. I might have to copy you," she said, changing the subject before the pair of them dissolved into tears.

"Yes, it would really make this corner of the common look fresh and welcoming."

He recovered, and they parted hands with a knowing smile and slow blink of acknowledgement.

"See you at the cafe, tomorrow tea time."

***

The Decadia lights were on. The welcoming smell of coffee brewing wafted from the kitchen.

"Before Faye gets here, I have a proposal," said Max. "Howie and I have been discussing it, and I think it would be a really nice idea to have a bench put on the common with a dedication to Ben on it. That way, Faye and Holly have somewhere to sit, somewhere to focus their grief. Anyway, I wondered what you all thought?"

They all nodded, "its a lovely idea," said Velvet, "we can club together can't we?"

"Yes, and I took the liberty of speaking to the parks department, we just have to let them know the wording for the plaque and pay them."

"I think she'll love that Max, well done," said Todd. "And before anyone wonders, I don't require the same thing for Moira, she has a resting place in her home town, and I think her family can do the honours there," he added. There was an awkward silence.

"Absolutely," said Max, "whatever you feel is appropriate Todd."

The door swung open, and Holly and Faye came in. Everyone shifted down the booth, and got up for a hug. They talked late into the evening, and Joe brought a couple of bottles of wine down from the flat, and before long, any awkwardness between them had dissipated. They made plans, they looked to the future, and the relief of normality swept over them.

Chapter 38 - Revelations

T he weather had cooled down to a nice, fresh twenty degrees. The residents of Kingshurst were finding a way forward after the shock of the arrest. The press had been sniffing about asking questions, but the town folk just wanted to be left alone - all except Ursula, who spoke to the reporters, setting the record straight about her recent outbursts and awful behaviour. They lapped it up, and the headline in the next edition of the local paper read "Actress Lures Battle Axe Killer to Justice" with a comprehensive article of how she prepared for her role, her past performances, her mother who inspired her, and her hopes and dreams for the future.

A week later she had an offer to audition for The Mousetrap from a London theatre company. Charles was so proud of her, he had been shocked to the core to hear what happened when he returned from his golfing break. She had been well and truly scolded, but he was proud nonetheless.

The Reverend was busy arranging a special service for the untimely departed. He knew his parish was in pain, and maybe by bringing them together and grieving as one, he might help to ease their suffering. Writing a sermon for such a solemn occasion would normally be a challenge, but he felt as if his heart would burst if he didn't get down on paper what he was feeling, and pages later in his little notebook he stopped, wiped the tears from his eyes, and felt satisfied this was the right thing to do.

Taking a break, he went to his computer and checked his emails. Amongst the usual round of church groups, Brownies and newsletters, was an email from the Bishop, dated today.

My Dear Reverend Fields,

I am full of apologies, James, for not replying to your request for holiday leave sooner. I neglected to tell you of a recent need for time away myself, due to a gallbladder operation, which I am relieved to report has been a tremendous success. I am now fully recovered and back to the proverbial grindstone. Indeed, I fully understand your need for a break given the unfortunate events that unfolded in your Parish last week, and therefore grant your request for a 1 week leave of absence, any more than this would appear, I fear, uncaring in the eyes of your congregation who may feel somewhat abandoned.

Please confirm the dates you wish to book and I will arrange for one of our marvellous lay ministers, or a curate, in need of a little dose of responsibility to contact you with a view to covering the parish of Kingshurst while you are away.

Yours in Christ,

+Phineas Carmichael

Bishop (SE London & Kent Bdrs)

The Reverend was utterly perplexed. He double checked the date and read the email again. He replied explaining that he had already been away, a few details of his holiday, that Reverend Jasper had kindly taken the reins in his absence, and had since returned briefly, that he was very sorry to hear of the Bishop's recent gallbladder troubles, but glad of his recovery and return to work. All he could think was that the recent bout of illness had resulted in the elderly Bishop being a little confused, although he didn't allude to such a notion in his email. There was no harm done, he supposed, but it was odd all the same.

A reply pinged into his inbox within minutes.

James,

I'm not familiar with the Reverend Jasper. Perhaps he came from another district? A relative of the Late Revered Carl Jasper perchance? An excellent young man who sadly passed to our dear Lord back in the late sixties, I believe it was Tetanus that did for him, after pruning the roses in your very church yard, of all things. I digress, I am fascinated to hear about your Byzantine adventures, perhaps we can schedule an evening meal and slide show of your photographs, if such a thing still exists.

Yours in Christ,

+Phineas

Dumbfounded, the Reverend stood up, pushing back from the small kitchen table and away from the words in front of him. With a mixture of horror and wonder, he cast his eyes to the Almighty and prayed for answers, then he prayed for the late Reverend Carl Jasper's soul, and his own sanity while he was at it.

***

Behind the Gallery, at the other end of the High Street, it was Howie's turn to make soup in the kitchen. Max had come down with a cold, convinced it was from standing around in the rain the week before. He'd been throwing himself around the place miserably, describing each of his symptoms in detail. Howie eventually pushed a comfy chair out to the shop behind the counter, and tucked him in with a blanket and a Lemsip.

"Now you just sit quietly, mind the shop and I'll bring you a mug of soup." Max did as he was told, staring gloomily into space.

The bell above the door clanged, and he groaned, knowing he'd have to rise to the occasion. It was a man dressed in edgy expensive casual fashion, a baseball cap and trendy thick soled white trainers. He'd parked out the front, his large Range Rover half on the pavement. Two serious looking henchmen hung around by the car. Max, alarmed that he was about to be robbed, stood up, knocking his Lemsip onto the floor, the eye winking concoction dribbling between the floorboards. Then the man opened his mouth and from the lopsided sneer, large white teeth and tone of voice, Max knew instantly who it was. The 'wasp' had kept his word and returned. Max buzzed the bell that linked the flat and the gallery, and Howie came through shrugging off his apron in the hall.

"Hi there, remember me? Coolio, six of your best abstracts my friend, as promised, I brought the Evoke, and the muscle this time."

After selecting the paintings he required to 'jazz up his work space', he pulled a large folded wedge of cash out of his back pocket, licked his thumb and started to count out the notes. This man was no appreciator of art, but there was room for everyone, thought Max.

After he left, "Ciao, stay cool Max, my man," with six wrapped pieces safely loaded into his fifty grand truck, Max beamed at Howie. "Can we get that soup to go? Let's take a drive out to that fancy hotel past Swanbridge, see if we can book this wedding?"

***

Over the common, Faye was just leaving the cottage. She nipped across the road, and onto the grass. It was a lovely little walk to work, when the weather was pleasant. She felt a lot better today, a week had passed, and things were starting to sink in, make sense and although upsetting, she felt somehow clearer headed than she'd done for a long time.

There had been a shower of rain early in the morning, and everything felt fresh.

Watching her step to avoid a small muddy puddle, out of the corner of her eye she noticed Fella, the Pekinese dog. She looked up, and his elderly owner was at the end of the lead, sitting on the bench nearby.

"Oh, good morning," she said, smiling.

"Good morning, Faye," he replied, in

his low burring tones.

Realising this would be a good chance to ask him a question, she took a few steps towards him. "I was just wondering, how you know me? Perhaps you knew my parents?"

He smiled and scratched his chin. "She was an exquisite creature, your Mother, and a fine artist, and teacher."

Faye felt the tears sting behind her eyes. "Yes, she was. Were you a teacher too?" She tentatively asked.

He sighed, "I was Headmaster," he replied proudly, "for a time... wonderful years."

Faye tried to think back, then the name came to her. "Mr.... Mr Govender?" She faltered. "I thought you had d... erm, I mean, I thought you were... that is to say, ummm. moved abroad." Then she glanced down at Fella. Memories flooded her mind of the little dog, he wasn't quite as ugly back then, and he certainly had enough teeth to keep his lolling tongue in place, but he must be absolutely ancient now, she thought.

A strange prickling feeling overtook her. She looked back up at her old headmaster. He had looked old when he retired, to her, a young girl. She remembered his last assembly, how they all clapped and he was handed a brass clock. Now his face, although lined and crinkled, somehow had an aura of youth exuding from him, one could say a glow. She felt a little lightheaded.

"Erm, I thought I had recognised you the other day, I hadn't really put two and two together....well, have a lovely day, I'd better get to work." She stumbled away from the bench and hurried across the grass.

Mr Govender leaned down and patted his dog, "time to go Fella," he said, and stood up and walked away towards Hunters Wood. Behind him, the sun glinted on the brass plaque attached to the bench.

IN LOVING MEMORY
OF
AUBREY GOVENDER
1935 - 1997
FORMER HEADMASTER
KINGSHURST PRIMARY SCHOOL

Chapter 39 - Community Spirit

Faye hammered on the door of the Decadia. Velvet obligingly opened it, and her friend burst in, her starfish hands and eyes full of confusion.

"What is it Faye, what's happened, are you alright?" Velvet turned the lock on the door and guided her friend to a seat. "Is it Holly? Todd?"

"Velvet, I know this sounds crazy, but I think, well, I think, I... I see dead people." Velvet burst out laughing. Faye looked appalled. "I'm not kidding Velvet, I've just had a real life conversation with a very dead headmaster and his goddam ugly ghost dog." She mimicked Fella's unfortunate face. Velvet laughed even harder.

"I'm not laughing at you Faye, well, I am, but it's just the "I see dead people" dramatic movie line! Faye, Faye, listen to me," Velvet moved in front of her, and held her hands. "I've seen them too, they are just people, they lived here in the past. Who do you think Stan the crumpet man was, and the lady with the coffee? They come in here so they can find their decade, they sit for a while, bathe in nostalgia then leave. I've been seeing them for weeks now, and I was so worried I went to see Elsa at that crystal shop, she's a psychic. She told me not to worry, to treat them like any other customer. She thought they'd come back to protect the village. I think she was right.

Faye sank into the booth, exhausted from fear. "I wondered why you'd gone there, why didn't you tell me?"

"Um, durrrr," Velvet gestured, to the harrowed wreck that was her friend. Faye continued "but Velvet, there are some things you're not supposed to see, to know, I don't like it, I really don't." But then she stopped, and a realisation swept over her face, "Except... well, I didn't tell anyone at the time," she took a deep breath, "but I think I saw Ben, on Christmas Eve. On the common, opposite the cottage, when everyone had left Holly's party. It was him Velv, it was him."

Tears erupted from her eyes, eyes that had cried so much already that week that they stung with another onslaught of salty tears. Velvet shed a few too and they held each other close. Velvet stroked her thick hair and comforted her friend as much as her tiny frame could.

"I think maybe we need to have a chat with Elsa, maybe get her to come to the cafe and..." started Velvet, "Nooo, I don't want to meddle, Velvet," Faye interrupted.

"Okay, okay, we won't ask Elsa," Velvet slumped back in the booth again.

"Faye, I'm sure they don't mean to scare anyone, you've got to remember, they are just people, they were people, before they..."

Faye interrupted "died! and had funerals, got cremated and buried - Velvet, they aren't supposed to pop back up and go walking their bloody dogs all over the village and ordering flippin' crumpets."

She folded her arms, mainly because she didn't know what to do with them. Her hands were still fizzing with anxiety. "Okay, Faye" said Velvet taking a new angle, "I think what we have to face, what YOU have to face, is, that they are here. Yes, walking dogs, sitting in the cafe, sniffing coffees, staring in windows. They are not here to do us harm, clearly, as they would have had adequate opportunity." Velvet squared up to Faye. She held her friend's tear stained face in her small hands.

"Faye, listen to me, its the living you need to worry about, not the dead. If the last few days hasn't taught us that, I don't know what will!"

Faye submitted to this point, and nodded. Velvet let go of her and rose to her feet. She resolved, "and if you want, you can just choose to ignore them. If it happens again in here, I will deal with it. You just take a back seat, a back seat, Okay?"

Faye repeated, rocking back and forth in the booth. "a back seat, a back seat, and you'll deal with it, okay." She finally looked up and into Velvet's dark eyes. "I can't believe we are having this conversation Velvet."

It wasn't the perfect distraction, but Velvet didn't have another plan, and it involved cake. She took Faye into the kitchen and started preparing ingredients for a morning of baking. She handed Faye a wooden spoon and bowl. The cafe was due to open in a couple of hours for lunches, and there was a lot to do. She put on some music, flicked on the kettle and prayed that none of her ethereal clientele would be in that day.

Faye was very jumpy, every little noise had her spinning around in her pinny ready to challenge the undead with her wooden spoon, her feelings as mixed as the cake ingredients in her bowl, and by the time the cafe opened, Velvet was exhausted from trying to keep her calm and focused.

She'd texted Holly numerous times with erroneous chores to keep her in the house. Until Faye had made it home and was safely tucked into bed with the duvet over her head and all the doors locked, she wouldn't be happy.

Fortunately, the afternoon ticked over with a constant stream of customers from the living community. Every time the bell over the door clinked its bright little ring, Faye looked nervously toward it, and by the time Velvet turned the closed sign around, she was calmer.

"I'm off now Velvet, I'm not going to be silly about this, I'll walk over the Common and if I see him, I'll just walk on by."

"Thats my girl, walk on by," and she broke into the song. Walk on by....," and added, "I can walk with you if you like."

"No, I have to be sensible. I'm an adult, I'm a mother, I can do this!" Faye said, bravely stepping through the door. "I'll see you tomorrow."

Approximately four minutes later she hammered back on the door "I can't do this, you'll have to walk me home, I'm freaking out Velve!"

"It's okay, I'm coming, I have to pop out anyway," Velvet swung her denim jacket on over her dress, and grabbed her keys and phone and paired up with her trembling friend on the doorstep.

"Come on, I need to talk to you about my order from the wholesaler."

"I asked you to accompany me, not put me to sleep, Velvet," joked Faye, her nerves having a brave stab at humour.

"Charming, maybe I'll go back inside!" Velvet threatened playfully, turning back towards the door.

"Noooo, I'm sorry, I'm sorry" cried out Faye screwing her face up and reaching out for her friend.

Up the road they went, talking of bags of flour, pounds of sugar and boxes of teabags. The merits of baking sourdough and whether their customers would appreciate the effort involved.

The walk across the common was uneventful, the only person out and about was Rick the rocker who was standing with Hendrix over by the woods. Velvet looked slyly over at him while Faye was chattering on, and decided not to draw attention to him.

She wasn't absolutely sure if he was one of the departed, the man had always looked more dead than alive, so frankly it was difficult to tell. He gave a mock salute and she nodded in reply, he turned and walked into the woods, Hendrix trotting by his side.

They reached the cottage and went in. Holly was cooking, the smell of tomatoes and onions wafting through the house. She stood at the cooker, stirring pasta into her sauce, her headphones on, singing along to her music. Into the kitchen came Faye and Velvet, bright and breezy. Velvet squeezed the young girl at the waist mischievously. Poor Holly jumped out of her skin, shrieked dropping the spoon, and Faye screamed loudly too.

"Faye, forgodsake!" Velvet exclaimed.

"Sorry, sorry, I don't know why I

screamed Velvet, I'm not scared," she said, astonished at herself.

"Velvet, I mean it, I'm really not scared anymore!" Her friend hugged her, "I told you, there's nothing to fear."

Holly stood staring at them, bemused. "When you two have finished being weird, can I get past you with my dinner?" she said holding a bowl of pasta aloft.

"Oh and Mum, next time you start chatting up strange men on park benches, can you actually give them your mobile phone number? I'm not your dating service, I've seen you in action and I don't want any part of it thanks!"

Faye looked at her quizzically, as they both moved to let Holly through. "Yeah, some guy, over the road, on my way home, literally called me by name and said to tell you he was 'sorry he missed you', or that 'he was sorry, and he missed you', something like that," she said, waving the fork around.

"He looked familiar, kinda skinny, but cute." She shrugged and loaded a forkful of pasta into her mouth.

Stunned, Velvet and Faye sat down at

the kitchen table with a bump. Faye started to laugh, poignant tears spilling onto her cheeks, and Velvet joined her, their bittersweet emotions rang out of the open windows, tumbled across the common past butterfly and bee, to where a stag stood alone and still, his nostrils flaring, fur lined ears twitching, absorbing the glorious sound. His soft brown eyes, lined with wispy golden lashes steadily focussed on the cottage.

The elegant creature, released from his role of bad omen, exonerated of all blame, turned, gave a flick of his tail, vanished into the woodland and all was quiet on the common.

The End

Acknowledgements

To my husband who ran down Memory Lane a good number of times to retrieve the words that fell off the tip of my tongue.

To my fabulous son, Tom Lawrence who inspires me every day with his energy and strength, and his heavenly brother Jack, who watches over us and wrote so beautifully, inspiring me to follow in his footsteps.

My glorious sister Merion Willis, whose loyalty knows no bounds and whose velvety tones will bring my characters to life in an audio book. Thanks for editing my schoolgirl grammar and keeping me alive with her baking.

To Findlay Willis MA for his Byzantine inspiration.

Harriet Willis for her equestrian inspiration and whose wicked sense of humour brought Holly to life for me.

My beautiful mother, Sonia Rees, her West End stardom and her passion for murder mystery a constant source of inspiration. To my step father Peter Cook for giving me three out of ten.

To Susan Denman, my dear sister-in-law who loved my initial idea one day whilst walking the dogs and has supported me all the way from Scotland and my dearly departed brother Mark whose knowledge of music and the natural world knew no bounds.

To Nancy Stanger, fellow author and friend, who made me promise to write something whilst under the influence of really, quite a lot of Prosecco.

To Celia Lawrence, 'special edition friend, now with eagle eyes', thank you for proof reading.

My dearly departed brother in law Gavin, for having a flat in Hastings and always showing us such kindness.

For everyone who inspired my characters, and talking of which, to Faye, Holly, Velvet, Nancy, Ursula, Todd, Howie and Max. As real to me as friends could be. I'm going to miss you terribly.

To all of my friends, old and new and my cousins who have supported me during this and other times in my life.

About the Author

Shani Denman lives with her husband, son and dog in a small town not too dissimilar to the one she writes about in The Commoners, her first novel.

She loves to sketch and paint, go to the theatre and cinema, read and crochet odd shaped blankets. She walks on the Common with her dachshund most days.

Following the sad passing of her eldest son, Shani was inspired by the bench assigned to him in the local park by his friends and the beauty of the surrounding countryside. Grief has shaped her life in ways she could never imagine. Friends have come and gone, but her ever constant family have supported her throughout her journey of bereavement and for this she remains eternally grateful.

Shani comes from a musical and theatrical family both of which run in her veins although she didn't pursue a career in either. This has not excluded her from creating the odd drama and on occasion making as much noise as possible without the aid of a musical instrument.

Printed in Dunstable, United Kingdom

68042709R00272